43 Fictions

Also by Steve Katz

43 Fictions
Steve Katz

SUN &
MOON

CLASSICS
18

Sun & Moon Press
A Program of
The Contemporary Arts Educational Project, Inc.
a non-profit corporation
6148 Wilshire Boulevard, Los Angeles, California 90048

First published in paperback in 1992 by Sun & Moon Press

10 9 8 7 6 5 4 3 2 1
FIRST EDITION

Some of these fictions were previously published in the books *The Exagggerations of Peter Prince* (New York: Holt, Rinehart and Winston, 1968) © Steve Katz, 1968; *Creamy and Delicious* (New York: Random House, 1970) © Steve Katz, 1970; *Saw* (New York: Alfred A. Knopf, 1972) © Steve Katz, 1972; *Moving Parts* (New York: Fiction Collective 1977), © Steve Katz, 1977; *Stolen Stories* (New York: Fiction Collective, 1984), © Steve Katz, 1984; and *American Made* (New York and Boulder, Colorado, 1986) © Fiction Collective, 1986; and in the magazines and newspapers *Boulder Daily Camera*, *Fiction International*, and *Guest Editor*.

The author wishes to thank the editors and publishers of the above organizations.
Biographical information © Sun & Moon Press, 1992

This book was made possible, in part, through a grant from the California Arts Council and through contributions to The Contemporary Arts Educational Project, Inc., a non-profit corporation.

Cover: Giacomo Balla, *Numbers in Love (Numeri innamorati)*, 1920

LIBRARY OF CONGRESS CATALOGING IN PUBLICATION DATA
Katz, Steve [1935]
43 Fictions
p. cm—(Sun & Moon Classics: 18)
ISBN: 1-55713-069-8
I. Title. II. Series.
811'.54—dc19
CIP 89-085477

TABLE OF CONTENTS:

FROM
*THE EXAGGGERATIONS
OF PETER PRINCE*

from *The Exagggerations Of Peter Prince*

Out of pity or boredom or despair, the cause was irrelevant, but the act itself counted, a way, for Peter Prince, into new modes of living when he set up house with Bebo to become the father, after her husband left her, of an Oriental orphan they had adopted, those new modes including selfless emotion and tenderness. Peter Prince felt a special tenderness for that child, though he had no special love for Bebo and at times resented the worst of her whining and hissing presence, but with a feeling for the child he knew must resemble fatherhood so much did a vague guilt swell in him sometimes like a cloud dissipating at its margins. In New York Peter Prince sometimes felt that all there was to separate his smoldering insides from the charred, sooty air was a pericarp of cold fire called his flesh and that reflected in car windows or in the polished marble and glass facades of the new buildings in New York he could see through chips in his integument the waste within himself, himself layed waste and penetrated by the wasted air, and though he didn't expect any more from himself than what others seemed to offer the world that self-consumption he contained frightened him. He needed to connect somewhere and make his disappearance known. To change and to change was the way. Despite these moribund self-evaluations Peter Prince seemed always happy enough. He never acted bored or desperate and was rarely self-pitying; moments of depression from time to time assailed him but he always found enough of what was left of life to be cheerful. He knew, however, that there wasn't much left, that there should be somewhere more available of life that he could get at, more loamy possibilities. A feeling of uneasy equilibrium, that one has in a house that has been robbed, came on him often in supermarkets and airline terminals and automobile showrooms and appliance stores, in front of TV, when he walked past the shopless facades of new office buildings that reflected dimly his charred going. It was all attractive stuff, not to touch; and his senses buzzed in it; but he couldn't help thinking it wasn't good enough, that someone, something had made a huge, incalculably stupid investment, and that Peter Prince, whose substance had been pirated to that end, was suffering from the receipt of ever diminishing returns. He moved against the flow, and had to keep moving, a flow that backed up against his desire and will, and he moved into it like a rescuer holding his victim above the flood, and those shoddy places: the shopping centers, airline terminals, showrooms, were not places he actually visited, but they most effortlessly swung down at him in the flood, coaxing him, softly battering his intentions. He consumed himself in this countering and he felt wasted, and that was why he chose Bebo, as if he could add substance to himself from the outside, something he could steer in his own direction, at least. Bebo and the child. He could learn something from that.

They moved the contents of their two small Lower East Side apartments out into the smoke and swamp of Queens. Their rented truck, a yellow and black mule, with gaskets blowing, stripped its differential on the Triboro Bridge, and Peter Prince, a load of alien household furnishings—frying pans slamming into the vanity, picture frames, a new freezer-frig combo—had to be towed off the bridge and he had to load each possession into another truck. He hated possessions, but the problems seemed necessary to him, the way to start off, as bad as possible, so one could appreciate the good times afterward and learn whatever the situation could yield him. He had invested his and Bebo's savings in a small co-op apartment, brand new, on the fourteenth floor (in a building that had no thirteenth) of one of the ten 143 family dwellings in the new Ma-Jo development (the name a synthesis of Marion and Joan, the first names of the wives of the two principal investors in the project). The options offered them were astounding. Rather than dull composition flooring they could choose a floor of wood veneer if they agreed to cover the kitchen floor at their own expense. For a minimum fee they could buy the burglar kit—alarm, pick-proof locks, window seals, and a one-way door mirror. They could choose to pay for air conditioning, which was built in to the heating system, or trade it for the price of plumbing fixtures. At a little extra expense they got continental light fixtures, brass hardware, slide-o-matic drapery pulls, the better Roll E-Z wardrobe doors, the Jingo Jalousies, extra Glo-Coat coats, deluxe cupboards, lux-o-matic drain covers, silky saddle toilet seats, all of which would have had to be removed if they chose inferior products. Peter Prince bought it all, feeling with this gesture the prosperity he knew he was entitled to as a citizen, a prosperity that the newly rich must feel when they first contribute to charity. He wanted Bebo, and himself, and their little Oriental charge to start out well.

"I'm so excited," said Bebo, as Peter Prince loaded with books came through the door, her soft tweed coat over his head.

"Grab some of this stuff," he grunted. She blithely swung the coat off his head and danced around the room. "It's so beautiful having a place. We're going to be happy." She wrapped her small shoulders in the coat and stroked one of the climatizers. "Winters and summers and springs and falls," she sang. "We'll have our own little weather here and we never have to be uncomfortable. I could chirp." She kissed Peter Prince when he straightened up from discharging his load.

"Chirp," he said.

He went back down the elevator, down the long hallway to the truck. The lobby was lined with divans and bureaus and sideboards waiting for the elevator. All the older folks stood by the windows down the hallway watching their children move in and conversing in Yiddish, in Puerto Rican, in Polish, obviously happy that their children could move out of the slums, and here it was so clean, they all agreed.

"There's what I call a real spirit here," said a huge woman in a black overcoat carrying a fry-pan and a plastic sack full of hair-curlers. By the mailboxes greetings and instructions from the managerial committee of the co-op were posted, each announcement ending with the slogan of the place: COOPERATION MEANS POWER.

A snappily dressed fourteen-year-old retarded son of one of the incoming tenants cooperated by holding the door open for the carriers, his shoes spit polished, pigskin gloves, felt collar on his topcoat. He laughed continuously and offered sprays of incoherent weather information and sympathy.

Peter Prince entered again with a load of records. "Wazzlo dhe sish Wockaroll?" The spittle glistened on the boy's lapel.

Upstairs Bebo was really chirping. She was small and pretty and her elation at having Peter Prince to carry her household in made her tingle with happiness. It made Peter Prince feel happily strong to see her. She was unpacking towels and blankets, pressing them to her cheeks as she carried them to the new linen closet.

"Don't go down yet," she said, after Peter Prince put down his records. "Rest just a minute." He folded his trembling arms in front of himself. She wiped the sweat from his face with a large, orange towel. "I want you to feel like a king." She formed a turban around his head with the towel. "Come to the window."

From their living-room window they could see the distant smoke of the city, and close by the construction of the new shopping center, their own, and the parking lot crowded already. The other houses of the project were being stuffed with families, the possessions swallowed by those buildings. Bebo took his hand.

"I didn't think I'd like this at all, I mean moving in with

all these squares, but it's really kind of exciting. Everyone seems so alive, as if things are better. I don't even think I'll mind being clean.'' Bebo giggled. ''I guess I'm about ready for the bourgeois scene.'' She turned a little latch and rolled back for the first time the Roll E-Z to the terrace. The air was a little sweeter here and they both breathed it and smiled. Jetliners came down in the distance over the low suburban homes, trailing exhaust like stretched shadows, and dropping into the black dust. They were hit suddenly from below with a crackling spasm of John Philip Sousa, drums rattling, brass bellowing out of tune. In the empty part of the supermarket parking lot a marching band from the local high school was practicing. The band was all Negro because the neighborhood before the Ma-Jo development had been all Negro. The development was going to change that. The band had purple uniforms and the white plumes of their caps bobbed on their troubled sound.

''They can't make that ofay music,'' Bebo said after they stepped back in and closed the Roll E-Z. ''My ofay king.'' She kissed him.

''I need to get this done. Then I can appreciate everything.'' His arms, freed from the weight of packages, felt as if they were going to float away from his body. He caught them in Bebo's armpits and squeezed her.

''Peter Prince,'' she said. ''You're doing so much for me. I don't understand why.''

Peter Prince closed his eyes because he felt tears coming to them. He rested his lips on the hot, pale curve of her neck, and the trembling in his arms floated inward till his heart rattled like an idling motor, and he squeezed her with recovered strength. "I don't understand why you're so good to me," she said. Neither did Peter Prince understand, but he felt this tenderness, a great necessity, moving into himself, and populating him where he lay waste. Thwang-Nuc, the child, was asleep in her own room. It was for that child.

The experimental use of napalm for psychological warfare by American advisers in her native province only half-maimed the child for whose sake Peter Prince really decided to "set up house"; one side of her was roasted and slightly paralyzed, her fingers gone, her body thick with scar tissue like callus. Because her cheek was destroyed and her mouth partly seared shut she had difficulty speaking her native Oriental dialect, and she could manage only a little whistling, like small sirens, out of the side of her mouth that could open, which she took to be the American language. She was bright enough, could write some of her own language, and was learning American, though she was hardly five. Her name, Thwang-Nuc, they had changed to Teresa; she was Catholic. Peter Prince didn't pity her, he loved her. When he watched her unscorched profile he saw how beautiful she might have been, and indeed was, a smallness of feature, a fine, narrow nose that had remained miraculously unscarred. She was changing, with some difficulty, from being naturally left-handed (the left side of her being the one destroyed) to using her right side, which would frustrate her sometimes when she was trying to draw, or balance blocks, difficult manual play, and she would swing the left side of her body around and beat on whatever she was doing with her stump, that was usually hidden in knitwear, knocking blocks across the room and smearing paint. Breakdowns like this would destroy the frail Bebo, making her tremble and cry, and Peter Prince had to comfort both of them, holding Teresa on his lap, and reassuring Bebo across the room that she was as good a mother as she could expect to be. Teresa had bad dreams and often kept Bebo and Peter Prince awake with a low, gurgling scream that she uttered in her sleep. That was Thwang-Nuc.

The spastic youth downstairs jumped up and down when he saw Peter Prince again. He shouted and pointed and hissed. Everyone stared at Peter Prince: the old folks, the young men with their arms full, the delivery boys. ''It's a crazy bunch moving in here,'' said the huge woman in her black overcoat, staring at the top of Peter Prince's head. ''There's gonna be an investigation.''

The boy drooled through his fingers that covered his mouth. ''Waffo tha . . . waffo tha . . .'' he asked touching the forehead of Peter Prince. Peter Prince saw the broken image in the polished doorframe of the orange turban still resting on his head.

''Whatta you, a maharaja or sumpin?'' said a man in coveralls who passed, holding up his end of a long, sagging couch.

*

''Deep one two three, Now one two three, Breathe one two three, Yes one two three.'' The gatherings of the Golden Mackerel began with breathing exercises, and all the trim, athletic men and women, dressed in dinner jackets and cocktail gowns winked at each other over their expanding and contracting chests, and so easily did the breathing come to them that they could manage to smile. This was where Peter Prince worked to support his home. The folks quoted their collective lung capacity at forty-three bushels or more, so great that the waiters, Peter Prince among them, had to hold the windows and doors during the exercises, to keep them from slamming. A few minutes of this ritual and the evening got going in a convivial atmosphere. The club accepted for membership aging young adults, full adults, and junior senior citizens, all of whom had wealth in common and a desire to keep fit. Each of them had his pet exertion like scuba and sky diving, rock climbing, yachting: sports the better advantaged Americans liked to invest in, sports that could keep them in tiptop condition well into their junior-senior citizenships. Each of them was proud of his condition and of his ability to maintain it though he smoked and drank. As Fellup Firrel once put it, describing the Golden Mackerel over closed TV to a Boy Scout jamboree, "We are a group of people young in energy who get together because of what we like to do, not because of what we think. *Activity* is our byword; *Do It* our only imperative." The Boy Scouts cheered and applauded, and the M.C., a smiling redhead, walked into the scene, applauding, "Yes sir, scouters," he said. "That's it. That's where the scouting spirit takes you, and that's why we know that Americans everywhere are the big daddies of the world." Peter Prince learned that what Fellup Firrel said was true. Though once in a while the conversation came round to philosophy or politics, and different persuasions were

voiced, and even some hostility rising from the elaborately spiced game and the organs of exotic beasts, that
hostility would subside again because in the American
Way the members of the Golden Mackerel kept their
sporting natures. The hostility was rare because the
breathing exercise was a cohesive ritual for their brother
and sisterhood, like the passing of a peace pipe, or a
fraternity handshake, or camp songs; the mingling of their
exhalations represented the bond uniting them. Often
when members met on the street or at parties they would
"take a quick breather," as they put it. It was a kind of
trust.

"Yes, I was saying about cats, they're my raison d'être.
Not so boring when I can train cats. Spelunking bores me."
Fowler Phelps watched Linda Lawrence nip her Nile Valley
legumes. He ignored Peter Prince the waiter who wanted
him to order. "The substance of life with cats . . ." Peter
Prince got his attention. "Creamed chipped Kudu," he
ordered authoritatively. "And a sable-fern salad, if the
ferns got here this morning. They clog my sniffer when
they're wilted." Linda Lawrence made Peter Prince wait.
"Cats. Cats," she murmured. "You'll find it delightful,"
he said. "A bit of the wild." "Skewered lark," Linda
Lawrence finally ordered, expecting it would come with
a pâté.

Peter Prince had the jargon and timing of his new
profession. "Koo in five and a lark skew." Old Wang, the
ageless Chinese broiler man, stared at Peter Prince and
tested his knife-edges on his wrist. "Listen," said Coombs,
an older waiter, just before he hoisted a tray and jolted
the OUT door with his rear. "It's just like oysters, a little

saltier, but they wash it out first." Peter Prince served the rolls, butter in a silver dish, and their favorite relishes.

"Old Wang wants to heave that knife at you," whispered Coombs, when Peter Prince got back. "He's touchy about casseroles, and don't cross him on a rarebit." It was dangerous, a conspiracy against waiters in the kitchen. There was the Kudu casserole cooling on the counter, and it wasn't Peter Prince's fault. He smiled at Old Wang whose expression didn't change. "Could you reheat the Kudu?" Wang hissed and grunted and seemed to throw a knife with his left hand, which Peter Prince ducked. The knife was in Wang's right. "You order the jelled salads too quick," said Flo, the salad lady. Peter Prince could, nonetheless, transform kitchen chaos into elegant service. He served the simmering Kudu, and gracefully slipped the skewers from the larks. Back at the bussing station he watched their faces for hints of satisfaction.

"Waiter," Linda Lawrence called without turning around. Peter Prince moistened one end of his towel just in case.

"Do you remember me?"

"I do, ma'am."

"Do you notice anything?"

In panic Peter Prince scanned the table. "The rolls," he exclaimed. "I didn't bring . . .".

"Not the rolls." She still wouldn't look at him. "But my pâté."

"Your pâté?"

"With my lark . . . pâté. Always pâté."

"Don't alienate the lad," said Fowler Phelps. "It's

never guaranteed pâté, my dear. Would that something were that certain, but never so. The lad will run off and do your pâté, if that's what you need. Run off lad.'' Peter Prince ran off. Hearing himself called lad, that cheered him up. With his Bebo and his Thwang-Nuc and his Ma-Jo apartment Peter Prince didn't think of himself as a lad any more.

"My lad," said Fowler Phelps, after Peter Prince had placed the pâté. "You mustn't let your pitfall be timidity. If you want something it's up and face it. Without that I'd have gotten nowhere training cats. That's so." Linda Lawrence darkly lipped her pâté.

"Your achievements are remarkable, sir."

"Right." Fowler Phelps half rose from his seat and pulled Peter Prince closer by his red lapel. "Now be good and take this back to the kitchen and have them heat it over. I've been talking so much that it's cooled and chilly creamed casseroles aren't worth eating. Gummy on the palate."

There is no terror, Peter Prince knew, like the fear of broiler chefs. Old Wang stood by the broiler eating his rice with chopsticks. Peter Prince dumped the chilly casserole at the dishwasher and ordered a fresh one. "That's from your own pocket," said Milly Malt, the checker, who saw everything in the kitchen.

"Fine now, fine. Fine." Fowler Phelps grinned over the freshly bubbling Kudu. "You're a fine lad and deserve special treatment. Some day at my private quarters you'll watch me work out with cats."

Even Linda Lawrence was smiling now that she had finished her pâté.

Thus Peter Prince became the darling of the Golden Mackerel. Of all the waiters Peter Prince was the favorite. No doubt of it. He was the youngest and had potential. They could call him "lad." They liked him so much that they would ask him to hang around after meals to meet their wives and daughters, and listen to sports lectures and travel tips. The people bored him, but he hung around anyway, though it made other waiters jealous and alienated him from the kitchen crew. He'd hang around, perhaps just to have something secret from the life that had developed for him in Queens, and from Bebo, who was jealous, more than anything, of his evenings at the Golden Mackerel.

*

"Sometimes," she said. "Sometimes you look so disgusted with me. Sometimes you look at me as if I'm despicable, despicable, as if you'd rather be with anyone else but me. As if I'm deformed."

"Fold this shirt," he said. He collected his black socks, his black shoes, his black suspenders, his black cummerbund, his black garters, his polished buttons, his cuff-links, his starched red jacket.

"I'm so miserable," she said, folding the shirt.

"Oh baby, please don't start this again. It wears me out."

"Peter Prince, I'm miserable. I'm miserable." She handed him the folded shirt and stretched out on the couch, pushing her face into the corduroy. In the other room Teresa's blocks were tumbling.

"Do you love me?" she asked, sitting up and holding a cushion on her head. "Do you think that you can love me?"

"That's a question you promised you'd never ask me."

"Do you think . . ."

"No. No. Shut up."

"Then why do you live with me?"

"Bebo, Bebo, please. That's a question I promised I'd never ask myself. I decided to live with you. That's all. I'm here."

Bebo hid her eyes. She was crying. Peter Prince pretended to look for grease spots on his black bowtie, but her sobs felt in him like fists pummeling his chest from within. He wanted to smash her. He'd better not care, he thought, and he left her to clean himself up in the bathroom. He hissed into the mirror at his helpless face. How did he get here? He couldn't give a shit for Bebo and yet he let himself be caught with her in this pressure cooker they called a home. The bathroom smelled faintly of ammonia all the time. He got at least that out of it, a clean bathroom. His shaving brush wasn't in the mug. Bebo often hid it. She knew how much he liked to shave, that it was one of his last intimacies with himself, the hot lather and straight razor, and she wanted a part even of that. It was like a comic routine. She bought him an electric razor, but he wouldn't use it; she got him all the varieties of explosive canned lather, but he couldn't stand them, like grease guns. She was desperate and lonely, he knew, and tried to enter his emotions everywhere, but how could Peter Prince spend so much help on her when the struggle was to keep himself from disappearing. He gave her so little, he had so little left, she was jealous of his shaving brush.

She had moved to the kitchen where she was listening to rock and roll music and pouting. "My shaving brush," he said. She didn't move. He looked in the cupboard, in the cookie jar, among the pots. It wasn't there.

"My shaving brush," he said softly, but firmly. It was a tender issue between them.

She slowly unbuttoned her blouse to reveal the badger bristles between her breasts. When he reached for the brush she kissed him on his elbow-crease. He touched her cheek with the brush.

"I'd like you," she said. "I want you to fuck me right now."

"In twenty minutes I go to work. You know that." He touched her breast with his brushless hand. "And Teresa is up."

"I know all that," she said, as she sucked on her lower lip. "I know all that but I still want to." She was looking at the ground with her hands in her apron pockets, like a stubborn child.

When Peter Prince lathered his face he could hear Bebo press against the bathroom door. "Peter Prince," she asked. "Would you still stay with me if I didn't have Thwang-Nuc? If she were dead?" He turned the faucet on full force so he couldn't hear her and shaved slowly, pulling the lather down with the long blade. He didn't want to have to leave her. He didn't want it to finish badly.

Bebo had turned the rock and roll up and was dancing by herself in the living room as Teresa watched, happily shaking and jerking in imitation. The Beatles: "I Should

Have Known Better," "I Want To Hold Your Hand," "All My Loving." "Why don't you," Bebo paused, and Peter Prince winced because it was one of those evenings when Bebo pummeled him with impossible demands. "You never take me with you to the Golden Mackerel. Couldn't you take me with you just one night?"

"Bebo, I work there. It's a private club. I can't just take you there."

"But you stay afterward for the parties."

"They aren't parties. Those people would bore you to death. They stink. They're the worst people you've ever met."

"Then why do you stay there late?"

"If they ask me to stay I can't very well say no. They feel like they're giving me a real privilege."

"I just want to be with people for a change. I want to have someone to talk to instead of floating here fourteen stories up."

"Bebo. Please."

She stared at Peter Prince. "You have some shaving cream on your ear."

Their little girl stared at the argument from the couch with her one good wide beautiful dark eye, her stump raised, as was her habit, to cover the mutilated half of her face. When they looked at her the child began to whistle and grunt, trying to speak American. Bebo took her back to her room and closed her up with her toys, where she was silent.

"She looks like she understands all this stupidity," said Peter Prince.

"I just need to get away from this."

"Bebo, buddy, coming down to that place won't do you any good. Besides, what about Teresa?"

"We'd get a baby-sitter. That's easy."

"We can't get a baby-sitter for her." It was hard of Peter Prince to talk about these domestic things; he threw his words twenty feet out in front of himself and watched them act. "You know the way she screams. We can't ask a baby-sitter to handle that. It isn't even fair to Thwang-Nuc."

"Fair to Thwang-Nuc. To her. To hell with her. Be fair to me for a change." Her face turned white, and she lifted her fists to her breasts.

"Bebo," said Peter Prince. "Be patient."

"I can't be patient. I'm miserable."

The wind shifted, and carried to their home from the airport the noise of rocket-assist take-offs that rattled the Jingo Jalousies and Roll E-Z doors. Bebo's misery nauseated him. He could hardly feel compassion for her tears, her fists beating softly on her breasts. An external, perfunctory pity, was all he'd admit, because he was doing what he could for someone he didn't love, and he couldn't tie himself up. He had to live the life of Peter Prince who was making his own lonely sacrifices. The woman tried to thicken his guilt, which guilt he bore because he loved the child.

"Sometimes I wish that we had gotten a good one," Bebo said.

"A good what?"

"I mean Teresa."

"Bebo. What an evil thing to say. You're crazy now."

"I don't mean what you think," she whispered. "I

mean it could have been so much easier if we hadn't had so much pity. We could have picked one without scars, one that was perfectly all right.

"Teresa is perfectly all right. I can't believe you're talking to me this way. Don't talk any more." He pulled his shoes out from in back of the mattress. "Here. Polish these."

She held the shoes in her hand as she hunted for polish. "I mean I wish I didn't have to pity her so much. Sometimes I think I pity her so much I don't have time to love her." She smeared the shoes with black wax.

"Don't say any more." Peter Prince covered his ears. "You're despicable." He went back to the fluorescents by his shaving mirror. His face looked like an apple skin, spotted.

"You see what I said in the first place?" She leaned around the corner. "That's the way you feel about me. Why don't you ever try to understand a fucking thing that I say, damn it damn it damn it. All you ever listen to is yourself."

"Christ," he shouted, and watched the color shift on his face. "What do you think I'm doing here? Why do you think I came to live in this screwy collective mortuary? Because I don't understand you? I took this whole fucking thing on myself." He splashed water onto his burning lips and cheeks. "And I don't want to hear you cry anymore."

"Peter Prince," she screamed, out of sight. "Will you let me come with you tonight?"

"No!"

"Shit," she blasted, on all her tweeters and woofers. He heard his shoes hit the shatterproof.

On the F train Peter Prince relaxed. He needed the anonymity. The subway was his place, it seemed, more than the Ma-Jo development or the Golden Mackerel. He felt at both those places only tentatively welcome; impossible as it was to keep Bebo and a small family happy, so much did waiting tables seem impermanent, a new sport he was learning; but the subway: the stench of passageways, greasy walls, men in the muddy light of change-booths, dealing tokens and sliding coins into pools. It was like a shrine, less likely to change than the city's surface. The subways would be overlooked because they were unprofitable, unnoticeable, a persistent sickness the city had grown used to, and the filthy quaintness wouldn't disappear for a while. It was reassuring, that rhythm of the express. Out of the chaos of his life in the Ma-Jo development, or the frantic worry at the Golden Mackerel of pleasing customers he would walk down into the subway, and from the subway he would emerge into a calmed world, the silence of the dining room at the Golden Mackerel before opening or back to his apartment, when it was quiet, Bebo almost asleep, the radio softly humming. It worked for him the way church must work for some people: He always entered out of the total disorder of his life, and left it to find peace in his life, as if something really happened in there to calm down the world.

Despicable. Despicable. Despicable. That word was caught in the rhythm of the subway car. It had issued from Bebo as if it grew onto her tongue out of her bloodstream. Poor Bebo. Despicable ran in her brain with a steady rhythm like the subway. Had he caused her pain? Could he prevent it? He had entered their relationship with only a limited commitment, to provide, and why did she test him then? Why the tasks, when he wasn't trying to win anything of hers? Miss Subways for that month stole his eyes, a pale and smiling Negress.

"How is it, baby? Man we haven't heard of you for so long, like you've been hiding." Hanging from the hand-grip above Peter Prince was a thin man with a spotty beard and long, ash-blonde hair.

"It's been fine," said Peter Prince, before he remembered who the man was. "I mean I've been hassling, but it's been O.K."

"Wow, what a drag. I mean such sadness in Queens, I mean trivial sadness." The man sat down beside him and put on his sunglasses. Peter Prince remembered him, a friend from The Snug, his old hangout, a painter. "How's Bebo? Like things are different without you two around. The groovy people all disappear, I mean it."

"Everything's cool," Peter Prince lied. "I've got a job now."

"Such tragic stories, all my friends lay such tragedies on me. Doing what?"

"I'm waiting tables."

"What a drag."

"I don't mind it."

"Yeah. I guess you always dug those funny scenes, but it's a drag you have to do it. Have you been working?"

Peter Prince read the headlines of the sheet a man across the car was reading: WIFE GRINDS KIDS, FEEDS HUSBAND. He wanted to find out more about that, he couldn't let it go by: the meat-grinder, the kids, the meal with both of them smacking grease from their lips, the ketchup.

"Are you working?" asked his friend again.

"I said I've been waiting tables."

"I don't mean that, baby. I mean working, you know. Writing. You said you were doing a journal thing last time I saw you."

"Yeah. I'm still working on that," Peter Prince lied again. It was that lie he left on the Lower East Side, and it was uncomfortable now to feel it catch him up again. His label, socially, when he lived there, was as a writer, but he never wrote. He'd sit down at a ledger he'd bought on Canal Street to use as a journal, but could only embarrass himself with the banality of what he thought. He'd carry it under his arm, the pages full of shopping lists written slantwise, newspaper cutups hanging out on paper clips. He'd get stoned with his friends and sit down later to write about it, or would try to write while he was stoned, enjoying the making of letters and the slow encouragement of ink marking paper. He rarely finished a word, and when he did he was too exhausted to start a second. That ridiculous inertia, that stupor he was in, made it right to leave with Bebo, and to rearrange his life. He would write some day, he had to, but that day had to come.

"It's a groove if you can keep working, like in Queens. I mean you have to keep working to stay alive anywhere, but in Queens. I can't believe what I see every time I go out there, those housing developments, like tombs. And people in madras, what poverty. It's the death of the eyes." They sat there for a moment, thinking it over. "The death of the eyes.'' Peter Prince enveloped that phrase and closed his eyes, opening them when the man spoke again. He had a gaunt profile, with small, curled ears, and loose skin that was impossible to shave. ''Look. I'd really dig it if sometime you'd make it with Bebo up to my loft. You could read some of your journal to me. And I want you to see my new work. You remember what I was doing? Well everything is changing, like I've exploded. I mean I'm building out of the canvas, and things move, I mean the imagery is the same but it's come alive, as if what I've been looking at all this time is finally talking to me. You have to see it. I mean come any time, and we'll blow some grass and sit around.''

''That sounds beautiful,'' said Peter Prince. ''I'd really dig that.''

''Yeah, I mean you have to relax some time. You must really be working, you looked so wiped out.''

Peter Prince didn't feel tired, but he could tell that worry was digging out its permanent design. It was becoming a father's face, a waiter's face. His bearded friend was right, it was time to visit the scene again.

''Listen,'' said the painter, rising, ''I split at Fifth Avenue. Could you lay five on me till I see you? I'm really hassling now, but I expect a job next week designing some toys.''

''Sure, baby, here.'' He pulled a bill out of his wallet.

''Crazy, you're beautiful, thank you. I'll have it back for you when you come to see me. Be sure to make it, please. Don't cop out.'' He went out the door at the Fifth Avenue station.

Five dollars. It was so easy to touch him for five dollars.

Tired Peter Prince was becoming simple and soft. His family made him tired, his job made him compliant. He didn't even remember where the painter lived. He'd have to hunt for him at The Snug. The five dollars was a down payment on his return to his friends. He'd have to strengthen Peter Prince.

On the way out of the station he bought the sheet that had the story of the meat-grinder murder, and he read it over coffee. It was disappointing. The woman was a giddy fool who was drunk, not hungry when she did it. On the story page was a photo of the husband crying over a pile of what was supposed to be ground child. It was an obvious montage. The husband was quoted. "I didn't know what I was eating. It tasted a little strange but it could have been anything so I asked her if it was horse-meat and she began to laugh and cry like she was crazy." There was no picture of the woman. That night at the Golden Mackerel business was stiff, with much special service: fish to bone, kabob to flame.

*

Peter Prince got home before midnight to find the apartment softly sleeping, a test pattern on their new TV screen, the kitchen lit by the refrigerator light, its door left open, the room filled with the odor of his Limburger. He peeked into the dark bedroom to hear Bebo breathe. She slept well. He would have some Limburger on Tris-cuits before he turned in. These were the moments he liked in their Queens apartment, this silence when he came home and the wind was blowing toward the airport.

In the adjacent apartments he could hear sometimes a
heavy-footed creature go from bed to the bathroom. He
could hear lightswitches, the toilet flushing, the bed
creaking. He sometimes thought about the places he could
take Teresa, dress her up and take her to museums and
gardens when she was old enough, and teach her about
the city, his girl. He wanted her to be something more,
something forgiving, lavish . . .

Teresa had begun to cry, small gasping whimpers at
first that slowly could grow into her furious fits of
screaming. Peter Prince wished she'd get over that, he
hated her screaming. If she wasn't calmed down she could
go on all night, shrieking. One night they had let the child
scream, hoping she would be cured by knowing she
couldn't get attention that way, but it didn't work, and
the next day the child, worn out, slept most of the time,
and every time she opened her eyes to see Bebo and Peter
Prince she would scream at them. The poor child had bad
dreams and wasn't able to speak.

Bebo was best at calming her, but she wasn't awake
yet, the pillow over her ear. He approached the bed
intending to awaken her and then saw the other man in
bed with her. It was a Negro, her husband in bed with her
again. The inundating notes of Teresa's fright drenched
his anger. She lay there with her head under the pillow
and he with an arm across her back. It was perfect, homey,
the way they breathed together and didn't move. The
room was damp, the air conditioner off. Peter Prince
quietly switched it on and turned it as cold as it would
go. Teresa's screams ran through his skull like a tape
recording, another time, away. He waited in the room

until he could feel the cold rising, and then he stepped out and closed the door.

He took the child from her bed and let her scream into his ear, while he whispered into hers her Oriental name. Her breath from fear smelled bitter like passion, and her body contracted in spasms like the reflex in a dead limb. He slowly calmed her, trying to hold her still, her forehead cracking against his till her fury subsided into sobs that she pulled from her throat like chains. She fell back to sleep in his arms, drooling on the back of his neck, and he put her down in her padded bed. A light rain had begun outside and the windows were smeared with moisture, blurring the lights from the highways in the distance. He watched the child and tried to listen for noises from the other room. He heard none. The child was sleeping now, a moist spot spreading slowly by her head. Peter Prince stayed to watch her sleep. He knew he should make some dramatic gesture, enter the other room and declare himself free of the mess of Bebo and her confused loyalties, her inability to understand the worth of Peter Prince, her desire for too much, for everything; but the child would be destroyed, that poor, neurotic victim. He felt for her an immeasurable guilt, a pressure in him that made any rational adjustment for him seem trivial. This act, he thought, looking at the maimed child, deserved retribution; this prideless act should be avenged. And Peter Prince let that vengeance be taken out on himself. His fault. It was his fault that Bebo destroyed the loving in herself. It was his fault the child's screaming, his fault the pain, his fault the earthless fourteenth-floor apartment, his fault the jet booms slamming the windows, his fault the mattress, his fault destruction, his fault Bebo's accepting her husband back again, who would degrade her again by leaving. His fault, and he deserved the pain.

Somewhere in the house a couple started arguing, screaming, and throwing things at each other, their running not shaking the house, but audible everywhere like an echo. "Keep all your goddam . . ." "You don't have enough . . ." "You asshole . . ." The whole house had been moving around earlier in the sounds of his argument with Bebo, like part of the atmosphere. Every sound made was heard somewhere: Teresa's screams, Bebo and her husband, Peter Prince's late arrivals. The noise released of memories, self-delusion, despair, like a sound track without a film, matching, overlapping, dispersing through the project, and Thwang-Nuc's screams mingled with it all. For all this Thwang-Nuc had been sacrificed to napalm, for these shoddy apartments, for this desperate communal note, for noise of complaints in housing projects sifting through the apartments like dust through rubble.

A door slammed that could have been the door to his apartment. Bebo was alone now, he could see, her head on the other pillow, still asleep. He turned on the light. She smiled abjectly, automatically. "It's icy in here," she said. She was naked, her bathrobe over a chair, a towel in which she wrapped her hair after she showered fallen by the side of the bed. "It's so chilly," she hummed again out of her sleep. He didn't feel the cold. It was just right. He pulled the covers off her chilly body. "Oooooooh," she muttered, showing her teeth in a sleepy smile. His cock was stiff and huge, as if he'd packed all his frustration into it. He undressed. She opened her eyes for a moment and smiled when she saw the cock. "That's nice," she said. "Warm . . ." He caught her mouth with his and pushed easily at her cunt, which opened with a hot explosion, like gas rising through the mud. He wanted to wound her, to split her in two from inside, but she covered his face with kisses and tongued his ear repeating, "I love, I love you, I love you," in a gentle, confusing patter. Her breath was bitter like Teresa's frightened smell. He clawed her but couldn't hurt her, and she bit at him, matching the fury of his anger with the fury of her lust. She screamed, they screamed together, and felt those screams dropping from apartment to apartment below them, and they came together, her teeth in his shoulder, his hands tearing at her ass.

He rolled over with the pillow under his shoulderblades and took a long breath through his nose. She reached over to finger his cock, which was still erect. "You're so strong," she said.

He closed his eyes. He wished it could be as good as it was, as it seemed. "As strong as *he* is?" he asked, not wanting to say it, the words muscling out.

"Who is?"

"Your husband."

She leaned over and tongued his ribs. "I can't even remember what it was like."

Leave it at that, he thought. "He was here," he said.

"What? Who was here?"

"Your husband was here."

"When? When did you see him?"

"You goddam bitch, don't fuck with my head. I saw him here in bed. Where I am right now."

"You're crazy. He wasn't here. I was here all night."

"I saw him, Bebo. I came in here and he was lying here."

"You're crazy to see such things. No such . . . For all I know that idiot is back in Vietnam. He re-enlisted. You know. Peter Prince, you made it up."

"You're lying." He sat up, afraid to look at her. Afraid he would destroy her if he looked into her face.

Her voice became suddenly sweet, playing a moment with the safety of coyness. "And what if he was here? What difference would that make, Peter Prince? He's still my husband, and you're not. He has a right to me that you don't even want."

"Bebo, I'm going to beat the shit out of you." He lifted her head by her long hair and slapped her face. "He was here."

"He wasn't."

"You just admitted it."

"You're crazy. I can't help it. Let go of my hair. That man is thousands of miles away. I was just lying here awake till you came because I wanted to apologize. I've been shitty, Peter Prince."

"You trivial cunt. Sleeping. You didn't even hear Teresa scream. Did you?"

"Teresa didn't scream."

"I suppose I hallucinated that too?" He jerked her head around till her mouth was twisted open in pain.

"Peter Prince, please."

He let go of her. "If this happens once more I'm going to kill you," he said, or he didn't say. He didn't want to remember.

But he did remember, and the memory embarrassed him, his outburst of stupidity. After that night Bebo met him regularly at the gatherings of the Golden Mackerel, waiting for him, dressed in spangled clothes, in the employees' lounge. They left Teresa with a baby-sitter, whom they could retain only by paying her double wages after the first night when she realized her duties were to keep calm a terrified child. Peter Prince actually enjoyed Bebo's company at the Golden Mackerel. To his surprise she really enjoyed the people, and knew how to act with them. She'd been brought up in wealth, disowned when she married a Negro, but her own social set had been very much like the Golden Mackerel set, and she could socialize at will, show interest in conversations, and rise discreetly on her toes in enthusiasm when the men described their sporting occupations. She wore glittering make-up on her eyelids and hair, and never complained to Peter Prince about her clothes, though he could see they caused her some embarrassment in the presence of Linda Lawrence, for example, who was always fashionable, and she would come home sometimes at night and throw her outmoded duds across the bedroom, causing Peter Prince to feel he provided inadequately for her. He needed to provide for her. It was satisfying.

"Poor Peter Prince," she said, when he started bringing new clothes home for her, "You're doing so much for me. I don't understand why."

Peter Prince couldn't come to terms in himself with that stupid jealousy he had felt to see Bebo's husband in bed with her again. He had no right to it, and he knew it was hypocritical. He had come to this new life choosing to bear little of the emotional burden of Bebo, to remain detached from her and to protect the child from too much pain. But his involvement was more than he'd counted on. He had come to dole himself out carefully, and to expect nothing. He had no right, even, to Bebo's loyalty. He wanted to be to her as a tugboat to its barges, pulling the weight, indifferent to the cargo, but that evening he had felt betrayed, though he knew he had no right to feel so, betrayed in some residual memory of family loyalties, because it was a household he had established himself that was violated. He'd been stupid, furious, blinded. He'd threatened to kill her. He had never known that violence in himself before, rising in him like sewage. He disgusted himself. He never wanted to be alone with her again. He wanted to prevent that anger from recurring. It was himself he despised and though he still felt a certain tenderness when they were with the child, and though he was comfortable with her at the Golden Mackerel, all his free time he would spend alone, haunting his old, downtown hangouts, and talking with old friends. He told her he was writing and needed the solitude. This was another turn he hadn't expected, thinking he could never turn back after the change to Queens, that his old life in those corners of indolence was over, and that he would never return. But he returned, and it was comforting, and he pitied himself.

It was a lavish pity in the subways, on the shadowy streets. Sometimes, out of self-pity, he'd spend the night with Milly Malt, the checker at the Golden Mackerel, when her boy friend was out of town. There were no complications with her. She liked Peter Prince in bed. She was taller than he and her sharp voice caused him some discomfort, her face was full of cosmetic scars. She wasn't pretty, but it was uncomplicated.

"I like it this way," said Peter Prince, fingering the fringe on the embroidered cover of her victorian love seat.

"It's strange," she said. "You're just like the last one Old Wang didn't like. Young, energetic, popular with the members."

"What happened to him?"

"He was blinded."

"How?"

"I don't know. He just didn't show up for work, and I was told he was blinded. Then they hired you." She kissed him. "You look scared."

"That scares the shit out of me. Old Wang has death in his eyes when he looks at me."

Milly Malt laughed. "A broiler chef with death in his eyes. Ha Ha. That's rich."

*

One night he searched out his painter friend at The Snug and spilled the whole complaint, cleansing and sickening himself at once. He tried to tell the truth about himself, climbing slowly the rises of self-deception, and dropping in cascading phrases into confession: Bebo, the child, his strange guilt, her lack of gratitude, his lack of concern.

"Oh baby," said the painter, "like that's the whole exploitation scene, that American chick. Like split, and leave it there. It's not your scene," the painter commiserated. "Look, baby, like there's no reason at all for what you told me, for what you just told me. Chicks will do that. They'll try to run your head. My wife played that bit with my work."

Peter Prince kept his eyes off the painter as he spoke and looked about the loft at the obsessive imagery of his work that lay around in disorder. The persistent image was a gun, or more frequently a bullet, done in a variety of manners, sometimes crowds of them with faces, conversing bullets, smiling, coughing, crying, singing. Two wrinkled bullets doing the Watusi. Bullets with wings and enigmatic smiles, bullets polishing their nails, bullets yawning and peeking from their gunbarrels like groundhogs, bullets in bed, bullets raining from the clouds, bullets in buses, on ferries, on motorcycles, bullets smoking pot, sniffing cocaine, cooking shmeck, bullets playing basketball, delivering sermons, giving guided tours, ice skating, bullets abstracted, gray and blue, riding through stripes of silver and gold paint, like Byzantine icons, motionless. Paranoia. And in the latest work they were beginning to fly off the canvas on springs, to hang down from the ceiling out of foreshortened gunbarrels, bullets on vibrating ribbons, some of them huge, with smiles and wings. The titles were, in some cases, painted right onto the canvas, titles, like: *The World Must Be Made Safe for Democracy*; *There Are No Atheists in the Fox Holes*; *Force, Force to the Utmost*; *Pick Out the Biggest One and Fire*; *I Shall Return*; *Let No Guilty Man Escape*; *The Sun Will Go Down on a Million Men in Arms*; *You Furnish the Pictures and I'll Furnish the War*; *My Spear Knows No Brother*. One of the compositions called, *The*

Chinese Must Go, was just a gun, neatly polished, like a trophy, with a bullet lying just outside its barrel, set on a long, white stand with a tape recorder hidden in it that constantly repeated this message,

"Knock, knock."

"Who's there?"

Silence.

"Knock, knock."

"Who's there?"

Silence.

"I know I should leave, baby," Peter Prince said. "But I'd feel like such a shit to do it."

"The chick doesn't even care. I mean she lays out there with that other cat, with her husband. Believe me, baby, once a chick has had black eyes there's nothing a white man can do. That chick will have him back, and have him back. She doesn't care about you, baby. You're colonized."

Peter Prince knew that the painter's estimation wasn't true. That vindictiveness wasn't Bebo's attitude, because she was pitiful, helpless in her way. She wanted to be able to love Peter Prince, if Peter Prince would let her, and to leave her old husband alone, if only Peter could have it that way, but he couldn't, he had to stay loose. "I've invested all this bread in the place; I mean I own that apartment, you know. And the kid. If you could see that kid. I was never sentimental before, but that kid tears out your heart. She's maimed and neurotic at four years old, and Bebo can't handle it alone, and with her husband it was worse. It's a sweet kid too, and there's something about its being Oriental. This might sound stupid, but I feel guilty about her. Like I'm American and it's all my fault. I never said that before. You know she screams in her sleep, sometimes all night.''

"What a drag."

"I don't really mind the screaming. I'm used to it. Like I deserve it. Bebo sleeps through.''

"Not the screaming, I mean being American is a drag and getting into the hang-up you're in. I think the worst thing in this world is to be born white Anglo-Saxon Protestant American. With all this guilt. To live in this horror show.''

"I can't believe that. I don't like to believe that.''

"Right. You don't like to believe it. Right. I believe it, though. I believe we've fucked up the whole world. I believe we're feeding our faces on the whole starving world. I believe that our interests on every continent do nothing but keep the Orientals, the Indians, the Arabs, the South Americans on every continent starving. I believe that. We support the few wealthy up on top with our aid, and turn our backs, not us, but a few of our fattest oil assholes, and murderous munitions producers. We use the oil interests, the natural resources, and fix the industries to our own profit, and nothing goes to the people. They eat the scabs off their arms. We sell them Coca Cola. And we exploit our own poor, foolish population. We dry out their brains. Even forget the spades, look at the helpless suburbs.'' As he talked he cut pictures out of old, glossy magazines and arranged them on the table in front of himself, never looking at Peter Prince, and Peter Prince couldn't look at the painter. "I know I sound like an extreme idiot, but I really try to understand it. I try, and

I can't. Look at me. I come from a wealthy family, really
wealthy. My father is like the biggest packaging engineer
in the country. He's the boss of those tabs that keep bread
bags closed, of that little strap that holds milk cartons
together, of the machine that seals strings of lollipops and
gum in cellophane, all that evil, efficient shit. But how
can I use any of that money? It's death. It's the death of
the world, of the heart. It's the death of the hands. Death
of the eyes. Death of the mouth. I mean New York City.
It's the best America has to offer, at least in culture and
taste, and what are they building? They're putting up this
glass and steel nightmare, nothing that a person can look
at and want to live in. It's the greed, the money of
America, the gluttonous few that deal out grief for
everyone. Everyone here is ashamed to look everyone
else in the face. Death. And the West Coast, holy shit; we
call the spread of that disease down the coast a sign of
energy. That's not energy, that's inertia, every house
down that coast built to the same pattern. Not enough
energy to change an idea, eight hundred miles of the same
boredom they build for themselves and call it prosperity.
Ha. Energy makes variety and pleasure, not monotony. I
haven't even begun to wail about smog, water pollution,
food adulteration, obsolescence, plastic idiocy. Baby, I
believe it, that we're naively making it impossible for
human beings to live, and that we're going to ruin the
world if we can. You feel guilty and want to help that
little Oriental victim, but what about the rest we're
destroying, and will destroy for pride and saving our ugly
face?''

    ''Stop talking.''

The painter was suddenly silent, and he looked at Peter Prince, and took all the pictures he'd clipped and arranged and tossed them into the air, and they fell like confetti: faces and car parts and fashions and bottles. "Stop talking? I say the truth, baby. I say it like it is. America is shitting on the world. We're all murderers."

"No," said Peter Prince. "I just can't listen to that kind of frantic wailing any more. It's not the truth. It's as hurtful as what it puts down."

"What is the truth?"

"Wow," said Peter Prince. "I mean all I'm trying to come to terms with is that somehow I'm in the world. I'm Peter Prince, and I'm in motion. That's all I can do. I think I can tell what's not the truth; what is? What is? Just keep ducking."

"Yeah, I see that. Like I could be a Communist but that's bullshit. That's not truth. Politics is all the same bag from any side. But I know we screwed up. We're doing it to the world. I care how the world looks. I pity anyone who sees what's happening, and you, and that poor kid. That's a big thing you decided to do. You're a big man, Peter Prince."

"Sometimes I want to scream like you do," said Peter Prince, looking around again at the bullets and guns. The painter took out a little medicine jar full of marijuana and began to roll joints. "But it's futile to scream. No one hears you. I can't do anything but a kind of silent penance, and there's no time to complain."

The painter put on a record by Jim Kweskin's Jug Band and they smoked in silence, coming to rest. Peter Prince could feel that she was there, Teresa, coming to him as a grown woman. She was whole, and beautiful, and she moved silently, with Oriental grace.

*

The kitchen crew was yapping and the waiters elbowed for position at the pick-up counter. It was a rush night. The pantry women cursed the waiters under their breath as they backed through the door and hurried into the silent dining room. Old Wang was unruffled, and seemed to work more efficiently as he got busier; he never looked up except, Peter Prince thought, to fix him in a yellow stare; it seemed to relax Old Wang, releasing the threat through his eyes. It was an especially busy night for Peter Prince because he was carrying his usual heavy station and a half of Coomb's station, who was having his piles operated on. It was almost too much for him to keep in his head. Bebo was there, besides, showing up in her spangles in the doorway of the employees' lounge to see if Peter Prince was finished. She was restless and made the crew more nervous.

With Bebo's visits work at the Golden Mackerel began to change for Peter Prince. The resentment the rest of the crew felt for his socializing with the members crystallized when Bebo joined him. She looked like a Golden Mackerel, thin, Anglo-Saxon, and she spoke with their nasal note. Because she was unaccustomed and uncomfortable around their coarseness Bebo could treat Peter Prince's colleagues only with the cold indifference and casual condescension she had learned as a child to use with other people's servants. They resented her, Wang hated her, and this feeling was reflected in their treatment of Peter Prince. He no longer got favors from the pantry girls; if anything, in fact, they would try to put his orders up a little bit off his timing. Peter Prince, however, had become so efficient, able to coordinate in his head so many orders at once, that the slight stubbornness in the kitchen didn't ruin his service; but he had to be, at all times, on top of his memory and in control. Only Wang rattled him, sharpening blades, glaring at Bebo when she appeared, the threat dimming his eyes, daring Peter Prince to make a mistake.

"Listen. Come by this evening after work," said Falkup Firrell who was making great demands that evening. "I want to show you my cats."

Peter Prince rushed past without pausing or smiling. He was swamped. He had to bone a partridge at a table on the other station, and do a crepe service. He was also behind on salads and relishes for his last table. He had to order a mixed game broil and a braised zebra tenderloin medium for he didn't remember whom. He felt chills inside himself, a pressure in his backbone that pushed cold sweat out his forehead. The members showed no sympathy, but were nervous, unfed, complaining. Charlie, his station captain, was nervous too, but he trusted Peter Prince to handle it in the end, to pull it through. Peter Prince didn't trust himself. He had stored up in his head an arrangement of his tables' orders in the order they had to be served, but he knew there were too many, that they were piled precariously and a slight disturbance would topple them beyond reconstruction. He could lose it all, all the orders, the timing, and be paralyzed.

"Pick up one bitty bird and two elk strips," he shouted at Wang as he hastily grabbed his salads, a relish tray, two roll baskets, and called for the crepe set-up. He avoided Wang's eyes that stared at him and pushed the crepe cart out in front of himself as he carried his stacked tray in his right hand. "You look like you're in trouble," said the checker, Milly Malt. He winked at her bravely.

He got there, served the elk strips, neatly boned the partridge, rolled the crepes in an elegant blue flame of brandy and Cointreau, served some relishes, rolls all around, iced some water glasses, and breathed.

Fallow Falcon tugged on his jacket, "We're getting hungry," he said, looking at his watch. "Can you take our order, old buddy." Peter Prince stood there while they ordered, letting the words register, dodging the dirty glances he was getting from a table of Coombs's regulars across the way. He took some relishes over to pacify Coombs's regulars, who didn't like him, and with his back to Charlie the Captain touched the cold sweat from his brow with his towel, a dining room sin.

All the waiters were lined up at the broiler and Peter Prince had to hold. Bebo was watching from the door of the employee's lounge, and he could see Wang glance at her quickly, furious.

"When will you be through?" she hollered.

"It's busy. Go back in. Quick." He waved her back.

"It's so late. I'm getting bored."

"Bebo, leave me alone. I have enough trouble now. Stop pestering."

He was the last at the broiler pick-up and swept his two orders onto his tray without looking at them. "Hurry up, please,'' said Bebo, as he accelerated out the door. He arrived just in time at his tray stand, because the customers were turning to look for the maitre d'. He set the zebra tenderloin in front of Felton Firko, and uncapped Linda Lawrence's dish saying, ''A little tardy, but delicious just the same.'' Not till he returned with the roll tray did he notice her face, frozen in displeasure, her hand playing with the comb in her upswept hair. He wanted to ask her why she wasn't eating, to tell her he didn't have time for her to not eat, please. There was something wrong.

She pushed aside the roll tray he offered her. ''You do recognize me, don't you?'' Linda Lawrence wasn't looking at Peter Prince, but at the plate in front of herself, and he too looked down to see not the mixed broil she had ordered, but the face of Old Wang grinning through a tender portion of broiled sea bass in paprika, with a nest of spinach and bacon. No. He had carried it out without checking, Bebo rapping in his ear, his haste cutting him down. ''Aaaaiiiiii,'' he despaired. The grin on his face threatened to rip into his cheeks.

''You do know who I am now?'' she asked.

Peter Prince looked at Fallen Feller, ''I'm quite satisfied myself,'' he said. He was chewing.

''Young man. Don't you notice anything?'' Peter Prince straightened up with his roll tray. ''Well, is anything strange?'' Her lips were drawn thin like bloody knife-edges.

He wanted to ask her if she would just once eat the sea bass and not send him back, but her stare demanded of him a professional response.

''I'm very sorry. I'll take it back to get your order. It's

a terrible mistake.''

"Who am I?'' she insisted, touching the top of his wrist with her painted fingernail.

"You are the mixed broil, madame,'' he said, and her lips relaxed into flesh and she let him go.

What Peter Prince should have done was to take the dish through the door, into the street, down to Third Avenue, to leave it on the doorstoop by a snoring wino. He should have said, "Forget it, to hell, I'm fed up.'' He should have put the dish down at Linda Lawrence's place with the fish still on it and told her to eat it, the trivial cunt, anyway. He should never have taken the extra half station. He should never have taken a job at the Golden Mackerel. He should never have moved out to Queens with Bebo. As he slowly walked out to face Old Wang, hefting the sea bass, he knew everything he should never have done, and would never do again, a pale lightning in his head like a distant storm, the calm now; he was calm, and he thought of Thwang-Nuc in her padded bed sad. He backed through the IN door into the stare of Old Wang like two thousand candlepower of blackness. He put the dish up on the counter. "Sea bass . . . my order was a mixed game broil.'' He leaned against a wooden upright and closed his eyes.

Old Wang smiled and waved his head on its stem like a swamp-flower and before Peter Prince could see his hands move, his knives were in the air. They revolved once in the yellow light and thudded into the pillar he leaned on and caught him by his excess jacket and pinned him there, the last knife into his crotch-cloth.

"Your mixed broil,'' said Wang, setting it on the

counter, as the whole kitchen crew watched. What could Peter Prince do now? He wasn't in an easy predicament, immobilized and facing a hostile kitchen crew. He couldn't shout for Charlie the Captain and he couldn't move too violently, afraid to rip his waiter's costume. Linda Lawrence, he knew, was devising pain for him while she waited in her hunger. Flo the salad lady, and Betty from the dessert pantry came up to look at him close.

"Look at him," Flo said.

Peter Prince could feel on his face the rancid breath of Betty from the dessert pantry. "He has green eyes; I've never seen that before."

Through his green eyes Peter Prince in desperation watched the mixed broil cooling on the counter. He was losing.

"Please," he asked the two women, "get me loose from here."

"What are you talking about?" Betty asked.

"I need to serve that mixed broil, badly."

"O that. Go ahead. Serve it," said Flo, and she turned to Betty. "You have to admit that there is something cute about him." They hustled back to their station when Charlie the Captain came IN through the OUT door. His face was swollen and discolored. He stopped in front of Peter Prince with his mouth open and seemed to be shouting, though Peter Prince heard nothing. He leaned forward from the hips waving his tongue.

"Please get me loose, I'll serve the mixed broil. I just need someone to get me loose."

Charlie the Captain slapped his own forehead.

"Loose."

Charlie the Captain closed his eyes, and clenched his fists, and gave up. He picked up the mixed broil himself. "Just pull these knives out," Peter Prince said. "I'll serve it myself."

"You're through here. That's it." said Charlie the Captain. He carried the mixed broil OUT to the dining room through the IN door.

"I told you," said Milly Malt, the checker, as she came around the pillar. "I told you trouble comes. Now you've really had it." She had the grin of a raven, beautiful, and he saw in her face his own destruction feeding on him and rising from the dust.

"Can't you get me loose from here?"

"I'm sorry, love, I can't do anything for you. It's your hang-up."

"Just loosen the knives so I can pull away."

"You're babbling. What knives? Don't be dumb. You broke down but that's never fatal. You'll recuperate, eventually." She returned to her station. What knives? He looked for them, but he couldn't see them either, but they held him, and he couldn't move. Milly Malt's cash register rang and rang and rang. He couldn't move and nothing was holding him. Nothing. He was afraid to go crazy, sweaty, licking the salt from his lips. Milly Malt's cash register rang and rang and rang. Bebo came by in spangles.

"Peter Prince, will you please finish up. I can't stand waiting any more."

The kitchen had suddenly closed and they were cleaning up, ignoring Peter Prince. He felt his weight bearing on the knifeblades, as if he were on a meat hook. The sweat from his forehead dripped into his eyes, burning them, making him cry, and he could see Bebo only faintly through his mist of tears.

"Come on," Bebo urged. "Let's get out of here." She was impatient to leave the damp kitchen because her hair, which she had teased earlier, was getting unruly.

"Can't you help me, Bebo, out of this predicament?"

"What predicament? You're so damned moody."

"Just help," he said. He felt pitiful, and confused, and embarrassed.

"Oh fuck it, Peter Prince, I'm going to go. I'll see you when you get ready to come out." She left him alone, and he stood there waiting to learn how to move again. They had mopped up around him, put everything away, and left him there in the antiseptic blue light they turned on at closing. He was alone, and he had stopped sweating. He stayed there, afraid, and counted to 52,943; then he decided to try to move an arm. It moved. A leg. It moved. His torso. It pulled away from the pillar. The reason he hadn't been able to move, he realized, was because he hadn't tried to move. It was simple as that.

By the time he had washed and changed almost everyone was gone from the Golden Mackerel gathering, and Bebo had already left, he was told. No one knew, for sure, where she had gone, but there were rumors of going to see cats. It was a kind of relief to Peter Prince that he didn't have to cope with Bebo right away, he felt light, as if he had more power than he needed, like a tugboat with its barges released. He had been through a failure, a defeat, he had not been able to face up to a challenge and it made him feel glorious. On his way back to the subway he dumped his black shoes, his black suspenders, his black cummerbund, his black garters, his polished buttons, (he kept the cuff-links), his starched red jacket into a trash basket. The last time he could remember feeling this good was when he didn't make his high school baseball team. To hell with it, he shouted, I'll go on relief.

The cleanliness of the Ma-Jo development struck him for the first time when he arrived that evening. It was pleasant. He walked beside the dim reflection of himself in the long window of the hallway and he saw through it the freshly painted wall. The reflection made him giddy outside the building, walking beside his own ghost, a transparency of himself beside him through which he could see the new decorations—one corner of the hallway, separated from the rest by a velvet rope, was a model sitting room, use prohibited to the tenants: a wavy mirror in a gilt frame, a few plastic, plushy straightback chairs around an imitation marble table top on a roughly gilt corrugated pinewood stand. A Canaletto reproduced: gondolas on the grand canal coming from the Rialto. He saw all this through his own reflection, and he liked it, the cheap emulation of foreign elegance. It filled him with a kind of gaiety and he kept repeating to himself, "I'm alive, after all."

"Wazah luh borboon kffit," the young, demented son of a tenant greeted him as he came through the entrance. The teen-agers were up late that night, with their portable radios on their ears.

He called Bebo's name as he entered the apartment but got no answer, though a light was on in the living room. He could see through her half-open door that Thwang-

Nuc was asleep, the light from the window reflected on her face a soft peaceful sheen. Bebo wasn't home, and he didn't see the baby-sitter; but under a light on the living-room couch a Negro man was reading. It was Bebo's husband. Peter Prince leaned on the entryway. The man saw him, and stood up, and backed around the side of the couch, and placed his left hand on the backrest. He was half in light. "I dismissed your baby-sitter when I got here. I'm waiting for Bebo." He took six steps to the wall and stood facing it, in darkness.

Peter Prince took four steps into the room and folded his arms across his chest, right over left. "I don't know where she is." He pivoted, took three steps, and pivoted again.

The man turned, took five steps toward Peter Prince, stood still and silent for three minutes, then lifted his left arm to point a finger at Peter Prince. He remained silent. Peter Prince moved around the upraised arm and back away from the man. When the chairseat rubbed the back of his legs he sat down. "Sit down," he said.

The man took eight steps diagonally across the room to a wooden rocker, decided he didn't want to sit in it, moved sideways five steps to the couch, and sat there, removing a book from under himself.

Peter Prince looked at him. It was the first time he had ever been able to examine Bebo's husband close up. He was surprised. He had expected someone thicker than himself, not this slender man, but a finger-snapping stud, something sweaty and sensational, not this fine-boned blackness, pink lipped, his voice tired and thin.

"You think I'm an ignorant, irresponsible black bastard

for leaving Bebo and the kid, but you make allowances for me because I'm a nigger.'' He let his right arm slide from the armrest and moved his left hand to his chin, touching it with three fingers.

"I never thought about that,'' said Peter Prince, he leaned forward from the waist, and placed his hands palm to palm in diving position.

"People tell you you're noble to take over this mess, and you probably expect from me some of the same recognition, the community opinion, since I'm called the cop-out in this case, but I won't . . .''

"I don't expect anything.'' Peter Prince extended, palm up, his empty hand, and raised it toward the ceiling.

"I won't because you're a white man.''

In three distinct motions Peter Prince rose, took nine steps to the window, and pressed his palms to the glass. The Negro rose too, arrived at the window in four steps, and put his right hand up to the glass, his left rested on the climatizer. They saw the lights snapping off all over the Ma-Jo development. They saw some cars on the highway. They saw planes leaving the city and arriving.

"You see I'm clean, because your guilt is so immense, white man, it washes the sin out of my desertion, and you're trapped in that guilt, and your guilt lasts forever.''

"I don't think . . .''

"I'm talking now, baby. It's your hour for silence. You see you know the weight of our flesh, and you're carrying it, tons of nigger-meat, and that makes us light. We move quick. Because that little yellow child, and you know it, could be my little sister that you hold on a pitch fork in the flames of the cross. You did that, over and over, and that's why you should be grateful that I copped out at all.''

Peter Prince turned from the window, took four steps to the couch, and leaned his belly on the backrest. The Negro moved two steps over at the window to where Peter Prince had been. They both pivoted to face each other.

"So don't expect this nigger to thank you." Left thumb to belt buckle, back of right hand to cover right kidney.

"I don't expect anybody to thank me." Right knee raised, left index finger inside shoe to scratch instep.

Right black index finger across pink lips. "Shhh. Keep your cool. I mean I understand why you'd want to move your complexion in on a darkie girl, to get all that passion." Black moves six steps toward couch, and leans on armrest.

Two white hands compress the air between themselves and a soft clap escapes. "Bebo isn't a, you know she's not a . . ." White stops talking without being interrupted. Black smiles, and scratches kinky hair with fingertips pinker than the backs of his hand.

"She isn't a nigger. Your powers of observation are a credit to your race. A credit to your race. To your race's credit. I enjoy saying that. But there's one thing you don't understand, or maybe aren't aware of; you see, the injection I gave her doesn't wear off, master. If I were you I would never let another nigger in my house."

White takes twenty-two steps to the refrigerator, and black takes eight to the rocking chair. Nineteen steps bring white back to the sideboard with two bottles of beer and two glasses. Black rocks. White pours one bottle into the glass on the right, the other bottle into the glass on the left. White takes two steps with the glass on the right and hands it to black. Six more white steps to the couch and white sits down.

"Why do you attack me?"

"What a display of corpuscles when you can call the truth an attack."

"I came to live here because I was fond of Thwang-Nuc."

"Simple as that."

"Simple as that."

"And I should polish your shoes for that simplicity."

"Why can't we talk to each other?"

"We are talking to each other."

"I mean as people. As people."

"We are talking as people. I'm black, you're white. That's people."

"I'm Peter Prince."

"I'm Coleman King."

"I want you to know me. Me."

"You're getting to know me, boy."

"But I know nothing."

"Bebo will get here, and she'll speak first either to you or to me. She'll look first either at you or at me. She'll want to ball either with you or with me. Black or White. The North Pole. The South Pole."

"Nothing."

At the laughter that followed Coleman King's last words Peter Prince rose and took five steps back to the window. It was nothing, and that was right. Venom over nothing, jealous over nothing, slogans to protest nothing,

Ma-Jo erected on nothing, the jetliners rising out of
nothing in the terminals—LaGuardia nothing, Idlewild
nothing—lifting their cargo of white bodies, no one,
going nowhere. The power defended, the power envied,
the power over nothing, which was the world, and what
was really there was the brink, always the edge on the
words, the beings in confrontation, their edges honed,
so many crowds rubbing along the razor's edge, generations in and out of nothing, of empty crowding, of the
noise-mass rising. He looked at Coleman King who was
rocking in the chair, and staring at nothing. He sat down
on the couch silent with Coleman King, and Peter Prince
stared at nothing.

He sat there all night sleeping like a bird with open eyes
and was awakened in the morning by the colored marching band practicing Sousa in the parking lot. The other
man was already gone, and Bebo hadn't yet come home.
He went to the child's bedroom to look at her for a
moment among the blankets. He loved to see her sleeping.
She was silent, she hadn't screamed all night, poor,
wounded child. Her face still held that strange sheen he
had noticed the evening before. Her burnt side was
exposed, the scar tissue shiny and stiff like wrinkled
ceramic. Something was different. He could hardly see her
breathing. He stared at her blanket to see it move just a
little in the blue shadows. The breathing was faint, if at
all. He touched her hand that was cold, the joints stiff.
Her face was covered by a fine, plastic membrane. Nothing. She didn't breathe at all. Peter Prince turned away to
the window where her room faced the repeated forms of
the rest of the Ma-Jo development. "No," he said, and

tried to tear the membrane from her face. It stuck to his hands like oil. It was a plastic cleaning bag (I told you to look out for that plastic cleaning bag). It tried to smother his arms. Nothing was there. She had been dead. Right. That was it. Nothing had come in a plastic sack and had roosted on her face.

*

"Ninety-four point three," said Philip Farrel.

"Both rectal and oral?" Linda Lawrence asked, sitting up with the sheet drawn to her chin.

"Both."

"Well," she chirped. "I guess it's alright. I guess everything's O.K. then."

"How can you say O.K., alright, can't you see what's going on?"

"It's normal, for me ninety-four point three is normal." She swung her feet down to sink them into the lavender fur of her slippers.

"Not that. I mean Peter Prince and the child, look what's happened there. How can you call everything O.K. with that going on?"

"Of course it's O.K.," she insisted, dropping a black slip over her head. "You're so gullible. If you look at things long enough and hard enough they're O.K. Just go back and read that section over, sentence by sentence. There are some nice sentences in it. What more do you want? Some nice style, some neat scenes. It's emotionally packed, but it's well written just the same. Read it some more. What do you have to worry about?'' She put out for herself her sequined yellow sheath and delicate narrow blue-gray, Italian suede shoes.

"I'm worried about Peter Prince. A few moments ago you were worried about Peter Prince yourself. How do you turn off so quickly?"

She did a small rotation on her vanity bench, holding poised in front of her face her eyebrush flecked with pale blue mascara. "It's not that I turned off, it's just that I know now."

"What do you mean, you know? What do you know?"

"I know that things will be alright because Peter Prince is leaving the country."

"When? How do you know this? When is he leaving the country?"

"In the next scene, you imbecile. He's leaving in the next scene. Don't you remember? It was written long before this last one. In fact it's been around to publishing houses, literary journals, Guggenheim foundations, long before Bebo was even thought of. It's archaic. In a sense you don't even have to worry about what's been happening so far, because as far as I can tell the story begins in the next scene. Of course if you're sick of the whole thing you can just walk out through Gottlieb's Exit on the next page, don't worry. You're free. As for Peter Prince, he's shipping out." Her last touch was the sparkle she sprayed in her hair, and she walked out through the door in a sputtering of sequins.

Philip Farrel waited till she left, and then turned around to gaze back through the pages he'd come. "Can't anybody do anything? Doesn't anybody have some control?'' he shouted down the mute, intractable corridors of sequence.

FROM
CREAMY AND DELICIOUS

Mythology: Diana

"**B**ecause Diana was the huntress, not the temptress," I replied. I forget what the question was. Anyway the ball on the 43-yard line in their own territory, fourth down, two yards to go, for most quarterbacks a kicking situation. For me a flick of the switch to another channel, and life or death in the soapy window. The machine is stuck—with an over-flow, and no change for another load. What to do? I got up in a flash and found another way through the closet where my winter outfit dangles. I had a date with my baby, I speculated. The sadness of my baby is ill-conceived, as is all primary emotion in our time. That suddenly caught me lonesome and I exited to the courtyard of our sanitarium where I loved to behold the birds when it wasn't raining. This time, the rain. I hid under the eaves by the window of Nelly Bloomgarden, the typhoid carrier, and was stopped dead in my tracks. She'd been in that room since 1897. I could see her through the barred window lying on her side and watching the TV a generous party had donated. She didn't like football. It was a first down with the ball on the thirty. How had they done it? The windup. The pitch. From behind a tree she tosses a mudball at me. "That's no way to do your hunting," I call, whoever she is. She's no temptress. I remember what he asked me now. He said, "What's the score?" That's a peculiar question to ask when the answer I gave was what I said at the outset. "The score?" The score is that nothing is happening in my heart, not even the action so familiar, you know, and one has to exercise those muscles to keep their tone. For a while I relax on the bus back, but when she has to get off she finds that I have closed my fist around the seat bar over her long and smelly hair. "Ouch. I missed my stop." She was sitting in front of me, unarmed, unfortunately, because I'd make a nice roast for her table. Why do they all make out she's a woman, anyway? Couldn't she be the great Jim Brown when she says to me, "Let's run off and get married just on the spur of the moment?" How do you answer a question like that without dropping her hair which my habit is to put in my mouth? We sprint off together like in the Musical Comedies and head right for a supermarket where we buy the aforementioned roast and by the time we're back at the place it's a marriage feast and we nibble on that. "Turn off the damn box," she says. "Are you a temptress or a huntress?" I ask. The ball has changed hands and those were on the offense who now are on the defense. It's time to go out and get blazing drunk, so I step to the threshold on my way and Blooey—I'm had in the arm in the back of the neck in the right loin. Next time you won't catch me marrying a you-know-what. The air is sharp and clear, the winds are crisp, the ground crunchy underfoot, a perfect day for the game. First, I hustle down to the market by the docks where beggars scoop fishscraps and I look around for a poor girl there because I want to fuck. Better to fuck a poor girl from the docks than a rich one who can afford weaponry. I dig one up covered with muck, the scales of carp stuck

in the dirt on her wrist and forearms, and I buy her from
her father for a song.

> *I'm sizing up your daughter*
> *Who lives here by the water*
> *I might save her from the slaughter*
> *When the other fishes caught her.*

And she delights me with some verses of her own:

> *One evening yet to come you will limp to the high*
>   *roof garden*
> *And bubbles from the lip of a peach will bust on*
>   *your sniffer.*

Ah, the twentieth century hustles by like a centipede, how
I love it, how we all behave in it as if it were the
twenty-first. Yes, it's exhilarating, it's a bulge in the flow
of events. All I need to do is turn my back and anything
will happen. It's happening now, but when I reverse my
field it will be too late. What happened? Well, I scrubbed
her with a hemp rag and she came out pretty and bright
as a nickel. When the medical student who lived below
us fell in love with her glands I released her to marry him.
"Be the huntress, not the temptress," I advised her; or
was it, "Be the temptress, not the huntress?" Anyway half
time was just over and I can't bear to hear a kick-off so I
turn down the sound and leave the glimmer. The air above
the atmosphere of the city is full of jets going South for
the winter. South. What a stupendous idea. I buy a
rucksack, Bicycle playing cards, a sackful of lotions, and

an automatic needle-threader, and head South myself, or rather with a free-living beauty I meet on the bum. We got to the beach and dropped into the water and lay around like cantaloupes getting tan. The girl was a bronze athletic type that you find sometimes on the beach and sometimes you don't. She met a Persian gymnast there and we all made love on a trampoline till I was out of the question. I looked at my watch and saw it ticking. "You're not a temptress," I said. "I'm a hunter," she said. I got out of there quick as a wink, arrows wobbling by, and to mine own self I was true. The game was finished, the final score 26-17, though I don't know who won, but those of you who know me realize it all adds up to forty-three, and so you've got it.

Mythology: Plastic Man

for Harry Rogan

Some people have all the money, some have all the luck, and some have all the brains, and those who have all three have luck, money and brains. I can't say it matters to me now because I'm too old, but for some people every door opens on wealth, fame or power and every road bends toward success. It's a good thing there is a different type of person too because I'm one of them, and that's a comfort. I can't say that I've had nothing, because I've had a bit; that is, I've lived this long and I've rarely been hungry, though I've been scared. The best thing to do is to keep moving, which I do, because then I don't have to pay rent, not that I mind paying rent if I like the place I'm at. I just don't like to pay it to Plastic Man, but that's the other end of the story, and we'll cross over to it when we've picked around a while on this end. I'm a prospector, you see, and that keeps me moving. I look for just about anything and sometimes I have a little bit of luck. That's not always so lucky, as you'll find out, as I found out too late in the game. At first it was just my "love of the great outdoors" and who cared if I found nothing or not? I was young. I could look time in the face and tell him to brush his teeth. I'd do it on foot, or take a horse and a couple of mules, stuff the packsaddles and go. I

could stay as long as I had grub, and then some. That living
went on for a while at a great rate, but whatever a guy is
doing, there always comes a time when he figures if he's
putting so much in he ought to be getting something out.
That was when I first began to see the sign on the desert.
I was crossing this wide, arid valley, nothing growing but
sage and tumbleweed, bronco grass, crested wheat,
chaparral, rabbit brush, mahoganies on the mountains,
willows in the canyons and chokecherry by the springs.
Suddenly a whole mountain sat in front of me that looked
heavy with minerals, sparkly outcroppings on it, and a
slide the color of doeskin. The sight of it yanked at my
feet and told them to step up. Then I saw the old sign
nailed to a wooden stake. It was quite faded, and looked
insignificant, so I didn't pay any attention to it though I
noticed it said: ALL THIS BELONGS TO PLASTIC MAN. I
thought that was amusing, probably put there by someone
with a sense of humor, who read comic books. I pushed
on into the hills and stooped at a spring to fill my water
bags and water my horse and my mule. When I cleared
the gravel off an old piece of tin that lay there in the spring
I noticed there was some printing on it, almost rusted out.
ALL THIS BELONGS TO PLASTIC MAN, it said. The
thought "perhaps this is a remnant of the ridiculous lost
city of Ult" crossed my mind, while the thought "This
isn't a Shoshone landmark" crossed it from the other
direction, leaving me without a thought. Nobody owned
that country, because nobody could need to own it, it was
so barren and so big. Hardly a road crossed it. Well, I
crossed the ridge and prospected for a few days and was
surprised to find, though I ranged pretty wide, that same

sign poking up here and there. I just went on with my prospecting. What I finally found was some outcroppings veined with high-grade cinnabar. I picked out some samples, staked three claims, and figured on heading for the assayer's and the land office in a couple of days. I'd take the sample and my map, get over the red tape, and come back as fast as I could. The morning I was to leave I took an early walk around my claims and noticed a fresh sign tacked up on each of the stakes. ALL THIS BELONGS TO PLASTIC MAN. Someone had come in the night, without my knowing it and had slapped up the signs. From where did they come? What did they mean by PLASTIC MAN? I decided to solve that mystery when I got back.

"Did you every hear about Plastic Man?" I asked at the land office. They looked at me as if I'd eaten locoweed.

"Did you ever see the signs he put up all over the desert out there?"

"Never been out there," said the land office man, and he looked for something in his drawer.

I registered the claims and took a couple of days to get rigged with powder, hand steels, fuse and grub and then I started back. I didn't expect I'd be leaving till the first signs of snow. It felt good when I saw again where I was going, like a home, except there was something peculiar about it, a kind of dull glitter from the distance, like a film of mucous over my claims. About a mile away my horse got jumpy and so did I, but not the mules, so we kept going. It seemed impossible. All three of my claims, from edge to edge, every rock, every bit of sagebrush was covered with a film of clear plastic so slick and hard even the mules couldn't get a footing on it. The big sign in the

middle said, ALL THIS BELONGS TO PLASTIC MAN. Well,
I thought, let's see. I figured I'd drill a hole to blast the
plastic out of there, but my hand steel wouldn't even
scratch the surface. I put five sticks of powder on the
surface with a two-minute fuse and took shelter down the
hill. I still don't know what happened to the grub, my
horse, the rest of my outfit, or to the plastic. I never woke
up till I don't know when and after I did I wasn't
anywhere I knew about. It was brand new, whatever it
was, and it smelled like a room, and was slick and slippery
wherever you touched it, and I was inside. Pretty soon a
piece of it pulled open like a door and a man in a gummy
suit told me that I had to get ready to meet Plastic Man.
He was in a bigger one of those chambers with softer walls
and everything there had the special glitter my claims had
before I lost them. Plastic Man was bent over like a U bolt
stuck in the ground. "Why is he bent over like that?" I
asked a man in a gummy suit. "Plastic Man can't straighten
up," he said. I sized up that situation and then asked for
an iron, a heating pad, or anything hot. While he went to
get it I rolled up my sleeves. Plastic Man didn't seem to
be in pain. He winked at me between his legs like the son
of a bitch that he was. "You see what happens when
you're made of plastic," he said. They brought me a kind
of heated rolling pin, and I began immediately to roll it
over his back. Pretty soon he straightened out just like a
bean sprout, and he wrapped each of his arms around me
three times as if he couldn't have straightened out himself
if he had wanted to. He apologized for what he had done
to my claims but told me I should have read the signs. I
told him I did read the signs, but that I didn't believe in

Plastic Man, so I paid them no mind. He laughed at that and asked if I believed in Plastic Man now. I laughed at that. We chatted for a while over fancy sardine sandwiches and lemonade and then he could see I was getting ready to mosey on. "Here you are, have a glittering trinket for your glove compartment," he said, handing me a glittering trinket. "There is no glove compartment on my mule," I answered. "Well, keep it for an hour, then give it to your kids." He shook my hand.

"Why don't you," he said, just before I moseyed along, "go in with me fifty-fifty on developing that property. Fifty-fifty."

"Thanks, Stretch," I said. "But no thanks." And maybe that was my big mistake, but I didn't want to have anything, nothing, to do with Plastic Man. "I'll just be on my way. I'll mosey along." Now, he didn't try to stop me from moseying, but since then things have never been the same. I keep moving but everywhere I go, far or wide, there's a sign that says, ALL THIS BELONGS TO PLASTIC MAN. Every little prospect I try to develop never works out anymore. He doesn't cover my claims with plastic like he used to, but this is what happens. Usually when I'm ready to put in my first round I suddenly feel his long arms wrap around me—gently—and I'm back having some fancy sandwiches and a Pepsi and the same conversation with Plastic Man. I don't know if he'll every give up, but it's nothing doing for me. I'm not one of those. So I keep moving because I don't want to pay the rent to Plastic Man, and though it can't possibly ever come out right, I hope to edge out of it some day.

Mythology: Hermes

The Head Librarian said he was a whiz. Hermes was the swiftest page in the stacks, who could remove a book for you almost before the request was in. And could he ever read. He finished a volume quicker than most people learned how to swim. Back in the old days they used to call him Hermes because he was like quicksilver, and one of the reasons was that he didn't eat. He didn't eat so much his girl friend got fat worrying about the leftovers, and it got so that Hermes could circle her forty-three times walking from his house to hers, whereas in the old days he could circle her only forty-three times, too, seeing how she got wider but also walked slower. Most living creatures on the face of the earth were no match for Hermes. They dropped dead of exhaustion, including the fabled Winnemucca centipede. Some people knew that he could outrun Swift Old Death, because Hermes was so old, but so was his girl friend, and she couldn't run at all. Some day maybe all the best stories of Hermes can be told, but you can't keep up with them they happen so fast. There is at least one that most deserves the telling, a story the Head Librarian likes to recount, and that story is still the one we'll tell, as soon as we get around to it. Hermes' girl friend was as slow as he was fast, and that was why she couldn't get him fed, but it wasn't her fault, because the only chance the girl had was when he fell asleep and he could get a good night's sleep in the blink of an eye, while the girl friend had hardly begun to stir the pudding, and she liked to lick the spoon. For all everybody knew Hermes could have eaten just the same, quicker than anyone else could see. The grub in and out so quick it never had a chance to change color; he just skimmed off the nutrition and left the rest on the table. That probably explains why everyone got slower while Hermes is always quicker. He can steal something, use it up, and return it in better-than-new condition between the time the owner decides to use it and goes to the closet to get it. He once stole a whole church picnic, hustled it over to feed a batch of Orientals, and got it back clean and empty so quick the church elders believed they must have already eaten it themselves. They rubbed their stomachs, packed up, and went home to watch the war on color TV.

The best story is still the one the Head Librarian tells, which we are coming to eventually. It was because of him, you remember, that automation never came to our library. That was the time they got up for us one of the slickest, quickest, prettiest IBM automatic book retrievers that ever read a book spine. It had blinking lights and buttons and I don't know what all, and it made the noise of a sweetheart. Hermes didn't care one bit. He just warmed up by running from here to Bogalusa, to Winnipeg, and back here, while most of us were eating breakfast. They brought down from the university one of the smartest men you ever wanted to see, one of those young, fresh ones with soft hair on his cheeks and two pair of glasses. You could see that there were the names of more books in his head than people who swim for pleasure. Everybody turned out, and they threw up a huge grandstand, and they sold lime juice in plastic cups. It was something. The professor with that bland academic sneer on his face looked at Hermes, who wasn't much to see, and signaled he was ready to begin. They plugged in their IBM beauty till it puckered up and started to blink like an army division looking for its contact lenses in an olympic-sized chlorinated pool. The pretty lady, whom we'll call the operator, signaled GO. It wasn't even a contest. Hermes took one look at the professor coming to the counter, disappeared, and reappeared almost immediately with seven books, just as the professor handed the request card to the operator (who wasn't a bad twist herself). Six of the books were those six written on the card, but when the professor saw the seventh his face turned yellow and then bright orange, his tongue went dry, and his eyeballs whirled in their sockets.

"This is absolutely remarkable, commendable, and straight-A work," he snorted. "This book is one I've had an interlibrary urgent search-and-find slip on for two years now." He reached over to shake Hermes' hand but grabbed only a slim puff of wind. Hermes' girl was bobbing up and down in a wobbly celebration. Everyone cheered, but no one was surprised, because everyone knew that Hermes could outrun even Swift Old Death, running him so fast through our town that he'd have to quit, and sit down on the outskirts, panting, and more often than no pass the people by. But the best story is the one the Head Librarian tells, which we'll come to present-ly, if not now, one which she tells to children from the porch of the huge old building that used to be the library, which faces our brand new blinker and hummer called The Information Central, that no one ever enters. It's the story of the great library fire, and how it happened, though no one knows how it began, but things have never been the same. It was Hermes, who is as quick with his nose as he is with his feet, who first smelled the smoke, and he speeded through the stacks to find the fire extinguishers, but the one on the first floor was empty, and on the second, and the third the same. The flames followed Hermes like a blaze through dry brush. On the seventh floor he found the only full one and spun around with the foam spewing to hit the Head Librarian flush. Well, I guess this story isn't so good, the usual silly slapstick from here on, and it's not worth telling again, and it has been so long since I rose up and told a story that I forgot. Goodby.

Mythology: Wonder Woman

Wonder Woman was a dike, but she was nice. If she hadn't been a dike she might have been nice, but she wouldn't have been Wonder Woman, and vice-versa. Of all the interesting stories about Wonder Woman, the most delightful is the tale of how she ended the war in Vietnam. When she started to end it it wasn't over but when she was through it was finished. Except nobody believed a dike could end the war. They went on killing like the bunch of rowdies they believed in. Finally everybody was crowded into the bloodshed till there was no one left on earth except Wonder Woman and one slow-moving little squirt with asthma. She met him on the road, where you meet everyone these days in case of emergency. He was trying to push his car uphill at a total stalemate when Wonder Woman surprised him.

"What's the big idea, buster," she intoned.

The car slid backwards into a warehouse of surplus feathers. "I'm not very anxious," he said.

"You're the last man here on earth so you should be bawling your ass off."

"You too should be weeping, for you are the last woman on earth as far as is imaginable." He leaned on the shoulder of the freeway.

"If you want to have the straight goop, I'm Wonder Woman, the dike." She blew on her wristlets. "But why do you insist on pushing around that old jalopy, when here for the asking are all these Cadillacs and Chaparrals?"

"My analyst is dead," he roared.

"Just hop in and drive one of them away, and don't bother me."

"There's no place I want to go. It's death, death, everywhere death. All the people are dead as doornails. I never thought I'd live to see the day."

"At least the traffic is light. Haw Haw." Wonder Woman fixed her comb and prepared to leave.

"I guess I could drive East through Canada. I always wanted to drive East through Canada, and why not? It's a beautiful country and a friendly place. Thank you for the wonderful idea, Wonder Woman." He reached a long arm out and dragged himself over to a solid blue Mercedes 300 and tipped out the ex-driver. The motor gurgled when he hit the switch.

Wonder Woman split for elsewhere. She visited the hangouts of her old consorts: Cynthia the Sphincter was dead, as were Julie and Fatty and Leslie the Mars Bar. She went to Pittsburgh. She headed for Santa Cruz. She got to Albany. She hit Moose Jaw. She stopped in Philly. She took in New York City. She crossed to Budapest. Copenhagen was empty. Damascus was empty. Kuala Lumpur was through. The little wheezer had been right. She journeyed to New Delhi. She hit Kyoto in the spring. She left for Singapore. She hustled to Djakarta. They all were dead. Everyone was dead. She decided to take in a movie. Best of all was a revival of the old blue whisker comedies, which she took in with a cup of buttered popcorn that tasted disturbingly fresh. Without her cohorts she fell into a fit of depression. Then she saw an airplane overhead and shot it down in her excitement. Luckily there was nobody aboard except for one newspaper. The flyer read TALK BUYS MUD FLACK and the headlines, REVERSE PUMP MURTY. The mention of Pump Murty kept Wonder Woman's chin up. "So," she thought. "Even at the end the old guy could wrap a rice patch."* Then she fell into a fit of depression. All around her heavy machinery was hanging out as if it had a contract to work. "For naught. For naught. For naught," she sighed and then hopped onto a Caterpillar D8 and started pushing everything aside until she uncovered the remains of a familiar solid blue Mercedes. She rolled it over and over down a side street. Poor little guy. "Fuck ambition," she screamed, standing up and waving her arms around. Suddenly the bulldozer veered out of control into a huge man-made wall which toppled on top of her knocking her for a loop, and squooshing her down in a pit or depression. When she came to she wasn't herself but was being cared for by a slowpoke with asthma. "There now," he said. "You had quite a seizure."

"Where am I?" Wonder Woman queried. "And what kind of special clothing is this?"

"You are Wonder Woman, the last dike on earth," said the slow one. "Admired and esteemed by the whole

---

*   special dike talk or professional dyke jargon

world, which is me.''

"Chubby chance of that, you handsome stud, you fistful of nuts,'' and she threw her weakened arms around his neck. He mopped her lecherous brow with droplets from a nearby rivulet. She began to sigh and swivel. He worked on her clothes with a hacksaw till they fell apart like a shutter. He was staring at the last cunt on earth. He untied from his leg the last cock on earth and when she saw it she sizzled. "Do something filthy dirty right away.''

"But you're Wonder Woman, the dike,'' he slobbered, holding his cock at arm's length. Just then she passed a sonorous and intoxicating flatus that drugged them into an ecstatic embrace, pumping and sucking like it was the end of the world. He wondered if she was still Wonder Woman if she wasn't a dike, but was so nice. She cooked his dinner and mended his sock and then they started to have babies, and the babies they had were made of gold.

Mythology: Thomas

A man there was called Thomas who in the aged long ago time before I was a boy was the man of many creatures, a many-creatured man in the hills before my youth of which one, and there was only one in the park across the street where there were no apple trees, no bushelfuls of apples to tumble to our baskets, though we held them up into the hushed evenings of hope when we were hopeless in the spring of asphalt freshets, and the earth abounded beneath it, we thought, and sang all hours of artichokes and pomegranates, quinces and loquats, though we had none, nor could we sing where the sun in the air like smoked crystal coughed, and the rivulets rippled through our Springmaid, chamber-tossed apartment and lapped against our father at his pinochle in the kitchen, who never saw him, who never would, our Thomas, where he stood in the windfall autumn light presaging school, which we dreaded as the vulture dreads the fountain of youth, when youth will go on forever until it becomes commonplace across the street to see kids, who can understand but will never care for the golden arguments of Thomas with his tedious assignment, for the tedium of youth is long enough to misconstrue when God is around, within, above, about, beneath and before us, in every marble, in every penny we illegally pitch, and he's under the steps, and in the bottle of Absorbine Jr. and

has forsaken his flock to come play with our championship sleepers and we called him, "Thomas," and he said,
"Hold your breath for a minute." He turned up his Zenith
to catch the score.

"Three up," he said. "Bottom of the sixth."

Maybe we had Thomas all wrong. Every week, after we
got our allowances, we'd sit around with him playing
draw poker and he'd tell us how he killed a man once and
served fourteen years of it, and how he'd do it again if he
had fourteen more years. He had more than that, though
we weren't smart enough to tell him. We were delighted
because he was the only guy we knew who had ever
murdered another guy, and we begged him to do it again,
but he was embarrassed. "Shut up, you shrimps," he'd
say and pretend to listen to the ball game while he skinned
us, but we didn't mind, because we were youths, and then
we grew up, and then he said he'd kill us, so we made out
we were kids again and played poker with him against our
better judgment. This time Billy won and Thomas pulled
a knife, but Billy had a zip gun and he killed Thomas, and
that's how Billy got his transistor radio which doesn't
work any more.

Well, to shorten this long story about Thomas let me
sum up: Ray quit school first and joined the Marines: Billy
disappeared and nobody ever heard from him again; Tony
went to college and became a science teacher; Andy has
got himself a line of girls and is socking it away; Tish got
a job as a runner on Wall Street and became a broker; John
Blue works in a machine shop; Phil is a junkie; Jack
Schneider drives a cab; Albert played Double-A ball for a
while but was too small and now works as a coach; Rico

became a pharmacist and still lives with his mother; Quinlan got a job down on Madison Avenue, but he's a faggot; Bert writes books; Rosey and Deuce run a filling station; Hubby has got a bunch of kids and works downtown at two jobs; nobody knows what happened to Plooky; Rosemarie was always one of the boys, and still is; Flynn went out West but now he's back and hangs out at the same bar his dad did; Milt owns a hardware store; Archie works in an office and fishes on weekends; Nick is happy as a dentist; Roger, Dan, Solly, Schultz and Norris all went nuts; you still see Powers around, but nobody knows what he does. I guess that's all, except for my gang, but this story is about Thomas.

A few weeks later Thomas shows up just when everybody thinks he's dead, and this time he's got a great big fur coat to wear with his beard and long hair. A few years later he asks me a question. "What happened to that kid Billy? He's got my radio." I tell him that I don't know, because Billy just disappeared and was never heard from again. Just then Billy shows up and Thomas pulls a knife and threatens to kill him if he doesn't give back the radio. "It's my radio in the first place," he says. But Billy's got a billy club and he beats Thomas across the side of his head and when he's down he takes the knife away and sticks him and then pushes his face in just for kicks so he's dead and then Billy disappears and is never heard from again. We all chip in to buy Thomas a good funeral with a big box, because he's the biggest man we know, and wanted to be buried with his coat on because he never really wore it enough.

When the war came everybody and his buddy enlisted

because we figured it was up to us to preserve our way of life so our kids would have it in the years to come, except Hubby didn't go because he had too many kids, so he went to work in a munitions factory that blew up and he died. Most of the gang died in the war including me, but first I have to finish this story.

On the next week after the war Thomas came back and everyone cried to see him because how come they died and he could come back afterwards? The neighborhood hadn't changed much except the Puerto Ricans were moving in and out so fast it scared the Germans. Everyone went to eat Chinks in Chinatown a lot and ordered the number three dinner for four. There were six of them. "I wish I knew what happened to Billy," Thomas said. "That kid who got my transistor radio that time." It couldn't have mattered much because he had a brand new shortwave transistor set he had heisted somewhere, and even one of those crystal sets we always played with when we were kids. Then Billy came back for good with the broken radio and he gave it back to Thomas and they both laughed. They have a lot in common now. They both listen to the radio a lot and you know it's them when you hear "Har, Har, Har," from Thomas. Billy says, "That kills me." They slap their knees and they slap each other's knees. Thomas has shaved and he cut his hair, but he's the same old Thomas. The old neighborhood seems just the same, otherwise. The guys stand in front of the candy store with Lennie the bookie, and Frenchy got a job as a soda jerk.

Mythology: Nasser

There was a small unshaven man in Jerusalem called
Nasser who worked at a cafe inside the Damascus
Gate. He carried cherry-red coals to your hooka when you
smoked. His clothes were a simple black smock tied with
a piece of rope around the middle, a black, gold-
embroidered skullcap and worn slippers. "War is ugly,
but peace is lovely," he shouted when he approached to
take your order. He kept your smoke bubbling through
the water by bringing his coals when yours were dim.
Though he always sounded angry, he wasn't, and would
get you tea or coffee, or whatever else you wanted when
you asked for it. He plays no more part in this saga.

Tim hiccuped and looked up at the apples. Applesauce
was a delicacy he admired more than trout, and that was
why he had decided not to fish long ago, though he always
carried a spear gun. He went to the carnival instead, a
rural affair with ostrich races, where he got twenty-five
big points. He hoped somebody was making a ladder. All
the sky was blue as Windex. Tim came to a shoddy stall
where a small unshaven man was selling rummage. Who
was this man and where did he come from and how did
he get to rural America? "Get out," said Tim. "Get out
and make room for a husky grownup." Tim examined the
goods and found what he wanted for the apple season: a
black smock, a rope belt, a black, gold-embroidered

skullcap. They weren't for sale. "Get out of here," said Tim, but the man didn't budge. "It's almost apple season." When the small man persisted Tim pierced his neck with a spear and now Tim plays no more part in this saga.

"War is lovely," said General Gon to his wife, who didn't like to cook and was stingy with oranges. "Only when you are winning, and you are always winning." A man in worn slippers entered with a pan of cherry-red coals for the General's pipe. Who, why and whence? He winked at the General's wife, who followed him out the door. The General smashed his wife's stringed instrument with a treacherous war trophy.

"I asked you never to do that," the wife piped up in the doorway.

"Now you'll spend more time strumming your instrument," mumbled General Gon.

Late that night a man in a black smock tied with a rope belt entered the General's sleeping chamber with a gold-embroidered black skullcap full of napalm with which he buttered the body of General Gon, and now General Gon plays no more part in this saga.

"I don't get those hawks," said Moriarity to his three-month-old son. "They've been up to that all day. Look at the way they dive down and rip out clumps of grass and carry it way up there and then drop it on each other like kids having a dirt fight. Who's ever seen hawks at play before?"

"Jeepers, Dad," said the child. "Your eyes are sharpissimo."

From around the corner of First Avenue and Forty-sixth Street Kagowitz appeared with his child in a perambulator.

"Slow down, Dad," said the child. "There's my connection."

The Kagowitz child was small and unshaven, and he started to shout, though of course he wasn't angry. Both fathers were gazing at the fabulous New York Grasshawks. The infant tied up with a stroller strap and his connection pulled a syringe from his plastic duck and now both the Moriarity and Kagowitz families are booted out of this saga and won't play a part in any other saga until they show some self-control.

It was Harry's giddiest job and a new experience, piloting a skywriter. On the ground he had a lousy handwriting, but in the air he was the most legible of them all. That's how he landed the position, though his Peace Corps record wasn't sweet and his dossier showed too many petitions signed. Could he spell? That was the unanswered dilemma in the minds of his superiors. Harry thought he could, but didn't know what would happen in a pinch. This was it. He was desperate and traumatized, in the midst of the worst identity crisis of the season. He cruised out over the city as if it were a suburb. "War," he embroidered on the atmospheric fabric, "is homely; but peace . . ." That's all he wrote. He bailed out like a punctuation, and too bad he disappeared, because there is a lot more he could do in this saga.

"Holey Moley," said Vincent, and he threw his gold-embroidered black skullcap at the wall. "I don't get it." He was a promising young violinist.

"What's there not to get?" Noland the potential literary critic, inquired.

"This work. This saga. It's goofy." He rent his black

smock to shreds and formed the rope belt into a noose.

"Give me a crack at it." Noland swaggered over to the desk.

"That's enough reading for me," said Vincent as he shoved the books into Noland's mitts. "I'm going to waste my time watching the boob tube from here on out."

Nolan read with the long hunger of a genuine book-worm until his cheeks were cherry-red. When he finally looked up there was an expression of nausea on his puss. "Why this is nothing but a . . ."

He never played a part in this saga, nor will he ever play a part in any other saga.

Mythology: Dickens

66 It used to be, 'hands off the blues and the yellows, Martha.' And I didn't think that was so bad, but things have turned for the worst since then and they aren't any better, not even at lunchtime. I can't spell any more. My heart feels like it's three inches above my head, and the elevator doesn't even work. I never started, and he expects me to stop, so what's the use? Work and work and he gets home and clobbers everything with his blundering personality which couldn't dope out a nuance if it was slapped in his face. What sounds do words make? Go on. He tells me to go on and points his finger and expects me to hop on it. Maybe for him it's easy when he does his breathing exercises and the rhythm cycle he bought when I can't afford a cup of hot chocolate. He calls me his trained flea just because it itches when I go by. I feel like a whore out of it. In the mirror I say to myself, 'You whore,' and then I relax and dress up funny. But he hasn't shown a puff of affection since six days ago last Wednesday a month. Is this what you call reality? The butt end of my string is on its way, so help me. Help me.''

Dickens stared through her at the wall behind which was covered with glowing wrappers, and he chortled deep and slow. She clutched her rucksack and sat with her mouth ajar because it was impressive to see him in the flesh. Many weary miles over the prickly deserts over the marshy swamps over the horny mountains she had made her pilgrimage to confer with the Dickens. Others went by jet or boat or train or used the special Dickens bus service, and no one found it disappointing. His cave, first of all, wasn't of the commonplace natural type found elsewhere, but it was a glittering artificial he had come upon in those years he had been wandering the wastes and wilderness. It was well preserved in what must have been a sprawling city of the ancients, near a huge body of water that is unexplored because still radiating. Strange monuments stand in the region as testimony to whatnot, and those who dare to dig can find things. This all sounds to the average person like hocus-pocus science fiction, but it's the realistic truth as far as can be told, and it's the mystery that makes it such hot stuff. People have come for generations in time of trial to see the Dickens.

The Dickens squinted at the woman over his quill, the plume of which he twisted in his bonelike fingers, and he rubbed his pointy chin and plucked a hair from his ear which grew like thistle-fur. He placed this along with the ingredients the woman had brought in the imitation stone lamp. Then he dipped the quill and made a few entries in his ledger. The woman closed her eyes, better to soak in what he was about to say. "Just look for the silver lining, whenever clouds appear into view," he said cryptically. He lit the offering in the lamp and the room filled with the sound of ukeleles. Dickens took the woman's hand, placed it on his desk, and rapped the knuckles seven times with a ruler he took from the scabbard at his side. She then asked him for his last words and he drew in a deep breath that seemed to be his last, and his boney cheeks turned the color of Nebraska on the map. "Pack your coat," his voice creaked, "and get your hat, leave your worries on the doorstep." He swooped into a trance as he spoke. "Just direct your feet, to the sunny side of the street. Tell no one what I have said here," he admonished her, as he does everyone.

The woman left the Dickens with a new lease on life. She did everything carefully according to his instructions, and died three years later of a peptic ulcer, though happily not in midwinter as she had always feared, but on a glorious summer day when she was swimming and had been dragged under by the lecher of the deep, a turn of fate for which she thanked the Dickens eternally.

Dickens signaled for the next pilgrim and hacked consumptively into a blue handkerchief.

". . . black warts on his neck and none on mine . . . turn a page, he turns it back . . . I don't drink but he's always polluted . . . and at sleep he'll be nibbling on my ear because he's homosexual and I'm not."

The Dickens stared through the two-headed man at the wall behind, and he chortled deep and slow. The two-headed man sat back with his mouths ajar and clutched their rucksack. The Dickens went through the usual ritual as if it were for the first time. "Just look for the silver lining whenever clouds appear into view," he intoned. "And remember that two heads are better than one."

The two-headed man guffawed with laughters. The Dickens made a last entry in his ledger, and then stood up straight looking angry. Then he pulled off his smock, revealing the creamy breasts of a young woman and a blushing abdomen. He lifted his face off as if it were a rubber mask, revealing such a perfect creature you would think this was a different story. Dickens then stepped out from behind his (her) desk and took the arm of the two-headed man and headed naked as a piglet down Hollywood Boulevard without even a toodleoo for the staff. "What the Dickens," they cried. The nude Dickens was immediately discovered by an ensorcelled talent scout and made into a star overnight. "Goodby, reading public," was the last entry in the ledger.

Mythology: Sampson

The phony politician eyed the cruel landlord who bought off the cop but the fishy columnist was able to obscure the plot of the rotten practitioner who wiped his filthy tongs on the thigh of the oppressive strawboss's syphilitic mistress who had told the crooked dealer that the jig was up so the sly administrator could pack his embezzled fortune and board the plane which was high-jacked by a sadistic colonel who had conspired with the perverted scientists that now rule the world. Tactless Sampson solved his problem by emptying his pockets. The trials of Hercules were child's play for such a nitwit as he made himself out to be. There was enough to run a store in those pockets, and he made good use of it. He only feared that someone would interrupt his reading. He preferred books, but the caustic temptress had suddenly appeared from nowhere. Had she been hired by the conspiracy of charlatans? "Yes," she said. "I am your sexpot." He lifted his arms in the nick of time and leaped from the cliff in a graceful swan-dive and sliced the water like a knife through hot butter. The three intrepid hoodlums followed him on their bikes and the motors sizzled when they hit the lake. He did three hundred yards under water and came up on an enormous deserted sandy beach where there was no one to see him for miles except a huge woman in a black tank suit beneath a green awning who sucked on a leaky persimmon. She gazed out to sea. Sampson gulped and gripped the sand, fatigue rippling his massive thews. Not a thought ambled through the teeming brain. Were those voices he heard in the underbrush? Overhead enemy search-planes carefully combed the area with their devil-may-care pilots. Sampson's strength slowly percolated back through his sinews. He parted the underbrush and beheld strangely painted people with awful rituals. They ate pastries. Sampson whipped out a camera and snapped a rare photo before a young brave rushed over to tell him to knock it off. Now they had him. They poked his gut with their nightsticks and tied him to a camel and dragged him to the office.

"They like to call you Sampson," said the big Prince. Slowly Sampson began to perceive where he was. It was a small yellow anteroom in a larger blue anteroom in a wing of a castle surrounded by a moat full of high-voltage eels high on a promontory overlooking a glassy plain. The man he was facing sat on a throne of nibbled balsam.

"What do you want of Sampson?" Sampson gagged.

The Prince chortled and tugged a silken purple cord. Down the hall a man in kilts flipped open a latch and whispered to an inner guard who hurried down a stairway to where a stone wall could be rubbed so as to reveal a lengthy chain which a splendid Nubian could wrap around a pulley, turning it with a tremendous clank as the portcullis rose revealing a carpeted foyer in which a dark eunuch stood oiling his belly. The eunuch tiptoed over to apartment 3-A and knocked. When the woman answered he whispered to her and she immediately looked in the phone book under D. The elevator was coming fast.

"The labors of Hercules were just up your alley, you tactless nitwit," the Prince intoned.

"I always read books," Sampson wobbled a tricep.

"Well I want you should meet someone, since you're such a nice boy."

A woman entered, curtseyed, pivoted, lifted her skirts, tossed her hair back, smiled coyly, blushed like a virgin, swung her perfect hip and extended her hand that was as white as all get out.

"Sampson, I want you to meet Miss D.; Miss D., Sampson."

Goodness, Sampson thought, this is a day for déjà vu.

"*Ciao*," Miss. D. murmured.

It took smelling salts to keep Sampson from passing out with desire, he found Miss D. so intoxicating.

"O.K.," said Miss D., as she leaned over him in her boudoir where the discs spun like dervishes on her turntables and her breasts smelled like cardamon. His sweetmeats were trembling. "But no French kissing till you brush your teeth." Sampson straightened up like an icepick. Never once had he ever brushed his teeth, or anything resembling dental hygienics. "Never once have I ever brushed my teeth," he said.

The revelation hit Miss D. like a shot from the blue. "But they're stuffed with grimy, smutty gunk," she said sincerely.

Sampson gazed at her with resignation written from top to bottom. Must I reveal it again? he thought. Is a French kiss worth a power failure? Will my secret never be safe? Miss D. wriggled like a voluptuous owl.

"It's in the teeth," Sampson confessed. "That's where

it is. Everything I've got in my cruddy teeth."

"You're putting me on."

"It's right there." He let loose such a filthy smile that Miss D. fell back in agony. She immediately hurried out to her unscrupulous cohorts and immediately hurried back with an uncivilized plot. She came topless to the couch of languishing Sampson. His enormous musculature quivered like a melting table-top. She sat on his massive lap and he saw her open mouth as her face drew near and he winked as if at his buddies because he was rounding second and headed for third. Their lips plunged together and from behind her lower jaw she nudged a capsule into his mouth with her tongue. One feel of the ticklish little tip and Sampson was out. He came to in the dentist's office. "Didn't hurt," said the dentist. "Never does." Sampson swaggered to a mirror, and then paid for the cleaning at the receptionist's desk and took the abortionist's elevator to the street. It sure was refreshing. The rain stopped immediately and with the sun came a new lease on life. He took three steps at a time whenever he could.

"Sampson. Sampson," the voice of the choirboy chimed in from across the street.

"Howdy," said Sampson.

"You're just in time," said the well-trained voice.

"I always am," said Sampson, and he put his fist through the window of a nearby shop and heisted the pocket-watch he had been admiring for weeks.

"Your fist is bleeding," said the voice.

"Just my hand," said Sampson.

"You were right on time," said the voice.

"Trust me," said Sampson, and he lofted the pocket-watch over the huge cupola and stepped off the curb into the perpetual darkness of the endless night.

Mythology: Homer

Homer was a writer par excellence. He could write in midstream where others would have to paddle. He could write spread-eagled or upside down or skinning the cat. He could write a poem with both eyes shut. He could write like the wind. He was an all-around writer of the old school, with a pinch of the new school thrown in. The kids wrote in his senior yearbook that here was a man who was supposed to be top rung. The writings he wrote in his teens would shame a man in his twenties. Almost at the drop of a bucket he wrote ten books. Their titles were: FRIED CUCUMBERS, BUTCHERED CARROTS, PRESSED WEENIES, WATERED ALMONDS, BOILED PERSIMMONS, TORTURED MUSH, MIXED CHOPS, FAITHFUL OKRA, RINSED MELONS, AND THANKS. He wrote so fast he hardly had time to help himself until he suddenly noticed that all the editors were saying, "No dice," and he realized it was up to him, so he printed up seven thousand copies of a book he called THREE SQUARE MEALS A DAY LEADS TO HAPPINESS AND HEALTH AND OTHER STORIES, but they all burned up in a distillery fire, except for the one his Uncle Ted stole. The writings Homer wrote in his twenties would shame a man in his thirties. Soon all the editors sat up and took notice, and they accepted a brand new novel of his called CRUNCHY. Unfortunately he left the manuscript in a briefcase on a train and never found out where it got off. The editors decided that his reconstruction of the manuscript had no zest and canceled his contract and in that period he wrote his two gloomiest books: SPUN SUGAR and FLAKES OVER THE ORANGE PIT. At the former the editors turned up their noses, and they said thumbs down to the latter. Homer decided then he was running out of luck, and his case was the one on which the new regulation about writers is based, that the law immediately publish the first three books of any new writer until he turns famous and relaxes; then he is told to improve. Homer might have been born too soon, but the writings he wrote in his thirties would shame a man in his forties. Too bad he had to become a daredevil pilot.

As a pilot he was a real daredevil because he couldn't figure how to navigate. Words were his specialty and he didn't know many numbers. South south east suggested to him the titles of three new novels which were called LOQUAT, THE NOISE OF THE PRICKLY PEAR, and TAP ON THE MAPLE, and he wouldn't put the plane down anywhere till the three books were thoroughly mapped out in his brain. That made him a daredevil pilot, especially when he landed blind on the enemy landing strip in the midst of confusion and was hustled immediately to headquarters, where he swiped a ream of paper and started to write. He never looked up once despite the vicious threats, but through thick and thin got well into the second narrative by the time the air strip fell back into friendly hands that all applauded him, but it was too late because the enemy had already swiped the manuscript and they published it immediately, disguised under the title of

SMALL FRUIT. Homer, flushed by sudden success, defected immediately, but you have to realize that the writing he wrote in his forties would shame a man in his fifties. After he learned the new language and understood that for them he would have to write books like POTATO, SOUP, CARROT, BREAD, he realized that the enemy wasn't his bag and stowed away on a freighter to a little South Sea island where he lived for many years without a care in the world among brownish folks who couldn't read. He scraped his stories on the rocks and carved them on the trees. There was where he invented the characters for which he is most beloved today: Blotio, Mercopaylayadine, and everybody's favorite, Ellipsedos. Many of us have memorized passages from the sublime ELLIPSIDOTE by heart these days: ''Spurning the leaden wave-crush they planted their oars like onion sets in the loamy sea, and plugged in to the purple night of Starnadine to once in the end confront the blushing Terror of the Deep. The hearts of the men were heavy as pan bread when the woman turns her back on the oven and lets the dough sit too long, causing it to fall again, so it won't rise in the baking, in the pan, to produce the light fluffy crusts of bread for which the islanders are notorious, for which they lick their chops.'' Passages like these, so rich in tender figures, in the peculiar metabolic metaphor such as ''blushing terror'' typical of the late Homer, and the last remarkable extension of image where his genius runs rampant, combining the emotions of men with old-fashioned home cooking are what we love him best for and is why we say that the things he wrote in his fifties would shame a man in his sixties. The life of utter pleasure paled on him after a time so he decided to head for home where he could settle the old scores. He found there that a younger generation was entrenched writing new novels called BUST THE FROZEN SPINACH, COUNTDOWN TO GRAPEFRUIT and ELECTRONIC LEMON PUCKER, exhibiting evidence of his influence, though his work was unknown to the people. He got the cold shoulder when he asked around what was up because he was such an old-timer, except for Mary True who fell in love with him though she was only seventeen. She went to live with him in a styrofoam hut on the beach while he wrote his penultimate oeuvre which he called BLUE FIGS BLACK FIGS YELLOW FIGS PINK FIGS MAUVE FIGS GREEN FIGS PUCE FIGS OCHRE FIGS AND THE PORTABLE CHAIN SAW. Everybody sat up and took notice and embarrassed Mary True, who left him for a dock worker, breaking his heart and shearing ten years off his life. She now lives with two weight lifters in Spokane. With his final, most complex, most revealing and least palatable book, LURD CHOMP, he became a beloved author, and we say of him today that the things he wrote in his seventies would shame a man in his twenty-fives.

FROM *SAW*

Leroy

Eileen grabs a subway and heads for Van Cortlandt Park. What a park. Anything you want is there. Cricket. Lacrosse. Ladies' softball. "So enjoy yourself," mumbles Eileen, as she slides to a seat near the mucky window. The woman in the seat by the door reads the *New York Times*. Eileen hates that newspaper and all its contents. The pup she has hidden under her sweatshirt is wiggling. "Nice pup you got there, lady," says a black kid, edging toward her along the seats. He is wearing a baseball uniform, and The Marvels is the name of his team. "I've got no puppy here," Eileen replies, knowing pups are illegal on the subway.

The kid sends some gestures and winks back to his teammates at the other end of the car. "You've sure got something that whines and wiggles like a puppy under there."

Eileen ignores the kid. The IRT rumbles on down the track and busts into daylight, heading for the Bronx. The boy tries to pet the hidden pup with his first baseman's mitt. "I told you there is no puppy under there," Eileen insists, turning aside and looking hard out the window. Flat-topped buildings stick up all over the little hills of the Bronx. "If you don't got no puppy in there," says the kid, "with all that whining and whomping around in there, then you something boss, lady; you got the jivingest jugs in the world.'' The kid goes back to his teammates and they slap each other's palms and roll baseballs up their arms.

Eileen sets the puppy free in the park, and it yerps with joy. The sun is good and hot. She slips out of her sweatshirt and strolls up the paths toward granite cliffs and bushes. Her tight bell-bottom jeans make her feel free at the ankles, and her purple jersey polo shirt grazes the nipples of her small, braless bosom. She feels giddy and loose. The little pup jumps at her and scampers around and growls: a lively white and black beagle crossbreed pup with a warm tongue. High above them the sun lights the wings of a hawk that glides in wide circles on the air currents, not a twitch but for its head that flicks from side to side. Van Cortlandt Park, in New York City, is most famous for its hawks. They hunt there for pigeons and squirrels and other small stuff running on the rocky slopes. They swoop down on baseballs. They snatch the caps of nurses. A sandwich isn't safe. Eileen steps across the grass, skirts the baseball diamonds, keeps one eye peeled for the circling hawk. She heads for a point of seclusion and comfort up in the rocks. The sun is strong; the wind, fresh. Jet streams crosshatch the sky. Hawk lazes in his circles overhead, casual enough to make us foolhardy. Eileen pauses high on a rock to gaze south at Manhattan poking up through the smog. The city is a dumb bunch of things, she thinks, so filthy and crunchy in its thick sauce. Then she hears the puppy squeal as the big hawk yanks it off the ground in its talons. ''Good boy,'' she says, and salutes the hawk who carries the pup to the top of some rocks.

Below her some stoned-out people swallow handfuls of pebbles for kicks. She certainly could never be one of them, nor one of any group she ever knew about. That was why she came to New York. She stretches her back out on a flat stone and a lovely depression floats down to settle around her like a heap of leaves. "Whatever my life is," she whispers into her mood, "nothing I do will ever add up to anything. No accounting. It's all for the moment, for the good moments. I'll never get to a conclusion. I won't reach a climax."

Hawk drops down softly to a fallen limb by her knee. "Thanks a million," it says. Eileen sits up. A bit of puppy gristle clings to the hook of the beak. "It sure is swell of you to keep on bringing me those tender pups. They make me feel so good. A hawk in New York is like a fish out of water these days. No eats here. Everything comes frozen or in cans."

Eileen smiles. "It's because I'm an Aquarius. My friend Corinne at the office is a Virgo, and she thinks what I do is hideous. But I don't balk at the law of tooth and fang. I tell my friends to feed the hawks and they think I'm a freak. I mean I believe violence is your predicament. It's in your nature. Once you make a hawk into a friend you can begin to understand him."

"I like you a whole lot, lady," says the hawk. "Otherwise I would let you know how stupid you are, because you are stupid. Violence is not even a word. We're up there for the circling, making circles, that's where it's at."

"Maybe that's true, but I want to tell you something." Eileen is enthusiastic. "I really need to blow up the *New York Times*. Everyone would be much better off if it were a bunch of cinders. And then maybe some TV networks. Get rid of all of them. But it's the *Times* that's my biggest nemesis. Everybody reads it and stuffs his head full of information. What good is information to the people? All it does is prevent me from becoming an adventuress.''

''Forget those half-assed ideas. I tell you, if human beings could learn to fly in circles of their own volition, life would be calm for them and information would fall away, and meaning would fall away, and wisdom would follow them like a stream of song. You humans are really out to lunch. There is no such thing as adventure.''

''You yourself told me that the hunting was bad.''

''Listen carefully. You're a nitwit. Hunting isn't worth the prey of a mantis in my estimation. It's not what you get. It's not the catch. It's the circling itself, those long arcs you can make without creaking a wing. I mean I like my food, lady, but that's not—''

''You should call me Eileen.''

''Okay, Eileen. But there's nothing the matter with it if I don't eat. It's my least care. Usually one gets something to eat, and if he doesn't he just keeps circling and circling into the most exquisite dreams. Those are the circles I make, and those circles are my life, which is the moving circle of my horizon as I fly, which makes me harmonious with my world, the sphere. And the Earth arcs around the sun, and the universe warps out forever. I know all that. I didn't have to study mathematics. Eileen, my dearest human friend, you live in a box, and that's why you always get those headaches.'' With that final remark the hawk stretches his wings and a few powerful sweeps bear him aloft.

So she gets headaches, how does a hawk understand that? He gets into the air easily, and that's admirable, but what he has to say is just so much hawk breath. So she gets headaches. What does a hawk know about aspirin and the even more potent remedies? Pills are little circles in themselves. So what? Take all your hawk theories along with all your man theories and put them in orbit and what have you got? Solar garbage. What she still wants to do is burn down the *New York Times*. Hawks make easy assumptions about human life without ever pausing in their circles to examine the complexities. If she were shaped like a wheel things would be different.

Eileen strolls on the paths around the baseball diamonds. This is the first really "good" day of the year and she knows that something extraordinary is about to happen to her. If this were not LEROY but was instead a cheap movie that featured her, she could expect to make a stop at some storefront fortune teller on Second Avenue and have the old fraud read from a crystal ball, or from the tarot, or from the stars, or her palm, that she is obliged that day to meet a remarkable and confusing stranger. What a bore on a day so warm and sunny to be constrained to have conversations with someone remarkable, and lot of superstitious nonsense anyway. Such hocus-pocus impresses the faint of heart, people who walk into lampposts and sit on wet park benches. All she wants to happen is something that keeps her from ever going back to her job again, that persistent nibbling just below the heart she has to call her "work." She loves to lie in the sun. She could be a professional lizard. Work is a stupid idea, a desiccating poison that people in this darkest of dark ages inflict on themselves.

"Hey lady, where's your pup?" The Marvels are on the playing field she passes, warming up for a game with the incomparable New York Bullets. "A hawk snatched it," she shouts back. "Right on, lady. We play The Hawks next Saturday." She feels something observing her. The boys toss around last year's baseballs, wrapped in black electrician's tape. They shag flies, do some pepper drill, practice sliding, bunting, learn to chew tobacco. Something is moving in the bushes, like a cloud. She heads for some flat rocks she knows about where she can lie down with her belly to the sun and no one will see her. There's a rumbling noise somewhere, like a jet plane, but it seems to be on the ground. She rises through some sumacs, some scruffy willows, some sycamores, and arrives at her flat place where the sun heats up her belly when she slips off her shirt and stretches out. She yawns, and almost dozes. Jets in great profusion rise above her belly from Kennedy, La Guardia and Newark, dropping poisonous smoke. She hears something else, like a large metal wheel cracking the gravel. "Who is it?" She pulls her shirt down. A big sphere rolls her way over the flat rocks. It's as high as she is, and full of a milky iridescence that looks like life. This is the most remarkable thing that has ever happened to her, and then the sphere begins to speak.

"I could have been quieter, but I was afraid that would alarm you completely. I've been gathering mushrooms."

"I'll bet you have," says Eileen.

"This time of year the morels pop up all over, and I know a spot that's just chock full of them. Nobody gets there before me. The month of May is so nice, just because of my favorite mushrooms."

The sphere makes Eileen smile. Almost immediately she forgets the fact that it's nothing but some big geometry with a voice. "You've got no way to pick mushrooms. You haven't any hands," she observes.

Waves of crimson, like a smoky blush, drift through the sphere's interior, and he says, softly, "You would notice something like that right off. We all have limitations, but perhaps you noticed that I said 'gathered,' not 'picked.' It's a question of semantics."

Eileen sits there stymied for a moment beside the sphere. City noises rise in her ears. She doesn't understand what is going on. Here she is in an extraordinary situation and she reacts no more than as if she were bored by it. She's numb. A chill descends in her and she looks at the sphere and wishes it had some arms to throw around her immediately and comfort her. "I'm terrible company," she whispers. "I have so little to say."

"Don't let it bug you," says the sphere, rocking back and forth. "You get through to me without words. Conversation went out with the trolley car and the glass milk bottle, anyway." The sphere rolls a little closer to Eileen, as if to get more intimate. "Back then I used to talk all the time. I used to make predictions, like a clairvoyant, and I liked to tell them to people; for instance, my basic prediction was that in 1965 southern Japan and the Philippines were to sink in an horrendous earthquake that would give birth to seven new chains of populous islands. California was to rise twelve feet higher out of the sea, causing a man named F. Scott Fitzgerald (not the writer) to become fabulously wealthy from the treasures he finds heaved up on the extended shore by his modest beach house. How do you like that?''

"None of that ever came true, did it?"

"No. Of course not. But that was only part of it. Listen to this. The Galapagos were supposed to pop off the Earth like a cork and spin into orbit, shattering the moon and causing a dispersal of satellite fragments that would orbit the Earth like one of Saturn's rings. Half of the Pacific would flow into the hole left by the Galapagos. South America would stretch out. Atlantis rediscovered. The hollow Earth theory proved correct. Within the Earth such pressures would build up that geysers funnel out all over the globe: Poughkeepsie, Tel Aviv, Kuznetsk, La Paz, Oslo, Christchurch—everywhere—a thousand feet into the air, spewing out quantities of strange steamed artifacts, whose use couldn't be known on the surface but which clearly must be the product of some form of intelligent life inhabiting the center of the globe."

"That's it." Eileen points a finger at the sphere. "You're from the center of the earth."

"You're right as rain. Very smart," says the sphere. "I left to escape the cataclysm, and also to see if the rumors of intelligent life on the outer surface were true."

"Were they?"

"Partially true, as far as I can tell. A lot of coquetry, willfulness, anger, and confusion. How about this prediction: By 1970 every city was going to have moving sidewalks, so nobody would have to walk to the store unless he wanted to get there twice as fast, and other people would get about on what looked like jet-propelled pogo sticks, making densely populated areas look like popcorn machines.''

"That didn't come true either.''

"Nope. But I predict that Mao Tse-tung and Chiang Kai-shek will be dead by 1985.''

Eileen smiles. "There's a chance on that one, anyway. But I'm really more interested in you. Do you have parents in there? What are they like?''

"Of course I do. They're just some parents. Authoritarian. Rigid. Dense. My father was a pyramid and my mother was rhomboid. The last thing they expected to have was a sphere, and they had no idea how to cope with me. As soon as I could roll off on my own I put distance between us.''

"Don't you ever have a hankering to return to the center of the Earth, to be with your own kind?''

"Rarely. I don't think that way. I am my own kind. I prefer isolation. It amuses me to be out here, and there are mushrooms, like little friends. The little fellows grow on the inner surface as well, you know. I guess they grow in pairs.'' The sphere starts slowly rolling up the hill, and Eileen follows. "But let me finish giving you my major prediction. You see, that catastrophe was supposed to wipe out most of the population of the U.S., leaving only teamsters and athletes to pick up the pieces, with some high-ranking military. They start again through a tribal system. They remember only sixteen letters of their alphabet, rendering the three books they find hermetically sealed in a capsule less than useless. *The Best of Broadway: 1954, Aion* by C. G. Jung, and *Born to Raise Hell*, a study of Richard Speck, the mass murderer, are the books. None of this came true, however, Does it bother you to hang out with a sphere whose predictions don't come true?"

"Of course it doesn't." Such a gentle presence is the sphere she walks beside. Variations of color that she imagines her eyes invent appear in its interior as it speaks. She strokes its surface affectionately and it quivers like a membrane. "No sphere has ever spoken with me before."

"Isn't that odd," says the sphere. "And you, what were your parents?"

"Just poor Midwestern people. My mother was pretty and my father handsome. I inherited their looks, for whatever it's worth. I lead a stupid life. I'm nobody."

"If you are nobody, what am I? Just geometry in your world. No body."

"I'm sorry," says Eileen, blushing deeply. "That was a dippy thing to say."

They come to the top of the hill and the sphere stops. "Amazing," it says. "Remarkable."

"What is?" Eileen looks around.

"Your city. Look at the way that Manhattan has disappeared down there. It has disappeared. That's miraculous." The sphere spins with excitement. "You know, one of my predictions was that Manhattan would disappear in the late sixties or early seventies. I predicted that it would dissolve in its own air and wash away, and now look. It's gone. My prediction has come true and I'm so happy. You are my good luck charm."

The sphere is right. Manhattan does seem to have disappeared, though she knows it isn't gone for good. Just a storm has swaddled it in clouds, rushing in off the Atlantic and sending a thick tongue up the Harlem River towards the Bronx. "That's just the rain on the city. You can hear thunder."

"Oh thunder. Right. Rain. There's always some damned explanation. I'm still not used to it here. Well, the rain can have Manhattan, damn it. I'm wrong again."

"I would have been quite upset," says Eileen, "had Manhattan actually disappeared. I would have been left without anything. Not even a friend."

"Well, then I'm glad my prediction didn't come true. To hell with it. I won't make any more. But I still think something is going to happen, and I'd like to know what it is."

"I predict we'll get soaked if we stay here," says Eileen, getting back into her sweatshirt.

"I don't get wet," says the sphere. "I can be impermeable."

"Maybe I sound fussy, but I'll get soaked and chilled, and I just got over a cold. I'm going to get to the subway before it rains."

"I even like the fresh water on my surface," the sphere says.

Eileen feels reluctant to leave the sphere. She knows the encounter will seem another of her daydreams once several hours have passed. She wants to touch it some more and to hear it talk. "Please . . . umh . . ." she finds the words difficult to release. "Please come home with me to my apartment if you want."

The sphere bounces around in place as if it has been bobbled. "I was hoping you would ask me to come. I haven't seen many interiors."

Eileen strokes the sphere with both her hands. "Well,"

she says. "One doesn't often find a sphere in the park she feels she can invite to her home."

Eileen loves the people of her adopted city. If she turned up with a sphere in her hometown of Swisher, Iowa, the whole population would call her a Communist Hippie Beatnik and they would never have a minute's privacy, but here she gets only a few glances over the shoulders from New Yorkers who shrug. Eileen is actually the only one who pays attention to her unusual escort. She gets a sense of vertigo from its rolling motion, because she imagines it continually turning its head over and getting dizzy. That clearly isn't the case. The mental parts, where the senses are, from which it communicates, is probably at the very center where she guesses it is soft, but the surface is tough, though she notices it can vary its texture for her touch, changing from soft to slick to plush to rigid. What a companion it is for her hands. She still feels dizzy with it, like a little girl doing cartwheel after cartwheel on the lawn. The sphere pops up and settles on the seat opposite her and remains there despite the jolting of the IRT.

"How do you stay up there?" she asks.

"Stay up where?"

"On the seat, when the subway jerks? You look like you should just roll off."

"I never think about it," says the sphere. "I have no reason to roll off, so I don't roll off, but I can understand why you wonder about it. When I first started living on the surface I used to wonder how you kept balanced on those two posts. I kept expecting you to fall off, but you never did."

Eileen's life seems as if she is finally having the experiences she bargained for. Spicy. If the sphere, once they get home, makes a pass at her, well, that is what she has come to New York for, to get away from the humdrum routines of monotonous Midwestern life. They get off at 79th Street and Broadway and walk the few blocks north to her apartment, under a sky that is clearing as fast as it has clouded up, the smell of ozone, the washed air, the sunlight flying down on glowing buildings. Her little apartment house is wet and luminous.

"You taking such a thing with you to your apartment?" asks the lady with a little yellow dog, that Eileen frequently greets on the street. "To your apartment? You must have a big apartment."

"It's coming home with me like a friend."

"What should it be?" The old woman slips on her glasses. "What kind of a thing do you call that?"

"This is my friend, the sphere, Mrs. . . ."

"Lubell. Mrs. Lubell, mother of Harry Lubell the TV producer. So what is this, anyway? Is this what you kids start to see from squirting the mayonnaise into your veins?"

"I'm hardly a kid, Mrs. Lubell."

"I didn't mean you, darling. But those kids, they get these hypodermics and then they jab themselves with cranberry juice and chloroform. Who knows what else? There's one of them in my house and what he sees is a special thing."

"Well, you see this sphere, don't you?"

"I don't see nothing. Don't ask me what I see. You're better off if you don't see nothing these days."

Though it's too wide for the doorways the sphere fits through each one as if it doesn't exist. It pauses by the sill of her apartment as she switches on some lights. "I've never spent any time in one of these interiors before," the sphere says. Eileen is suddenly embarrassed. The place isn't herself. She has never done the decoration she always promised. The dead walls are covered with a dog-eared poster of Lenny Bruce, a dull batik hanging, a picture of the Rolling Stones. Nothing herself. The sphere moves around, humming and glowing like a detective's device, then it pauses before a little fishbowl full of brightly colored transparent marbles. "This is just amazing," it says. "If you had these where I come from you'd be locked up." The sphere stops moving and talking. Silence rushes in on them, separating them with the random noise of the building at dinner time. Eileen chews up some bread and cheese she has brought from the kitchen. The sphere seems to be watching her. It rolls onto the coffee table and amuses itself by balancing on the edge. It must be taking some account of how she has fitted out her life, and she doesn't know how to explain that this place isn't what she really is, but just a way station, a watering hole she was stopping at on her journey to wherever. She begins in the silence to feel the panic of losing contact. Nothing is right. Her own apartment is unreal, like the lair of a hibernating beast. She shuts her eyes for a moment and feels herself rolling over and over, as if the sphere has got into her. "Don't you ever feel peculiar?" she says, when she opens her eyes. "I mean you're here on the surface of the Earth, where you don't belong, without friends, or hope of anyone to understand you."

"That makes little sense to me." The voice of the sphere projects a calm that slows her uneasiness. "Everything I do is interesting to me. I have everything I need. I have myself. I don't stay still."

"I am . . . I have nothing," Eileen says slowly, wholeheartedly, as if she is blowing a great weight off her tongue. "You're so lucky not to be made of this flesh. All I feel in myself is an endless dissolution, like I'm run through with nematodes and being carried away from myself in little nibbles, off into a void. I know despair is fatuous, but every face you look at is destroyed by troubles, and behind those troubles lies an abyss. You're lucky just to be a visitor. Nothing is strong enough to hold me together. I don't even know what I'm talking about, and why I say it to a sphere. What are you, or what am I for that matter? If there were another world I'd like to go there and try it for myself, because I don't sit very easy in this one. I want to know some whole people, but there just don't seem to be any. Just nerve bunches, like transmitters running with shapes inflicting pain. Everyone is suffering, and it's like that suffering is a skyscraper built around us in our sleep and only a certain dream we can never have in this life will remove it. I'm so unsettled. I need to blow up the *New York Times*. I need to go away. My friends talk revolution. The only revolution can be a breakthrough to what's real. I care about that. Something durable has to come clear. What's to become of us? I feel something supreme and horrible is happening on the Earth, and we will be excluded. Flesh. How did you ever get into my house, you roly-poly? This must sound so stupid to you. It's like car horns. People talk like honking taxis. Honk. Out of my way. Blast. This is ridiculous to a sphere. I don't know what I talk about. I just want to find any other world, someplace calmer. I want space to unload, anywhere. You find me tiresome."

The sphere rolls toward her till it is touching her and it moves around her softly grazing her clothes. "You get so serious," it says. "Just relax. You should laugh a lot. Flesh is flesh. It's like the air. Some day you'll get along without it but for now there is no way to step outside, because it's inside of you. You have it and it has you, like a lover, or a talent. Relax. There's nothing to resist." The sphere keeps rubbing her while he makes gentle philosophy. She begins to feel sexy. Perhaps the sphere is just handing her a line, she thinks, and wants only to get her into bed. She feels a pleasant tingling all over her skin. It can't be just a sphere of philosophy that makes her feel this way. The doubts and troubles she has fetched from deep within are slowly displaced by a round, rising dreamlike motion in herself. "You . . . you touch me like . . . like this," she says.

"You need to be touched. I know that," says the sphere. "Those feelings reach me quicker than words. Perhaps through the language understanding may grow, but knowledge descends through touch alone."

"I know what you are," Eileen says lightly. "You're a spherical make-out artist, playing out a line for me."

"A line?"

"It makes no difference. Forget about it. Did you ever make love to a human woman before?"

"In the park once I made love, if that's what you call it, but that was long ago and I think it was a young human male."

"You think it was a 'young human male.' What are you, a female?"

"Of course not. I'm a sphere, as you see me."

"A queer sphere," Eileen claps her hand over her mouth. "You would do it with men or women."

"Of course I'd 'do it' with men or women, or with dogs."

"With dogs?"

"They seem to be everybody's favorite. In the park you see men with men, women with women. You see everybody with dogs."

"Golly," Eileen blushes. "Sometimes I forget I'm just a hayseed girl from Swisher, Iowa, but it's true. My friend, Lester Stueval, used to talk about doing it with young sows. He was far out." Eileen begins to circle the sphere. The sexiness she feels is uncontrollable, but nothing sticks out on the sphere, nothing to grab or stroke. Its surface slowly changes texture in the most pleasing way, and as she strokes it she feels mild electricity flowing just under her skin. She starts it rolling toward her bedroom, her excitement whetted by questions that stroke her mind: How can this sphere penetrate her? Would she call it sex with a sphere? If her experience were ever jotted down by a writer, could it be called pornography by the millions?

Once in the bedroom she quickly undresses, a strange activity before a sphere, who seems to get naked from within, its most intimate substances seeping to the surface. The skin is so inadequate, she thinks, in order to be genuinely naked she would have to remove it. The sphere rolls toward her and she spreads her arms as it touches her. "Do something," she says.

"I want to," says the sphere. "You're so sweet and gorgeous."

Her body feels shot through with refreshing, vital warmth, and she swoons backward onto the floor, but something soft breaks her fall. The sphere rolls up and down her body in a perfect, gentle massage, slowly intensifying its action and making her feel covered head to toe with a warm, satiny fabric, and all her bones feel as if they have been turned loose in her muscles and rolled down a hill. Suddenly the sphere seems to be not only on top of her but under her also, rolling in two directions at once. She feels a minute massaging just under her skin, and begins to let out little shudders of sighs and screams, and she suddenly feels safe inside the sphere rolling over and over down a long hill picking up speed like a juggernaut in ecstasy. She opens her eyes on the marvelous incandescence of the room generated by the sphere who is setting itself off in pale vermilion bubbles toward the ceiling. In a moment her eyes close again and she falls asleep and continues to talk with the sphere in a dream. "Have you ever been in love?" she asks. "What is love?" it responds. "Have you ever been hungry?" "What is hungry?" "Have you ever been tired?" "What is tired?" "Have you ever been angry?" "What is angry?" "Have you ever thought of marriage?" "What is marriage?" "Have you ever had the religious experience?" "What is experience?" In the dream Eileen and the sphere circulate in empty space, and they never touch, though they resemble each other, and Eileen feels closer to the sphere than she has ever felt to father or lover.

By morning the sphere has fled but Eileen isn't disappointed. She feels permanently changed, lifted like a wing off the planet onto another realm. She is curious to go outside and see what it is all about again. A fringed buck-skin miniskirt, a yellow silk tasseled blouse, thin-strapped high-heeled Italian sandals, a lime-green silk scarf around her neck, in the mirror she looks too appealing to hit the street. She feels divine. Out she goes. A rare crisp morning after a night of rain has clarified the air. The people take long strides or short quick steps with dogs bounding at their sides. No one looks lazy. Up and down Broadway troops of colorful people walk their dogs and whistle. Eileen heads north, thinking of something to buy. She has left her purse at home with no money in it. Old people walk their Pomeranians and Schnauzers. Pretty girls heel their German Shepherds. Hookers walk their Doberman Pinschers. Drag Queens strut with Great Danes. Elegant ladies with Afghan and Borzoi. Chummy animals, all of them, and full of teeth which they bare at Eileen because they hate her. Eileen has already taken her step off the Earth and she drifts up Broadway, sexy and vulnerable. They look her over, the stoned young couples, the old women in loose cotton dresses, the young men from behind their shades. They're like snipers. They're wallflowers taking tithes from her skin. How glad she is to have left behind this life of sinister presences, this uptown Broadway hanging out, this looking through sunglasses, this weather. She is being followed. Seven blocks and the same male behind her. What could she want now with a male? A confusing pursuit. She walks more quickly and he continues to get closer. He is just behind her. She can hear his clothes. She turns around.

"I am The Astronaut," he says. He is a small, handsome man.

"What's your reason for following me? I have nothing for you."

"Now that I am here you no longer can be the main character of LEROY."

Eileen is startled by such a twist, though not upset. She has no ambitions to be the main character of anything. Now that the sphere has changed her life she would prefer more time to herself. Her sphere is gone forever, she realizes, and she feels ready to weep. "What do you mean by that?" she asks.

"Don't let it trouble you. I am here now and must replace you as the protagonist of LEROY."

Since she has come to New York City, Eileen muses, each thing that happens to her has been stranger than the last. "If this is true, what do I do now?"

"You do what you please. You may leave, or remain in LEROY as a secondary personage. I should like to see you from time to time."

"How do you know this is what happens?" Eileen asks.

"I have the ability to read ahead."

"Why do you claim that you are The Astronaut?"

"That's who I am. There hasn't been space yet to explain how it happens that I am, but I am always The Astronaut."

"I guess it's quite simple and clear-cut, except that before you take over I'd like to ask you to help me with one thing."

"Certainly," says The Astronaut. "As long as we can take care of it on this page."

"I still need to blow up the *New York Times*."

"That will be no problem," says The Astronaut. Eileen is jubilant. She shoves her arm through his and they head for the downtown IRT. Forty-three minutes later the *New York Times* is a heap of rubble.

FROM *MOVING PARTS*

Parcel Of Wrists

In this morning's mail I received a parcel postmarked from Irondale, Tennessee. It was wrapped in heavy, glazed brown paper, like thick butcher paper. The box was of even dimensions, two feet high, two feet deep, three feet long, and it was packed from top to bottom with human wrists.

The wrists were clean and odorless. They had been prepared so neatly, without a trace of torn flesh, that it occurred to me they might never have been attached to hand or forearm. I held one for a moment in the palm of my hand, a small one that might have belonged to a child or a frail girl. It seemed to flex itself there slightly, perhaps in reaction to the warmth of my hand, as if the person to whom the wrist could have belonged were just beginning to wake up. I put the wrist back in the box, closed it, and went downstairs to the luncheonette to get some breakfast and mull over the strange detour my life had taken as a result of my opening the morning mail.

For breakfast I had a toasted bagel with what in New York City they call a "shmear" of cream cheese, a glass of fresh orange juice, and a cup of coffee, regular. I kept repeating to myself the phrase, "parcel of wrists." I could say it rapidly ten times, without a slip. I also said "box of wrists," "carton of wrists," "package of wrists," "shipment of wrists," "bundle of wrists." I am often prone to distractions. I sometimes read twenty books at a time. I leave them at different locations in my apartment so that I have something to read wherever I pause. I don't concentrate. I don't usually focus well. What I noticed at this moment, however, was that I was absolutely locked in on the problem of "wrist." The word kept firing in my mind like a spark plug. I had been instantaneously and profoundly affected, and I realized that before I could return my life to normal I would have to find the answer to the question of the wrists. I decided to go to Irondale, Tennessee.

I invested first in twenty-five pounds of topsoil, and buried each of the wrists in a flowerpot. There were forty-three pots in all. That I had been sent an odd number made the whole matter seem even more curious. The pots took up a good third of one room of my small two-room apartment; in fact, it had become so crowded in my home that I was glad for the opportunity to get away for a while, out into the country. I tore the return address and postmark off the wrapping paper. C. Routs, Irondale, Tennessee, was the return address, printed rather carefully. I packed a change of clothes, grabbed my sheepskin coat, and left. It was October. The leaves were probably turning. It always seems to me one of the unaccountable luxuries of this hideous second half of our century to be able to take trips on one's unemployment compensation.

I hitched to Washington, D.C., looked around for half a day, and was happy to leave. I took the Greyhound to Nashville, Tennessee. I picked Nashville even though I have never looked at a map of Tennessee, and have no idea what's close to Irondale; but what other alternatives

were there? I just couldn't conceive of myself in Knoxville, and Memphis has the sound of a place to raise a
family, whereas Nashville seems like a place you can go
to, look around at it, and leave again. Until recently I never
had much love for country music, but I thought it would
be delightful to step off the bus into the heart of the
country sound. Not so. Not a murmur of it. A dreary bus
station. Blue walls. Years of piss stench. Drunks prodded
by police in starched uniforms. I consulted a map under
a piece of dirty glass on the wall.

"Irondale?" said the man at the ticket window. "Now
you've got a problem there." He looked me over once
and then went back to studying his tally sheet.

"I need a ticket to Irondale, Tennessee," I repeated.

The man put down his pencil, and smiled, and
scratched his nose, and shook his head, and looked at me.
"There is no such place as Irondale, Tennessee."

His accent made me realize I was in the South. I hadn't
been thinking about going south, what that meant. The
map in the bus station showed Tennessee to be just north
of Mississippi, Alabama, and Georgia; what most New
Yorkers assume is enemy territory. There was no Irondale, Tennessee, on the map. I didn't know what my next
move would be. Generous hospitality and sheer brutality
were the two polarities I had stored among my Northern
preconceptions of the South. I wanted to make no friends
and intimidate no one: utter neutrality was my goal. For
that reason I went to a barber shop as soon as I left the
bus station, and since that shave I have not grown back
my beard.

Vincent D'Ambrogio was the barber's name. It was strange to meet an Italian with a Nashville accent. "You're 'bout number three fer the day."

"Number three what?"

"Number three longhair I clipped. They all come to Nashville to git their hairs clipped."

"Say," I asked, after a pause. "Did you ever hear of Irondale, Tennessee?"

Without hesitation the barber said he had.

"Where is it?" I asked.

"It's in West Virginia. Irondale, West Virginia."

The postmark on the wrapper clearly indicated Irondale, Tennessee. I wasn't about to go to west Virginia. I stopped at a filling station before I found myself a room to get a Tennessee road map. The attendant had a St. Louis station on full blast, Johnny Paycheck singing:

There are things to do in Knoxville
There are things to do in Nashville
And Rock City is a place you ought to see;
But if you want to visit my town
You won't find it on the road map,
I can't say much for Heartbreak, Tennessee.

"Yew want to buy that Mustang sits out there?" the attendant asked, pointing at a yellow car. "It's a running machine."

"No."

"Don't have a car, do yer?"

"No."

"You sure could use that Mustang."

As soon as I hit my bed I fell asleep, with the map of Tennessee unfolded on my face. When I woke up there was still no Irondale on the map, though I did find an Iron Hill, west of Nashville, and Iron City, southwest, on the Alabama border. I decided to go to Iron Hill first.

"You don't want to go there. Ain't nothin' there." The ticket agent at the wicket of the Louisville and Nashville line was myopic and leaned far over his counter to try to see me. "Passenger train goes through but once a day on the way to Blondy and Hohenwald."

"That's were I'm going," I noticed I was starting to pick up the accent.

"Well go ahead, then; but you're going nowhere." He leaned back in his seat, fiddled with some papers, and in a few moments handed me a ticket, a long, elaborately franked piece of paper that guaranteed my transportation forty miles from Nashville to Iron Hill.

He was right. There was nothing at Iron Hill. It was a water stop. Just a tower. No buildings. An unimpressive hill with some sparse growth and a rusty outcropping of rock that probably gave the place its name. I climbed to the top of it. The land flattened out to the west, and was dotted with sharecroppers' shacks. Cotton country. It was hazy and warm and I was sweating. I didn't know when another train was coming through. I sat down under an old pawpaw and watched the leaves fall around me. Wild peanuts were dying on the hillside. I guess I dozed off because the next thing I remember is the sound of giggling kids and the pressure of some small hands on my shoulders. Three of them, waking me up; a boy and twin girls. I don't remember their names any more.

"You want to come home with me?" asks the little boy.

I look up and down the railroad track. There is no sign of a train. "Do you know when the next train comes through for Nashville?"

"When you hear a whistle, that's a train," says one little girl, and her twin sister cups her hands over her mouth and whistles a long, mournful tone, that if I were not observing her do it I would think the train was already upon us.

They said nothing more, but silently led me through the woods for about two miles into a complex of buildings like a small factory complex from the turn of the century, built of bricks and wood. The children disappeared behind some buildings and left me there, in sort of the center of things. People appeared in windows, on porches, from around corners. They had stopped their business to look at me. None of them was armed. I wasn't afraid.

I realized I had been led into the heart of a flourishing commune. Everyone looked extraordinarily healthy. The women's faces shined under their bandannas, their breasts pushed out around the bibs of their overalls. The men were all bearded, longhaired, and vigorous, and made me feel strange in my new state of hairlessness. The kids who led me here had taken off all their clothes and were hiding behind some grown-ups. A short, robust man, wearing a railroader's hat and carrying a clipboard under his arm stepped off the porch of the main building and approached me. His face was red under his beard. He was all business. I was smiling, but he wasn't.

"If you want to stay, you'll have to work. Your first twenty hours a week give you the privileges of room and board. After that you get credit at the commissary." He pointed at a small wooden building I guessed was the commissary. "My name is Lith. you'll have to accept the name we give you. We don't allow you to keep your old name while you're here. What is your old name?"

"Steve," I said.

"We'll choose a new one for you. You can stay in that building over there."

I went to the building I was assigned. It was late, and I wasn't sure, anyway, I could find my way back to the railroad tracks that evening. I was curious about the name they would assign me. The wooden building was an old sawmill. It was spotless, not a trace of sawdust. I doubt that the equipment had even been used. It was that elegant, turn of the century, cast-iron machinery: big heavy cog-wheels, counterweights, belt drives, stiff, old leather belts, all of it rusted but ready to go just the same. I loved the look of it. The big, circular steel blade of the buzz saw attracted me especially. Though I have no doubt it was from the same era as the rest of the equipment, there wasn't a spot of rust on it. It had the perfect, bluish glint of newly polished steel. I touched it. It wasn't cold, like steel, but seemed to transmit no temperature, like plastic, or something else; and its balance was perfect, because my slight touch started it turning, glinting and turning, and for all the time I was staying in the mill that blade was never still.

I hardly had time to notice this before my host, Lith, arrived with an older woman. She carried a pile of burlap sacks over her arms, and was smiling. Lith was all business.

"Your name is Seven," he said.

I was disappointed. "That's not very imaginative."

"It has all the letters of the name you gave us, but we substituted an 'n' for the 't.' We don't like 't,' and when you make a small substitution the letter substituted goes to the end of the name, making your name 'Seven.' "

"That's just a number."

"It's your name while you're here."

He handed me a list off his clipboard. It was a breakdown of the commodities available at the commissary in exchange for work:

1 pr. Coveralls, men	26 hrs.
1 pr. Coveralls, women	29 hrs.
1 lb. Green Tea	07 hrs.
1 red bandanna	01 hr.
1 spoon cocaine	31 hrs.
1 lemon	01/2 hrs.
1 lid uncut Colombian	08 hrs.
1 pr. Men's Workshoes	47 hrs.

"You have two days a week to get high, any days you choose. The rest of the week you work. If you want to save your high days, as many of us do, you can work six days a week and do the forty-eight-day trip at the end of the year. We have a separate retreat for hat. And I don't mean to say that you have to use drugs."

While he was laying this all out for me the woman spread the burlap sacks in one corner for a makeshift bed. She sat down on it. She looked nearly fifty, but had a lovely, slim body noticeable under her shift.

"You might decide by morning what kind of work you'd like to do around here," said Lith, as he left.

"What's your name?" I asked the woman.

"Marie," she said, standing up and laying both her arms on my shoulders. Her smile was nice.

"What was your name before you came here?"

"Marie. My name was always Marie."

"Didn't you have to change your name?"

"That's Lith's trip. It's a power number he does. He's always doing that."

"You mean I didn't have to change my name. My name can still . . ."

She put her fingers over my mouth. "Seven. Seven is a nice name. Don't worry."

We turned once in the closing darkness. For the first time since I received my parcel of wrists I feel an emotion stronger than my curiosity. It's frightening. I know it won't last.

"It's so weird, you staying here. I mean like no one else has ever stayed in this building I mean, you know, I wanted to make it with you the first minute I saw you, but I don't think I can get it on with anyone in this building. No way." She releases me and backs off, shaking her head. Her voice is young and sweet and troubled as a trippy teenager's. It is strange to watch this lovely white-haired woman, carrying her years so well, but spouting an anomalous youthful jargon. A bell rings in the yard, like a Chinese gong."

"Food time," she says. I follow her to the mess hall.

When I got back to my building the blade was still turning, and though it was dark it still glinted, reflecting light from some invisible source. I moved my bed of burlap sacks into the semicircle of reflected light. When I lay down the turning light flowed over my face like a cool fabric. I slept well in the light, as if I were back under the streetlamp outside my New York bedroom window.

The work I was going to do at the commune had already chosen itself. As soon as I woke up I began to check out the machinery. It was stiff. It wanted a good dousing in penetrating oil to get it turning. The belts were brittle and needed to be soaked in neat's-foot oil. I had to rehabilitate an old generator to power the operation. Other people at the commune, once they saw what I was up to, pitched in. They realized the sawmill was a possible source of income, if they could cut selectively and sell the abundant hardwood in their forest. I worked continuous-ly, finding in myself a capacity for hard labor I had never felt before, and an aptitude, even inventiveness in dealing with this machinery that seemed to be so clear, con-tinuous, and elegant a process of cause and effect—this shaft turns that cog drives that belt—that it was relaxing to contemplate, and exhilarating to work on. The result would be (I relished the prospect) that I would have the privilege of watching that wonderful blade, that peculiar-ly elegant presence that reflected, or perhaps even generated, the light over my sleep; I would have the privilege of being the witness to its first cut.

I haven't felt so good ever in my life, eating fresh soy beans and squash and collards and okra, feasting on whole grains, taking milk and butter from the goats kept here. If my life were mine to choose I certainly would choose to live this way. Marie has gotten over her phobia about staying in the mill now that it seems populated, although she still refuses to sleep with me under the light of the blade. When she arrives we move the burlap into a corner and make love with a tenderness I've never known before, and a mutual appreciation that makes every touch, every stroke exquisite. If she stays away, or if she leaves when it's still dark, I move my burlap back near the sawblade that has become my obsession now that I live on this commune.

I don't know how long it took me to get the mill into working condition, but I got it done. In the evening at dinner I announced the completion of my work and everyone at the commune cheered. Lith rose, and in a quite old-fashioned way, proposed a toast to me. He raised his glass of carrot juice and carried on about how Seven came, and Seven worked, and Seven was now one of them. They all clinked glasses. Someone proposed they allow me a bonus of twenty-five hours' credit at the commissary. I accepted. I traded that windfall for a pair of leather suspenders, made in the commune, tooled with a pattern of daisies and swastikas, which I wear even to this day.

The mill was to be launched on the following afternoon according to a ritual of their own devising, which Marie described to me as a Cherokee Thanksgiving ritual modified by Shaker austerity. She thought I would appreciate it. Part of the austerity, she explained, was that she abstain from making love with me the night before the inaugural. I lie on my mat alone in the saw-light and stare at the blade. How tempting it is to start the works and make the first cut myself. This is not my commune, I think, but it is my mill, after all.

I stand up and go outside. The moon is full behind a nappy blanket of bright little clouds. I heft a piece of the black walnut tree I cut that afternoon out of the woods. A certain energy seems to fill me. To hell with it, I'll do it. I pile a lot of sacks around the generator to muffle the sound and start it up. No one seems to stir. I enter the mill and lay the piece of walnut on the saw-table. The wood is cylindrical, about three feet long, and two feet in diameter. I don't know why, but I anticipate that the first cut from my saw will be something special. I pull the lever and engage the gears. All the wheels in the room start to turn. I throw another lever and without a hum the sawblade picks up momentum. I feed the small log into it by hand. There is no sound as the blade easily rips the wood. It is like drawing a line across a sheet of paper, as if the blade were inking the separation of the wood into halves. They fall apart. I shut off the blade and generator. The two halves are perfect, shining as if they had been minutely sanded. They look like two surfaces of polished stone. There is no sawdust left on the table.

I put my bed back in Marie's corner and left the mill. I expect the commune has made good use of it since my departure. I climbed into the truck that went early every morning to Hohenwald and fell asleep, hiding under some mats. By 7:00 a.m. I was in Hohenwald, and by 3:00 p.m. that afternoon I arrived at the Nashville station.

"You're the fellow from Irondale," said Vincent D'-Ambrogio. I was learning the luxury of being shaved by a barber familiar with your face.

"Yep, I'm from Irondale."

I bought the yellow Mustang for seventy-five dollars. It was in pretty good running condition; at least, good enough to get me from Nashville to Iron City, where I was headed next, and back again if it was necessary. To get to Iron City you take Route 431 out of Nashville to Franklin, where you get Route 31. Take Route 31 to Columbia until Route 43, which you take to St. Joseph, and from St. Joseph you take an unmarked dirt road to Iron City. That there had been 43 wrists in the box I received in the morning's mail, and that I was to take Route 43 to get to Iron City, seemed to me no mere coincidence. I was sure I was on the right track.

There's not much happening in Iron City, Tennessee, but it has got a Post Office. It's the small, Deep South town I always imagined I would get to some day. It's on the Alabama border, equidistant from Lawrenceburg, Tennessee, and Florence, Alabama. I felt, when I got out of my Mustang, that I had better not move too fast and call attention to myself from these people who moved so slow they seemed submerged; they lifted their heads and slowly raised their eyelids to register my presence. Black people, white people, they all looked like Southerners to me. They almost smiled. They weren't used to strangers. I could feel my heart beating so quickly and erratically it seemed to rattle in my chest. I sat down at a little lunch counter called Louise for breakfast, and she served me grits and golden eggs and the thickest, sweetest bacon I have ever tasted.

It took me a while to get up the nerve to go to the Post Office across the street. A few people sat around over

there, saying some words, among the four squat Doric
columns that fronted the building. I had no sane purpose
for being in Iron City, Tennessee, especially since the
wrinkled piece of wrapping paper I had carried in my
pocket from New York City was postmarked without a
smudge, from Irondale, Tennessee.

There was just one wicket in Post Office behind which
no one seemed present in the vast, empty space used for
the receiving, sorting, and holding of mail. It's clear that
not much mail comes through Iron City, Tennessee, an
observation that makes me hopeful the postmaster will
remember such a parcel of wrists as I received in the
morning's mail, if indeed it was sent from this place. I saw
no one anywhere behind the wicket. For several minutes
I read the Wanted posters tacked to the dark brown wood
paneling. America is full of fugitives it seems to me. No
one appears. I step outside. Several people sit on the porch
of the Post Office. ''Is there anybody working in the Post
Office?'' I inquire. Everyone turns to look at someone I
take at first to be a young man, but who I realize after a
moment is a young woman, very attractive, although
dressed to disguise her beauty in a pale beige uniform like
a state trooper's without badges, her long black hair coiled
in a tight braid against the back of her head.

''I'm the postal clerk,'' she says. Several other people,
a young boy, a smoky old man, an old woman in a long
cotton smock, all get up to leave, as if my presence is too
much for them to handle.

''I need some stamps,'' I say.

She smiles. It's the first real smile I've noticed since I
pulled into Iron City. ''I think we've got some left,'' she

says. "I'll see you inside." I enter and watch through the wicket. She gets in through the back door. She seems more handsome every moment, erect, yet mobile and graceful. She unlocks her stamp drawer and thumbs through the folder more like a collector than a postal clerk. She grins at me.

"We have several 1-1/2c stamps, three 17c, and one 90c. There'll be a new shipment next week. They seem to disappear as soon as we get them."

I laid my piece of wrapping paper on the counter in front of her eyes. "Do you know this person?" I asked.

She looked at my face, taking in my short hair and my blue eyes. I noticed something in her dark eyes beyond Iron City, Tennessee.

"Are you a detective?"

"Yes," I replied.

She examined both sides of the paper and handed it back to me.

"This is postmarked Irondale, Tennessee."

"There is no Irondale, Tennessee," I said.

"O. I didn't know that," she said, scrutinizing the paper again. "I thought that if there was a postmark there always was a place."

"Not in this case," I said. "But if somebody by the name of C. Routs lives in this town I would like to speak to him."

"So would I," she said, coyly. "But I never heard of such a name, and I know all the names. Can you tell me what was in the parcel you received?"

I looked away from her, down at the brass counter. "Forty-three human wrists," I said, almost gagging on the words.

When I look up she is smiling at me as if she really likes me. "Were they gift wrapped?" she asks.

"No. No." I say. "Not at all.

"That seems even more peculiar. You'd think if some-one sent them, went to all that trouble, he'd want to wrap them nicely." She locks up her stamp drawer. Everything suddenly seems easier for me; if not clearer, at least less complicated. "Do you have a car?" she asks. I say that I have a yellow Mustang.

"Good," she says. "I'm closing the Post Office for the rest of the day, and I need a ride home."

A crowd had gathered around my yellow Mustang while I was in the Post Office. I made my way through them and got to the car door. "Wouldn't you know it was a Yankee," said a man in the crowd. Then I saw what had made the crowd gather. A large bird, a buzzard, had somehow got into the car and was perched on the driver's seat. I had locked the car up before breakfast at Louise and had no idea how the bird could have got in.

"How do it feel ridin' shotgun to a buzzard?" asked someone under a straw hat. I opened the door and the buzzard lurched once, tumbled out of the car, and then with laborious grace lifted itself above the crowd where it circled easily. The crowd dispersed. I thought to myself, "How strange."

I could hardly keep my eyes on the road with the postal clerk beside me. Cynthia was her name. She was from Mobile, Alabama, but had gone to school in the North and had shed some of her accent there. As we rode into the bronze shade of tobacco country she began to let down her braid and slowly comb it out. Her hair was very long and very black, and I kept losing my eyes in it. Only her hand, occasionally touching mine on the wheel, reminded me that I was driving.

"This is home," she says. Just as I pull into her red-dirt driveway she wraps around her forehead a brightly beaded headband of exquisite design. I don't know what to expect next. I don't expect anything. The day composes itself minute by minute.

Cynthia lives in a large, circular house of yurtlike construction set in off the road among some loblolly pines. The sharecropper land around their place is in sorghum and cotton. A bearded man steps out of the front door and comes toward us. I am disappointed. He takes my hand. "It's good to see you, man. It's really good to see somebody." He throws an arm around my shoulder and leads me into the house he has built himself. "I tell you, sometimes I'm so strung out here. It's lonely, man. Nobody. I'm a city boy, and this is a strange trip for me, though I love it somehow, sometimes; but sometimes I think I've got to get away."

I won't describe the elaborate ornaments they have made for their circular home. They were both accomplished craftsmen. While Cynthia was changing her clothes her boyfriend, named Kevin, told me their history. He and Cynthia had come as Vista volunteers, had been dismissed because of budget cuts, and decided to stay anyway, bought a little piece of land, and because of her father's political pull Cynthia had landed the postal clerk's job, a real plum in Lawrence county. It all made me yawn. For so long I had been indulging myself in my own luxuriously inexplicable activity, that the utter mundanity of this beautiful couple's history made me want to sleep. When Cynthia appeared again in jeans and a Pakistani blouse I realized I preferred her in her trooper's uniform, so ephemerally possible underneath. In this youth culture outfit she was just another pretty girl.

"Let's go," she said.

"Where are we going?"

"We've got some distance to travel," said Kevin. "There's something you need to see."

"What is it?"

"You'll see it," said Cynthia.

I smiled and slapped my toe on the gas. That was an exchange of information on a level I found pleasurable. We traveled East for miles, into more mountainous country. Kevin kept a Jew's harp in his mouth which he plucked at random on the way, while Cynthia leaned against him and hummed. It was late afternoon. The shadows were deep in the foothills. "I think it's just over the next hill," Kevin kept saying. I took his word for it and drove. It wasn't over the next hill, or the next one. What we finally came on looked to me at first like a gravel pit for the highway department. Except there was a difference. People were swarming throughout the excavation, among the idle bulldozers and graders. They were scrounging in the rubble. They were ripping at the perimeter of turf. Hundreds of them. An old woman, emaciated Appalachian lady in a dress of patches, rushed by us, cackling. She carried what looked like a bone of some sort, and a lame old man followed her shouting weakly for her to let him see what she had. The place was full of poor mountain people come down here as if to perform a ritual of disorder in this excavation.

"It's a Cherokee burial ground," said Kevin. "They just came here one day and bulldozed it up. This is on the trail of tears, man. Hundreds of Cherokee starved here, man. Died."

"I'm part Seminole," said Cynthia.

"It's horrible. They just came here and opened it up with bulldozers. It's been full of these people for weeks." A young man ran around in a circle in front of us brandishing what looked like a piece of human jaw. He was really happy.

"I haven't slept," said Kevin. "Since they excavated this place. I don't know what's happening, but we've got to get away from here."

"I'm part Cherokee," said Cynthia.

I wandered away from Kevin and Cynthia, in among the people grubbing for relics. Things weren't as chaotic as they had first seemed. Territories in the pit seemed to be tacitly assumed by family groups. That organization made the activity seem not quite so horrible. Everyone: children, adults, old people, were working furiously at unearthing whatever was there. The mountain air was full up with delirious vibrations, like the screeching of brakes. Their faces were full of it, the demonic glee of Americans unspeakably poor suddenly getting for free something that might be valuable, that they insisted on making valuable with their own intensity. They rushed around waving skulls and legbones, showing fistfuls of arrowheads and pottery shards. One family had planted a post, and on it they were carefully reconstructing with bailing wire the complete skeleton of a Cherokee youth. They were such a poor family, such a flea-bitten lot of enthusiastic kids, and they lavished on their primitive archeological project so much attention and love that I surprised myself by starting to weep. How long it has been since I last wept. I watched them carefully trying to fit bones into place, their own arms so thin, scarcely more than some bones to begin with.

I had enough. It is almost dark. People are leaving in old pickups and junk cars and tractors with carts. I look for my car. It's gone. Kevin and Cynthia have escaped. I'm alone. It doesn't get me mad. It's not so bad that they took the yellow Mustang. I was through with it, and it was through with me; but my sheepskin coat is in the car, and now I'm cold. It's dark. I'll have to stick it out for a whole night in these mountains, by this excavated Indian boneyard. I climb to the woods above the hole and scrape up a pile of leaves to crawl into for warmth, my boy scout notion of survival in the wilderness. There is no way I can get to sleep in this place. Down there the people are digging through the night. They are orange with huge, swaying shadows in the light of fires they have lit to illuminate their work. Some play harmonicas and banjoes and sing spirituals. Their music is subtle, lustrous, like something valuable. I consider prayer for myself. What can prayer mean as I remember speaking it as a child, spoken by my voice in this location, in the fix I am in, among the homeless spirits of the Cherokee that wander abroad this evening?

I got on the road and hitched back to New York in the morning. My long evening awake had made me do a lot of thinking. The possibility that most nagged me was that I had been wrong about the wrists. Perhaps I had mistakenly perceived wrists, and there had been something else entirely in the package: some flexible plastic cable or some kind of sausage. It was important that I get back to my apartment and dig one up; after all, forty-three is an odd number.

The New York I returned to was not the New York I had left. There was such an hysteria in the air, such broad currents of ill will inundating the faces of people in the streets that I hardly recognized the place where I had spent the most exciting years of my development as a human being. As soon as I opened the door to my apartment the telephone rang. That was a sound I hadn't heard for a while.

"Steve. I'm so glad you're home. This is Nikki. God, my voice must really sound different. I need to talk to you. Michael's in the hospital."

"Get him out of there."

"He was stabbed. We were mugged."

I glanced into the other room where I had left my forty-three potted wrists. Something had happened in there while I was gone. I couldn't say a word into the telephone. I tried to get my coat off. Something green was happening in the other room.

"Are you still there?"

"Yes." The word peeled off the top of my palate.

"I need to speak to you. I need to see you."

I was peering into the other room. I began to shake

because I suddenly had the premonition that of all the strange changes that had come down since I received my parcel of wrists, the most shattering were just beginning to develop.

"Are you there?"

"I'm there." I'd forgotten I was holding the telephone.

"Listen. I have to come over. Will that be okay?"

"Come over," I said. "It's okay." I hung up. Without taking my eyes off the other room I put my coat away. There was certainly a presence in there. I reached around the doorway and switched on the light, and without entering at first I scrutinized the contents. What I saw filled me suddenly with a feeling I can only call joy in our language, but it was a terrifying joy, a feeling that seemed balanced in me on the most delicately equilibrated pinnacles, and my premonition was that if I refused to nurture this feeling I would totter off into an abysmal silence. Happiness settled from nowhere on my chest, and rushed out as pure laughter from my parted lips. In each of the forty-three pots something had sprouted. My room was full of greenery.

They were tiny, monocotyledonous plants that come up on slender stems, each so far producing a single large leaf with a wavy margin. Each of the pots had produced one of these graceful plants, and there was no way I could bring myself to disturb any of them at the roots. I couldn't dig one up now. I touched the soil. It was very dry. My first responsibility would be to water them. I needed some grow-lights, some fishmeal fertilizer. Larger pots for transplanting.

I open the door to leave for the plant store and find

myself face to face with two women. "You have a sixth sense," says Nikki.

"Why are you wearing your overcoat and carrying that teapot?" asks the other woman.

"I brought Linda. I hope it's okay," says Nikki. "I'm afraid to go out in the street by myself just now."

It feels as if I never left the city. Linda is the woman with whom I was having a rather desultory affair before the arrival of my wrists. She is smart and pretty, a promising young editor at a small, prestigious publishing house, one of the bright, young, independent women of our time; but when we are alone together each sucks the other into such emptiness, such a vast, unremitting indifference to one another, each of us pledged to his and her own vague ambitions, that our relationship is an excruciating game that we both find to be evil, and therefore addicting. We are seen together. We are presumed to be together. Indeed we are still attracted to each other like some barely luminous plankton in the great, tidal, disjunctive movement of life in New York City. Enough of that.

"Last night it was raining, you know. We were walking down Broadway without an umbrella, just getting wet. It was nice. Michael noticed two guys with an umbrella fall in step behind us as we turned down 78th Street. I could feel Michael's arm get tense. I turned around and saw them. They were two black guys. Michael knew what was coming. He picked up the pace and crossed the street, and we started back for Broadway where there would be some people. It was too late. They backed us against the wall. One held the umbrella and a gun. The other had a straight razor that he kept at Michael's face as he took his wallet.

They were smiling. They didn't say anything. I became hysterical. 'Don't hurt him. He's a great writer. He's your friend. Rape me. Don't hurt him.' I spouted all sorts of self-destructive nonsense.''

"That's your negative sexism. It's pitiful," says Linda.

"Whatever it was it didn't work. The guy with the umbrella thanked me for the invitation. He was young and really fine looking. I was actually weirdly attracted to him. Maybe I really thought I could win him with love. I don't know. Anyway, the guy with the razor slashed Michael's face twice, in an X right across one eye, then he ripped his stomach. I'm sure they would have done something to me next, but a patrol car turned the corner, and I screamed, and the dome light and siren went on, and the two muggers sprinted, and now Michael is in the hospital. He's critical.''

While Nikki is telling her story I prepare some tea on my hot plate. I always take a lot of care with tea. I like it. This time it is Mormon tea, or squaw tea, made from twigs of the creosote bush, mixed with a touch of damiana, a Mexican herb, for its aroma. You drop that tea into the boiling water, then shut off the heat. Nikki stands up as the brew is steeping and starts to cry. She embraces me. A shudder travels up her spine, connecting with me at the navel and loosening my knees. "I'm sorry. I'm sorry. I'm sorry," she says. I say something perfunctory. She sits down. I pour the tea. Linda sips and watches both of us. I am trembling as Nikki is trembling.

"I've never been mugged. Almost all my friends have," says Linda. "It's just never happened to me. Must be my vibes.''

I've neglected what is going on in the other room. I glance momentarily at the bedroom door, and then at Linda. She smiles slightly and lowers her eyelids. She thinks what I mean is that I want her to stay the night. I don't know how to refute that assumption. Nikki sees our exchange and understands the same thing as Linda. She sighs.

"I'll take a cab home. I guess all I wanted was to see a man I knew. I'll be all right."

"I think I can visit Michael tomorrow," I say.

"It would be good to go together. I'd appreciate it," says Nikki. I take her hand as we're flagging a cab. The hand is so cold it's almost painful to hold it.

When I got back to my apartment Linda had opened the door to my bedroom, and was standing just inside, surveying my growing patriarchy.

"Steve," she said, turning to me. "I didn't know you had such a green thumb."

I was amazed. What a few moments before had been nothing more than a few limber seedlings were now, all of them, healthy plants, almost two feet high, splendidly leafed out, and they had grown that fast without fertilizer or grow-light, just a little New York City water. "It's not that so much," I said. "They just grow."

"How did you get them?"

"They came in the mail." I almost told her about the wrists, but decided it would take too much energy to explain, and she would think I was putting her on in some male way, or that I was going totally nuts, as she had always anticipated.

"Amazing," she said. "I never get anything in the

mail." She stared at me. "I like you without the beard. The hair could be longer for my taste, though."

We turned off the light, undressed, and immediately started to make love. It was horrible. So little did we love each other that we couldn't tolerate any mischief, any foreplay, any giggling conversation. We went at each other and satisfied our needs. We had each other, and stopped. Linda fell asleep under the blankets. I lay awake on top of them in the light of the mercury vapor lamp on my corner, casting pale shadows from the leaves of my garden across my body. The shadows felt warm. I didn't dare sleep. Two children's stories kept playing in my head: Jack and the Beanstalk and Pandora's Box. They were the potential nightmares that kept me awake.

Linda left before breakfast that morning, and I rushed out to buy grow-lights, fertilizer, and the larger pots, which I already needed. I also got a botanical key, and a book by Thalassa Cruso on potted plants. It took almost all my money, but there was no way I could scrimp on this new responsibility. Was it a hobby? Was it an avocation? Was it my new path? The plants had begun to so appropriate my energy and integrate my time with their welfare that my decision had to be that this was now my life. I should have hated the idea, but I didn't. I knew that I would have to get a job, and keep it, no screwing around any more if my plants were to survive. What a novel and exhausting cause has arisen to absorb me. What a fool I am.

There's very little more to tell about it. I got a job writing ad copy, and it brings in enough. From that evening on I allowed no visitors to my apartment. The plants have expanded their territory from my bedroom to the living room and kitchen. They have grown to be quite the little trees. I haven't yet been able to identify them. When they were small I thought they might have been some sweet viburnum or nannyberries (*Viburnum lentago Linnaeus*), but I learned that except for greenbriers most woody plants are dicotyledonous. As the plants grew the new leaves became thicker and deeper green, as if they might be related to the lemon or some other citrus. I thought, when blossoms began to appear, that I would finally have the decisive clue to the identity of my plants, and perhaps to the mystery of my parcel of wrists, wrists that since I received them in the morning mail have never been off my mind, lying there like the skies above me full of little clouds.

Not so. The blossoms were quite unusual. They were odorless. Although the forty-three plants were superficially identical, they each put out a different blossom, and each of the blossoms on the same plant differed one from the other in some small particular of shape or size or behavior; I could describe them forever. Some grew in clusters, some singly, some drooped, some erect. One of the flowers was made of insects, tiny grey-golden flies clustered around a stem like lupine or larkspur, that scattered when you got close, the flower seeming to disappear in a scintillation of these little flies, then reappearing when you withdrew. One that looked like Indian paintbrush would curl itself around your finger if you tried to touch it. Another, like a small peony, would lean towards you as you got close, and seem to pucker up as if it had the urge to give you a kiss. Each flower was a different color; not just a shade, but a distinct color. My mind now is full of ten thousand colors, colors that are nowhere visible, that even Fra Angelico could never have touched to canvas.

That they were invariably odorless made me uneasy, because there's always a certain aloofness about a flower without a smell, as if there is something they want to hold back from the world of men.

As demanding as the plants were while they grew and flowered, they complicated my life even further when they began to bear fruit. I had begun to like the way things were shaping up for me. Granted, my territory in the apartment I share with my forest has been reduced to a corner near the bathroom, where I have my bed, my telephone, and my hot plate; but everything is very compact, and I like it. I come home, spend a few hours watering and observing the brood, and go to sleep. I have come to like the noise the plants make at night, as if they are inventing a wind for themselves, but now the fruit begins to appear and the relative simplicity of my life is changing.

I got home late after visiting Michael in the hospital, and having dinner with Nikki. Michael not only lost the sight in one eye but also lost the ability to control the movement of the other. Nikki was very upset, and blamed as much as she could on me. She mentioned my aloofness. I'm not compassionate enough. She told me I don't give enough time to my friends. She mentioned a group that she and Linda go to that she thought I ought to join. They all get together, men and women, and rap about their problems, getting it all out in the open; and then they have their problems out there in the open, ready to share. It has been a long time since I thought of myself as having problems, although I do recognize as problematical my time-consuming charter of responsibilities. Nonetheless when I got home I was quite upset. There is nothing, not even death, so unnerving as a close friend suddenly blinded.

I have difficulty falling asleep; but just as I have about broken through all the fine charged wires of consciousness, and am nearly away, I hear a loud thunk, as of a large book dropping on a table, and my eyes snap open. It was one of those noises that you can't locate in space. I thought it came from out there, but its reverberations remain confined to my skull. I lie there looking out, expecting the noise to repeat. It doesn't, but I'm awake for the duration. I turn the lights off and wander into my forest. At first I don't notice anything has changed, except the unusual quiet. Then I notice that all the petals have fallen, all at once, not a hint of flowers on the trees; and then, as if my eyes have suddenly adjusted to the peculiar sight I am obliged to witness, I notice the kind of fruit my parcel of trees has begun to bear. I work my way toward a slight whisper in the corner. There, one of the trees has produced, on slender, flexible stems, like an abundance of cherries, a crop of human lips. They are all moving, cleverly using the leaves nearest themselves for tongues. As I get closer to them I hear them saying, "Find me some teeth. Get me some teeth."

Perhaps I am dreaming. It's the kind of dream I would have, the way my life has been going. Two things happen to assure me I'm not. I feel a sudden blow on my rump from the rear, and the telephone rings. I turn to see that I have been kicked by a tree whose limbs are weighed down with a crop of human legs, like bunches of bananas. It seems like such a ridiculously slapstick apparition that I break out laughing, and I am still laughing as I pick up the telephone.

"Do you always wake up laughing?" Linda asks.

"I've been awake," I say.

"I always think I'm the only one who isn't able to sleep," she says, and she goes on talking as I survey my forest of parts. There is something else on each of the forty-three trees: noses, armpits, navels, knees, vaginas and penises, pelvises. The sight is terrifying and exhilarating.

I agreed to meet Linda for dinner in the evening. She hung up, and I stared into my woods still holding the receiver. Sleep came on me suddenly there in the wooden chair, my eyes open.

Michael seems somewhat unnerved to have me pop in on him at the hospital on the next day, but I have no choice. I have the means to help him, and if a friend has those means he should use them whatever the sacrifice.

"Of course I want to see. Are you crazy? I still like to see."

He isn't prepared for me. He hasn't been properly tranquilized. I can feel hysteria near the surface of his skin. There is a bandage over the socket of the eye he has lost, and over the wandering eye is a black patch to help him avoid the confusion of seeing. He lifts the patch and tries to look at me. I can't be but a blur, some streaks of color in the random, rapid motion of vision. The eyeball jerks around out of control in his skull. I put my hand on his forearm and feel the sobs coming from his belly.

"I'm sorry," I say.

"It's not your fault," he says. "I'll get used to it."

I feel the time is right. "I think I've got something to help you." I reach into the bag in my pocket and pull out one of the eyes I just picked fresh this morning. Only the brown eyes have ripened so far but I feel it should still be at least a temporary consolation, even though Michael's eyes are blue. He seems calm for the moment. I hold the eye with the tips of my fingers over his own flailing eye and try to follow the movement so he can see at least for the moment, what I have brought him.

At this point something very unexpected happens. At first I don't know it's happening, but then I realize that my arm is moving, without my intending it; indeed, if I wanted to I couldn't do it. The arm is moving in perfect synchronization with what I imagine to be the random motion of Michael's injured eye. I am following it. It isn't difficult. I can feel in my fingertips the eye I have brought making minute adjustments of angle and focus. Then I suddenly perceive, or begin to understand that I am beginning to see through the palm of my hand. I close my eyes. At first I see only the surface of Michael's blue eye, in its absolute stillness; and then I begin to see through his eye, or behind his eye, the image clearing through my palm. What I see is a huge tree, like a giant lush maple, with a bifurcated trunk. One half of the tree is full of squirrels, chasing each other in circles; on the other half a great black-and-white hawk preens its feathers and sharpens its beak against the limb it is gripping. Behind the tree a sun, distended, ovoid, at the horizon, is either rising or setting. I don't have time to see if it's going up or down because someone has grabbed my arm and has made me drop the eye. All this time, without my being aware of it, Michael has been screaming. Two orderlies pull me back from the bed. I don't resist. I feel sorry for Michael.

"Jesus, Maria, look what he's got," says one of the orderlies, as the bag falls from my pocket and my eyes all roll across the floor. One of the orderlies lets go of me to scoop up the eyes, and in a moment of self-preservation I break the grip of the other orderly and get out of there, escaping through the emergency exit. I realize that now life is going to be very hard for Michael, unless he figures out how to help himself, and despite the fact that I have suffered no physical injury from now on life will be almost impossible for me, and there is no way I can help it.

Linda and I met that evening at a Japanese restaurant on West 56th Street. At first we had little to say to each other. We didn't want to talk about Michael or Nikki because we both already knew too much. She was too considerate to burden me with publishing gossip, and I didn't have much I wanted to tell her from my own life. We ate iced bean curd, and sushi, and pickled radish. It was a refreshing meal, and as a result we both were very relaxed. I sighed and she sighed.

"Steve," she said. "I wish I knew where our relationship was going."

I smiled and watched her face very carefully. She leaned forward and took both my hands, which I had carelessly left on the table. "I do love you," she said.

I have always been obsessed with watching Linda's mouth. It is her most expressive feature. It tends, in fact, to telegraph her feelings, to demonstrate them on such a level of exaggeration, so much sadness weighing down the lips, so much passion in their pucker, that when I was in a more intimate position not of watching her, but of being a subject of love, I would find myself hurtling off on long blind journeys of guilt or horniness just from noticing her mouth. That evening her lips seemed to flash a curious mixed semaphore of love, pain, despair, indifference, defensiveness, abandon: every nuance. I slipped one of my hands out of hers, and took from my inside jacket pocket a large billfold and picked from it one of the lovelier sets of lips I had gleaned from my tree. I leaned forward and attached them to her mouth. They made a world of difference.

"What do you call that?" she said, puckering up and working her mouth around, finally peeling the new lips off and dropping them into her hand. The lips immediately flipped over and kissed her on the palm. "What is all this you've got here?" she giggled. I already had another set out and was trying it on her. She wiped that one off and then dumped my cache of lips out of my billfold onto the table. They squirmed around there, kissing each other, and kissing her hand. She drew back, amused and horrified at the same time. "What are these things?"

I was too absorbed in the problem I saw in front of me to answer. I pulled a few chins out of another pocket. There is such a variety of chins. I tried to line a dimpled one up on Linda's face, but when she saw it she covered that face as if horrified. It was unfortunate. I pulled the noses and the ears on her. I had made a careful selection. "You're crazed. I always knew it would happen to you. You're absolutely insane." When she saw I was insisting on what I was doing she stood up at the table. "Steve, I'm going to leave before I start screaming and embarrass us both." She threw on her shawl and rushed out the door. I looked around the restaurant and the few people who had been staring our way went back to manipulating their chopsticks. The waitress, an older Japanese woman in traditional dress, who looked perpetually worried, started to clear the table. I gathered my produce back into my pockets, paid my bill, and went into the streets. Though I understood Linda's point of view I was disappointed. I had been hoping I could depend on a few old friends.

Old friends dropped away. Nothing I could do about it. My commitment wasn't the result of any decision I had made and for that reason was all the more binding. I was doomed from then on to make a kind of pest out of myself. Perhaps you have met me at one time or another in the streets, haunting strangers, insisting on the replacements from the pack of goods I carry on my back. You must know who I am.

Occasionally I do meet someone who knows who I am who has even come looking for me. It's gratifying and disconcerting. I remember a girl by the name of Susan Kentucky. She met me on the street, said she'd come all the way from Atlanta, Georgia, just to find me. She took me to lunch, not even ashamed to sit with me among all the flashy people at the Buffalo Roadhouse. She had a hamburger, I had a spinach salad. It was tasty. And it wasn't like being with Linda that time. She said, "You do have style, Steve. I really like your style." It was flattery, and I appreciated that in itself. I was far beyond the inclination to make the so-called "next move," but some move was possible because flattery is often more liberating than the truth. I did begin to lay out my goods for her, never imagining that someone who had looks as perfect as Susan Kentucky's would use any of it. She took a forehead, complete with temples, a couple of cheeks with variable dimples, one of my powerful brows, and I don't know what else. I was a success. She offered to pay for it all. How could I let her pay for anything? I was in love with Susan Kentucky, as I am secretly in love with everyone else.

I don't imagine I'll ever see her again. There's no reason for her to look for me any more, and if she has applied my parts to her features I'll never be able to recognize her. That's one of the hazards of my occupation, and one of the paradoxes not entirely taken into account by those who imagine mine to be a "power trip." Who is it? Who really exercises the control? That's an important question.

I sometimes try to put my finger on the one problem that caused this life that I have, to all intents and purposes, lived, to take the peculiar turn it did at a certain point. I think it's that I never really trusted the United States Post Office. I didn't really believe in it. If I had I would have done what I should have done in the first place when I received my parcel of wrists in the morning mail. Without thinking about it I should have wrapped it up again and shipped it back to C. Routs in Irondale, Tennessee, where it came from. When I consider it from this vantage I realize that could have made all the difference. If I had done that my life might have worked itself out by an entirely other set of priorities.

FROM *STOLEN STORIES*

Friendship

My friend Sadie was a closet cannibal and that was why I introduced her to Herman in the first place. At the time I thought it was best for people to get these propensities out in the open, at least on some level. Express yourself. Let it all hang out. I thought Herman might do that for her because among all my friends he was the one who tended to be most willing, even driven, to sacrifice himself.

"It's the 'iffiness' of this life we lead," Sadie once confided to me. "It's not even the old-fashioned ennui. That would seem better than this blank anxiety that we always feel. It's not as simple as plain boredom." Sadie pushed her long black hair back from her eyes. Those eyes had an enticing grey-green clarity, cat-like, startling. "It's this edginess, and what's worse, a fear of losing the edge because then you'd have nothing. You know what I mean."

"It's a long down drag, Sadie, but you've got to make the best of it, whatever." I've always believed that between friends a little banality is like a shot in the arm.

"Anthony, it's a total disaster. I'd rather live in some primitive society, in New Guinea, in a jungle, where my life was directed with certainty by some explicit rituals that defined the parameters of knowing the world, for myself and for everyone around me. Then there'd be no question of what to do. But we have all this choice. We live in this big city of feasts, and so you can never decide what's worth doing.''

"Sadie, we can't go back to the dark ages."

''If I didn't have my bodily functions: eating, getting up, sleeping, shitting, fucking; if I didn't menstruate I'd never know when to do anything. I'm like a dung beetle pushing around a crappy little ball of time. Not even that beetle can feel what I feel. How do you get through a month without menstruating?''

''Your problem is twofold, Sadie: you've got too much intelligence, and you're genuinely ridiculous. Just relax. Let it flow.''

''I know it,'' she said. She leaned over to kiss me. Sadie and I had a thing going, a fucking thing that happened two or three times a month. I can't stand it any more than that. She bites me so hard she sometimes draws blood. When she comes, she comes with her teeth clamped into my shoulder so deep that I start to scream. I hate it, but I like it too because she's my friend. When I leave her my body looks like one of those early paintings by Larry Poons, full of lozenge shaped bruises. I think when I finally close my art gallery I'll auction off my body as the last work of art. I never liked it in the first place. Gloria, my girlfriend, is a model. She never sees the bruises because with me she likes to pretend she is enormously fat and ashamed of her body. We make love in the dark and she has the soft slow style that I like best.

Herman moved in after seeing Sadie just a couple of times, and the change in her was almost immediate. I could see in her face that the potential of her life had expanded beyond her imagination. She forgot the whole line of bullshit she had been laying down for me about modern life and its general fucked-upness. Anthropology was her gig, and she started reading Levi-Strauss and Mircea Eliade again with a totally new set of eyes.

The change in Herman was slower, but I could see it happening to him too. He was growing, slowly pushing through his hang-ups. It's my biggest pleasure in life to get two of my friends together from different worlds, and to see them both begin to groove on each other. I used to think I loved art more than anything else in the world, but then it became my business. Now for me it's just another scam. It earns the bread and butter, such as it is. I realize now that what I really love is people. Friends. Keeping them happy.

"I wish I could thank you enough for introducing us. My whole life has changed," said Herman. "Sadie is the best thing that has happened to me in years; in fact, she's the only thing."

"Don't thank me," I said. I must admit I get a real glow from situations like this. "You're both friends of mine. I didn't do anything. Someday you'll find something to do for me."

"I hope so," Herman took my hand. His eyes were lit up like a fanatic's. "Her mind is so engaged. She has so much energy. She talks and I feel like I'm burning in the flame of her intellect. I haven't had so many thoughts since I was in college. I'm almost flattered to be allowed to listen to her."

"Don't underestimate yourself, Herman. Sadie's very

bright and very articulate, but you've got a brilliant mind in your own way. She recognizes this in you.''

Herman's grin was so wide he couldn't sip his espresso.

"What is it?" I asked.

He leaned towards me. "I didn't want to at first, but now I think I'll show you."

"What?"

Herman lifted his left pants leg to reveal a bandage on his calf. When he removed the bandage, I saw that a hunk of flesh was missing.

"How did that happen?"

"I gave it to her," he said, smiling even wider.

"You what?"

"I don't mind. She was hungry. She just wanted a taste."

"Wait a second. You mean you fed her from your own calf?" Although I mentioned when I started relating this anecdote that Sadie was a closet cannibal I must admit that I felt that analysis was just a figure of speech, meant symbolically or something, to help you get a quick fix on her. I never expected the cannibal to come out of the closet. I guess that's New York City. It pampers people to their extremes.

"This happened so naturally," Herman said. "The way everything else happens between us. We had just made love. She said she was hungry and there wasn't a thing in the house. I sat up to try to think of something and the blanket fell off my leg. She looked at it. I looked at her. She looked into my eyes. It was understood. It wasn't one of those intellectual things, although our intellectual compatibility is a help. She keeps a paring knife in her night table drawer. First she cut off a little piece, held it in her mouth for the flavor, and swallowed it like an oyster. She looked so delighted I didn't believe it. I was flattered. I didn't even notice my pain. 'Take. Take some more,' I said. She took another hunk, and that was it. She broiled it. I figure all that muscle doesn't make any difference to me in my line of work.''

He had a point there. Herman was a stamp dealer. I mean he was a heavyweight dealer in stamps. Better than $18,000 of philately passed through his store every week. He certainly didn't need muscle.

"You know," he went on. "If someone else did it I'd think it was weird, but I don't think it's weird because it's between me and her. Do you think it's weird?"

"If . . . if . . . if it's what the two of you want, Herman, who am I to judge? You're both my friends."

He looked so happy I felt like cupid.

For the two months I was in Germany I hardly thought about Sadie and Herman. Gloria came along with me, and between listening to her complaints about German food, and pushing my artists' work, I had plenty to think about. But the couple came to mind occasionally, as friends often do. I had two images of them that I could not reconcile. One was of this obsequiously happy couple, both of whom I loved, and the other was these two strangers performing a ritual I could never understand. You can bring friends together, I kept reminding myself, but you can't influence the way they're going to work out their relationship.

Gloria was getting even thinner, if you can imagine it, but at night she was into clomping around in some wooden shoes she had bought on a side trip to Sweden, and imitating the voice of an enormous hausfrau. She'd jump on top of me in bed and I'd pretend to be crushed. She did this in Munchen and Koln, but she nearly flipped out in Hamburg and I had to send her back to the States.

I concentrated then on selling art. At this point in time the Germans have real avant-garde taste. Very analytical. Like my taste. They take it minimal, crisp, conceptual. That's what I've got in my shop so I do okay over there. I keep the paint squiggles on canvas, the bunch of junk welded together, all that vomit of the ego, out of my gallery. I've stayed away from figurative too, even though it sells. I hope before I have to peddle any of that I go out of business. Anyway, I go to Germany and get the Marks. With the dollar sinking that isn't bad business.

I went to visit Sadie once more after I got back. She was so effervescent, so gay, so untroubled when she answered the door that I hardly recognized her. She had chintzed up all her windows, covered her couch with an embroidered antimacassar, polished the ashtrays. It was unbelievable. It was strange. She kissed me lightly, a little tic, hardly the kind of wide-open sucking of my tongue she used once to threaten me. I sensed the thing we once had was probably over forever.

"You look so splendid, Sadie," I said.

"I am splendid," she replied.

I noticed another woman, a bull-dyke type, with a d.a. and baggy pants, eyeing me from the easy chair, over her copy of Steppenwolf. "That's sister Nathan," said Sadie. "She's an old friend."

"And Herman."

"He's here. He's here. He's been asking about you. You'll see him. First I'll make some tea."

I didn't like the way that sounded. Sadie always took forever to make tea. It was a production. I tried, without being too conspicuous, looking around the apartment for Herman, but he was not to be seen.

"Come on," she said, finally bringing the tea. "Herman talks about you all the time and he's just going to be so happy to see you."

She led me to a closet in the hall, and I had a chilling premonition of what would be in there. I felt like I had stepped into the Twilight Zone.

"Don't make any wise-ass remarks about praying mantises or whatever. This is something that happened between us. This is the way we like it," said Sadie, before she opened the door.

"You don't need to be defensive, Sadie," I reassured her. "Remember I was the one who introduced you in the first place."

There was such beatitude in Sadie's sudden smile, so much peace, that I felt I could allow her any transgression. "You're so great," she sang, and pulled open the closet door.

"What a treat to see you, Anthony. It's been months," said Herman. "So much has happened." I could see that. Herman was in the closet; at least, what remained of him. His carcass, carved up neatly, hung from coathangers, and was talking to me. "Isn't this great. I feel like a million dollars. Sadie's a terrific cook."

I didn't find the sight repulsive; in fact, if I remember at all what I felt it was a sense of utter absurdity. My own friends. For once I was at a loss for words.

"Have you been selling any stamps, Herman?"

"The business takes care of itself, Anthony. And if it doesn't, I've made enough money in my life. It's about time I started living."

"You said a mouthful, Herman." She had just cut the filets off of him, and had left most of the stuff around the vital organs. The bones were all there. She hadn't eaten the liver. She hadn't eaten the heart. I wouldn't have believed it if I hadn't seen it with my own eyes.

"It even feels good this way, Anthony. It's good for the head. It's relaxing. I'm conscious of so much more. I'd thank you again, but I don't want to sound insincere."

"It's okay, Herman. I only introduced you. I can't take credit for anything else." I started to close the closet. "I'll see you around."

"Anthony," said Herman, just before the door shut. "Will you do me a favor?"

I pulled the door open a little, "What?"

"Will you speak to my bookkeeper? I really like the guy."

"What'll I tell him?"

"I don't know. Make it up. Tell him philately isn't everything in life. Tell him to sell the one penny magenta and the tete-beche collection. Tell him to sell all the stamps and to go to the Seychelles Islands. Give him my regards. Give him a bonus."

"I'll do that, Herman," I said, and finally closed the door.

Sadie had the tea poured in the other room. "That's heavy," I said to her.

She turned on me, obviously expecting my strong

reaction. "Look. Different people work out different trips." A look passed over her face so dark it reminded me of the Sadie I once knew, and then I realized how far she had come. That discrepancy seemed to justify everything, if everything needed justification. "It might be heavy," she said. "Certain people work out heavy relationships. That's the way they do it. Other people have to accept that. But if it works, it isn't horrible."

"No. I guess it isn't horrible."

"We know what we're doing. We're adults. We're consenting adults. It might not work for everybody, but for us it's a fine thing."

"As long as the two of you are happy."

Her mood had passed. She asked me if I wanted some dinner. I could tell by the intensity of her question that it would be a breach of friendship to refuse. I didn't. She cooked up some kind of meat patty. We offered some to sister Nathan. She said very gruffly that she didn't eat meat, and went on reading. I didn't ask her what was in it, but it tasted quite good, and I told her so. As I left she threw her arms around my neck and told me how happy she was now, and how good it was to have a friend like me. Her kiss was like a little moist peck on my cheek. I didn't need to worry about her any more.

I don't intend to think about those people ever again at all. Friendships come and friendships go. People grow out of each other. I don't feel responsible for what happened. When I think about it hardly anything at all seemed to have happened. It was natural. Two people followed their propensities into their own kind of happiness. This is the seventies. You've got to get some happiness while you can. They were better at working it out than most of my friends, but as far as I was personally concerned they were into something I couldn't relate to. Friendship, like everything else, is not forever.

When I got back to my place Gloria was burning incense in the dark and strumming her koto. She came over and sat down on my lap. She was like a feather. The only light was the glowing tip of the joss stick fanned by the air conditioner.

"Am I hurting you?" she asked.

"No. Not at all." I wasn't thinking.

"I thought I might be too heavy for you," she said, surprising me with a kiss on the eye.

"Well," I said. "If you'd just shift your weight a little, so I don't get numb."

That made her very happy.

Two Seaside Yarns

I

GREED

The other day as I walked my dog down the beach and watched him sniff the breeze I happened to cut my foot on a piece of rusty iron that was sticking out of the pebbles. Sandpipers scooted, terns flew back and forth, stabbing at the water. I was bleeding profusely, but I thought that before I treated myself I would perform an act of good citizenship and rid the beach of this hazard. I strained my back a trifle pulling at the old piece of iron, but there was no way to free it. I got down on my hands and knees and scraped back the pebbles to see what held the iron fast. It turned out to be an old barrel ring, attached to a very old barrel, that had probably been buried on this beach years before they built the breakwater, and only now was the barrel being uncovered. On its lid one word was burned: AFRIQUE. I rushed back to my campsite to get a tool that would crack open the barrel. My two kids and my wife came back to satisfy their curiosities as well. They were quick to call divvies on whatever sunken treasure we found. With great difficulty we freed the barrel from the stones and turned it upright. It weighed a ton. I pried at its lid with a tire iron. It wouldn't budge until suddenly it flew off, and the tire iron slipped from my hands and crushed my wife's nose. We were all astonished at what we found within, all of us except my three-year-old daughter. We hadn't noticed the tide was rising. We lost her. A big wave pulled her off her feet, and a riptide dragged her out to sea. There was nothing we could do. I still haven't got over it. the barrel was full of tiny, delicately carved ivory elephants. Some of them were still alive, and when they saw us they climbed over the backs of the dead ones and marched around the rim of the barrel like their big counterparts in the circus. Naturally my dog went crazy when he saw the creatures. He treated them like rats, crushing their delicate, hollow ivory skulls in his big jaws. The only way I could stop him was to club him with the tire iron. He was finished, and it's a shame. In every other way he was a nice dog. Dead or alive those elephants were worth a mint. The three of us looked at each other. We didn't dare say it, but we felt like profiteers. And we were rich ones. We closed the barrel and slowly pushed it up the bank to our Chevy. Each of those elephants weighed only a few ounces, but I wouldn't want to estimate the weight of a whole barrelful. One time the barrel rolled back on my son. His legs and pelvis were crushed, but we got it up the bank, and into the Chevy, and deciding that discretion was the better part of valor we left in a hurry, not bothering to even pick up our tent and camping gear. We headed home with our find. When we were stopped at the light a colored man approached and started to engage us in conversation. I didn't catch everything he said, but something to the effect of, "Hey, jive turkey, you peckerwood toejam motherfucker," was the gist of it. "If you want to get anywhere in this life," I suggested to him, "You'll have to improve your English. Take this, my good man." I gave him one of the elephants my pooch had crushed. "Hey, motherfuck," he said, as our Chevy pulled away. "I'm gonna motherfuck you motherfuckin' motherfuckers." I had forgotten completely about my wounded foot. It wasn't until after we got the living elephants into the birdcages at home that I tried to treat it. By then it was too late. I lost the leg, and decided on a peg-leg instead of a prosthesis, because it seemed appropriate. The elephants sold out—four hundred a piece for the dead ones, eleven hundred for those still moving. Now we've got lots of things. Traded the Chevy for a Caddy. Bought this yacht. My wife is happy. She wears a veil, but lifts it when she shines up my peg. We have more fun now, even as a family. I had a wheelchair made for my son out of the very barrel-staves our fortune came in. We have three little elephants left. One whistles like a canary. The other two are lovers. What I enjoy now is things like when I put a rollerskate on my good foot and stick my peg into one of the holes on the deck of our yacht. Then my son comes by in his wheelchair and pushes me around. I spin like a top. It's better than working. Or my wife attaches some muslin wings from my arms to my belt and I turn like radar in the wind. I did that for them at Gibraltar and they loved it. We love it, too.

II

NEED

That's the sea. Finally. Now you have to do without a beach chair and an umbrella. No cabana for you, darling. After all you bought that little white elephant from the black man and spent too much money. Sure he was nice and polite and poor, but I still say he was too damned expensive. And what use is a little white elephant? Anyway, there's our sea. We can't go any further in this direction. If we turn around it's back to the mountains, and what can you do there besides jump on the rocks? You go back there if that's what you need to do; I'm going to stay right here and watch that there old raven peckin' at the wrack. Look at his buddy trying to coax him away, swooping up and down, but my old raven figures these big waves are bound to wash in something. That's the way I feel about it. Stand by the waves long enough and you'll get some good stuff. Wait a second. What's that riding in on that big wave? There goes the raven. Whatever it is, he doesn't want it. I think it's coming in for us, honey. Let's climb down this bank and get it. Wait a minute. Look at here. Just what we need. This is a great big penis, and riding on that penis is a gorgeous mermaid. Put away your elephant, honey. You take the penis and I've got the mermaid. Now I bet you're glad we came to the ocean. See you later. Hello, miss. Pucker up. Ouch. You've got scratchy scales. Keep your tail to yourself, and let's just talk. Must get lonesome riding around all day on a penis. Come on, you could stab a man to death with those fins.

What I was saying was that a penis doesn't make a man, and a man doesn't make a penis either. Sure I could get fond of your tits, but I need the rest of the anatomy to get roused up. If you've got a sister at home who carries the bottom half bring her along next time. Honey, you about done with that penis? Where'd you go? Good God. Your penis has jaws, miss, and it just ate my wife. That's not fair. I'm going to miss her. Once a man has a wife, he needs a wife. You get out of here and take your penis before anything else happens. Damned mermaid, ruins a vacation. There she goes on the penis that swallowed my wife. But I'm not one to cry over spilt milk. Mermaids aren't all they're cracked up to be, and neither are giant penises. I still believe in the seashore more than the mountains, but at this point nothing could be satisfying, and now I'm alone. Hey, what's this coming in now? It looks like a bed. It is. It's a waterbed. Too late. Thanks a lot. Now we've lost each other and now I've got this waterbed. Hello raven, watcha cravin'? What the hell. Have an elephant. No? Okay, see you later. Fly away. Can anyone believe what has happened to me on my vacation? I feel empty. All that's left for me to do is sing my song:

Hello.
My name is Steve Katz.
Have pity on me. A giant
Penis ate my wife, and now
I'm left alone, with a tiny
Ivory elephant, and a waterbed
On the beach.

The Stolen Stories

To say they swoop, or drift, or glide, would be imprecise. They don't plunge. These turkey-buzzards are called John-crows in Jamaica. That they ride the fabric of the air as it billows downward to the bay is too metaphorical. Down there the cruise ship with one blue stack brushed against its moorings. A, an American author, swirled the ice cubes through his rum and lime, and clipped the end off a good five-cent cigar. He sat with his back to Montego Bay and talked to B, another American writer who, with his son, Rafael, was a guest at the house where A was spending a year as a Guggenheim Fellow.

"Down here you can't keep the image of Errol Flynn himself separate from his role in the Captain Blood movie. To most Jamaicans, like George Huggins for instance, Errol Flynn is Captain Blood. The movie was even set in Jamaica. He, himself, behaved like he thought he was Captain Blood. He owned the biggest ranch around Port Antonio, that his widow lives on now . . ."

B imagined the tour buses pulling away from the ship to visit those duty-free ships to which the tourists had been guaranteed they would be transported, price of tour all-inclusive. One of the tourists, he imagined, was Emily Monthaven, from French Lick, Indiana, a youthful woman in her middle forties, who was travelling with her mother. Emily didn't prefer to travel this way, on packaged tours;

in fact, she found it degrading. It made her feel juvenile, dependent, stupid; but her mother insisted on such tours, and while her mother lived it was her mother's money. Otherwise she wouldn't be able to travel at all. It was always her mother's money.

"Here's this story I told you I'd tell you about Flynn, that I heard through rumors and hearsay, but anyway it's a great story. He was partying on a yacht that a doctor friend of his had moored in the harbor. It was a long, drunk, decadent party. The doctor's son was visiting. He was a medical student at a some big, northern medical school. It must have been a mess of debauchery on that yacht. Flynn had an enormous ego, and of course enough money to have things his own way. At a certain point in this marathon festivity they decided that since the doctor's son was studying to save lives he ought to first be initiated by seeing if he could take a life. They decided that he should kill a woman. They only had to figure out how to get someone to the ship whose life wouldn't be missed."

B still gazed at the ship below. "So decadent," he said to A, then he turned to his son. "Aren't you glad you're not one of those tourists being led around on that cruise ship?" Rafael watched a green lizard on the wall flick out the flap of orange skin at his neck to attract a female hidden somewhere. "I guess so," said the son. "But I've never been on one."

B imagined the heat on the poorly ventilated tourist bus made Emily Monthaven uncomfortable. She was not a hot weather person, but her mother had said Caribbean, and Caribbean it had to be. The bus stopped at a row of tacky modern tourist shops, their obsequious East Indian proprietors grinning in the doorways and rubbing their hands together. She needed a straw hat, and had to get some perfume for a friend, and her mother wanted a small silver chafing dish. She didn't know what for. When she reached into her purse to get the money her fingers played for a moment with the six bottles of valium she had managed to buy in Cape Haitian, where the drug stores sold everything over the counter. Just touching the bottles made her feel better.

Lisa, A's eight year old daughter, announced, as she came out on the terrace, that she was going to write a story. "Go ahead and write one," said A. "Can I use your pen?" she asked B. "Use your own pens and paper. Don't ask grown-ups for theirs," said her father. The late afternoon light was pink on the white limestone in the garden, and a thin spiral of pink smoke rose from the blue stack of the cruise ship.

"It was early in the morning when they made that decision," A went on. "Flynn went into town and woke up a certain man, a butcher he knew there, who frequently got women for him, sometimes young girls who needed money, sometimes prostitutes. He didn't tell the butcher how they were going to use the girl, but just that they wanted someone for the young man. The butcher got dressed and went out to look for someone."

"I want to take a swim," said Rafael. "Before it gets dark." He left through the living room. Lisa came back with a pad and pencil and took the seat Rafael had vacated, and stared at her empty page, and chewed on the eraser.

"I guess it was too late. The butcher couldn't find

anyone in town. I guess all the young girls were in bed and all the prostitutes were occupied, so he woke up his own wife and convinced her to go to the ship and get the money. He took her out there to do what he thought was make love with the doctor's son, then returned to Port Antonio because it was time for him to open the shop.''

''You got to know yourself, B,'' said George Huggins, as he came onto the terrace with a spliff smoking in his hand. ''That's right.'' If you just measure him you might say that George is a slight man, but that isn't what you perceive when you look at him. His beard—the Rastas call a beard, 'stature'—gives his face magnitude, and his calm eloquence makes his presence quite grand. Prophecy is his preferred mode of speech, the Rasta mode. ''Yes B, and A, I-n-I know a man for himself, for what he is. The man must know himself as well.'' George handed the spliff back to A and returned to the kitchen. B watched him go. It was a pleasure to watch people move through the open spaces of this tropical house, as if they were the figures that came through the openings of your own memory. He heard a splash as his son dived into the pool. The light was almost gone, only a very brief sunset in the tropics. Emily Monthaven had returned to her cabin where her mother seemed content to stay all day and look out through the porthole at the town of Montego Bay. The old woman smiled when her daughter unwrapped the chafing dish. ''It's much too small for anything,'' said Celia Monthaven. ''But you asked for a small one,'' her daughter replied. ''I said small, not tiny.'' The mother, disgusted, looked back out the porthole. It was at times like these when Emily felt she could strangle her mother with her bare hands.

A drew on the spliff, held down the smoke, passed it to B. The marijuana was rolled in a piece of brown paper bag into a spliff about the size of a good five-cent cigar. B drew on it and coughed.

"I can't think of anything to write,' Lisa whined at her father.

C, A's wife, came onto the terrace. "B, you should watch George cook the veg. It's beautiful. He's like a zenmaster when he cooks."

"You have to make it up," A instructed his daughter. "That's what writing a story means. You make it up." Lisa took this hint and started to write immediately.

B went to the kitchen. It was a pleasure to watch George Huggins do anything. The Rastafarian's belief, like the Zen Buddhist's, committed him to utter attention and devotion to whatever task was at hand. The focus is now, on what you are doing now, and through that love is manifested. "Yes, B," he said when B entered the kitchen. "I cook dem, B. Dem be Jamaican beans. I cook dem rice and use milk from dem dreadnaught, B." The beans and rice were mixed in a pot, and he was arranging some carrots, tomatoes and peppers to cook on top of them. It was beautiful, and strong. "I-tol, B. Heavy I-tol. Don't eat no pork. Yes, B."

C sat on the terrace now, in the seat B had vacated. Lisa tried to show A the story she had written, while he and C tried to discuss the use of their van for the next day. B sat down in the seat Lisa had vacated. "That's very good, Lisa," A said, after looking at her story. Cathy, their six-year-old, strolled onto the terrace and stared at B with superior knowledge. "You're not asleep," she said, con-

tinuing a private story that was going on between them.
"Yes I am," he said. "Then why are your eyes open?"
She put her fists to her hips and shook her curls, in-
credulous and gutsy as the original Shirley Temple.

"Tomorrow afternoon I'm going to see Jerry and I-ya,"
C explained to B. "It's a long trampoose into the bush.
That's why I need the car."

"Jerry and I-ya?"

"I haven't told you about them. Jerry is a white Rasta
queen, and I-ya is the man she lives with. He's a brujo, an
Obie man, an herb doctor."

"How did you meet them?"

"When I think about it, it's such a strange one, I have
trouble believing it myself," said C.

"I don't interfere there," said A. "It's totally her story,
and her territory."

"I'll tell you," said C. "We were here last year for two
months, and in the market I saw this woman selling veg.
This was a white woman, and she had mighty dreadlocks;
I mean, Mighty Dreadlocks." C showed the volume of hair
with her hands. "And she was dressed like a Jamaican
market woman, and was selling her veg with the others
in the market, and she slept in the stalls with them
overnight. It was very heavy to see her. I tried to talk with
her then, but she wouldn't speak in English, only in thick
patois. I understood a lot less patois then than I do now.
And she was friendly, but she wanted to keep some
distance. I got nowhere, but it was still mind-blowing to
me. It's very heavy to see a white woman living like a
black Jamaican, and not just a Jamaican, but a Rasta queen.
I mean, that's unimaginable."

"Yes B, yes C, yes A," George Huggins sat down on the terrace with another big spliff he had just rolled. He lit it. "The veg is cooking, C." He passed the spliff to B. "You be in Jamaica, B. We open up your mind to the vibes here, to this space and time, in this cosmos." B passed the spliff to his son who had come in from swimming. "Ganja be good for you, B. Jah herb, Holy herb. It heavy, B."

"What else did you find out about her? Who is this woman? How did she get here?"

"Okay. I finally saw her again when we came back this year. She was selling her veg in the market and I talked to her again and this time she was very friendly. She invited me to her village, to visit her. I was very flattered. I knew I had to go there. Had to. No way I could stay away. But it took me a long time to get myself together to do it. And I needed George to come with me, just to mediate. No way I could go alone. They live in an I-tol village. I-tols are like Jesuits. They're the most orthodox of the Rastafari."

"I-tol very heavy, B. In troot and justice and Jah's name. I-n-I live in dem spirit, B. Live in dem spirit," said George.

"George and I finally did go out there."

"We trampoose, B. We go there."

"It's the first time I saw I-ya. He's one of those ageless older men—fifty-five, sixty-five. Jerry lives with him. She isn't thirty yet. We sat down together and she told me the story of how she got to live the life she did. How she got to Jamaica. She spoke in her heavy patois, only occasionally saying something in English for me. She's a total Rasta queen. There's no reason for her to speak English. That's why I didn't understand all of it, but I did get that she's from a middle-class Jewish family in Philadelphia. She was in college, and was always a very private person, but found herself becoming downright anti-social, depressed, withdrawn. She stayed in her room, saw no one for weeks at a time. This was a neurotic, middle-class girl. The family sent her to an analyst, to several analysts. Nothing helped. Finally the family withdrew her from school and sent her down to Florida for a rest, and she somehow went from there to Jamaica, to Negril, and one day with some people she knew she took a bus to Montego Bay. Those buses are really top-heavy, and they frequently turn over. This one did, and she was thrown into the bush, and was bruised a bit, but not bad. Well she was lying there in the bush, and from what I could understand there was this guy, these mighty dreadlocks, this Rastaman, just standing there, and he told her to follow him, and she followed him into the bush. And that's where she stayed. She disappeared. She lived for a year and a half by herself in a shack and spent her time learning I-tol cooking and herbs. And she really learned it; in fact, one thing we're doing is trying to write an I-tol cookbook together. Then she met I-ya, and spent several years trying to get him to live with her. Finally he did. You should see him. He's such a tiny man, and so black. I asked Jerry why she picked I-ya and she said, 'Look at him.' I-ya was busy, hopping around. His eyes were shining. He was smiling. He looked at you and you knew he was at peace. 'He's always like that. That's why.' Now she lives in this I-tol village, grows her veg, sells it in the market. She's a Rasta queen. She still paints, that's what she studied, and she tries to sell the paintings. They smoke herb all the time. It's so heavy, so far out. Sometimes I sit right there in front of her, talking with her, and I don't believe it's true.''

"It's like some romantic fantasy," said B. "She has no problem that she's white?"

"No, B. No problem," said George Huggins. "Look at my skin. My skin is not black. I am not a pure African, B. One of my grandmothers was a Jewish woman, B. And I look at your skin, and I see it's not white. The British are white, but not you, B and A, and C. The Africans will return to Ethiopia, to our homeland, and you, B and A and C, you are the descendants of the original Arawak Indians, and you will come back to claim Jamaica, your native land. That is the prophecy. Yes, B."

"Arawak Indians?" B repeated.

"Yes, B."

"This Arawak is getting hungry," said A. "The veg must be ready." B went to the terrace rail, next to his son, and looked out at the cruise ship with its lights lit from stack to bow. "Arawak Indians," he said. "It's really pretty," said Rafael. Emily Monthaven and her mother must have been in the ship's dining room now, waiting for their dinner. They listened to the accordion, saxophone and drums. Celia Monthaven felt suddenly happy. The old woman got up and started to dance with herself, hugging herself around the dance floor. Old bag of bones, Emily thought. The fruit cup was on the table, and her mother was acting foolish. It was embarrassing, even though nobody paid attention. Her mother was easier to take when she was cranky.

"Do you want to read my story?" asked Lisa, as

everyone started to go for the food. "Sure," said B. Lisa had reinvented a version of The Ugly Duckling, and had illustrated it. "That's a very good story," said B. "I know it," said Lisa.

That evening the two authors and Rafael went down the hill to the little store-pub in Anchovy, where the neighborhood people gathered to drink white rum, listen to the juke-box, dance, and play dominoes in the back room. A hung out down there with a group of men, mostly in their early thirties, who had all grown up together, and knew each other down to the bone. Gray, the furniture maker and upholsterer, was there, and so was Juke, a stone mason out of work, eternal optimist, always borrowing money, rarely paying it back. Juke is tall and powerfully built. That nick-name means slice or cut. It also means fuck. They say Juke does like to juke the women. Gray is a solid, witty man, whose small upholstery business makes him one of the few financially stable men among his friends. He lives alone, is a powerful player of dominoes, and lends Juke always less money than he asks for, but never expects it back. Benjy came in, looking glum. He is a waiter, out of work, who worries a lot about money. Since the election of Manley's socialist government, and the few over-publicized incidents of violence, the bottom fell out of the tourist industry in Jamaica, and work is hard to find. A hired Benjy to drive his kids to school every day, and that was his only steady income for the year. He also lent Juke one hundred dollars to have some cysts removed from under his eyelid, so he could pass the physical to go to work in the United States. The operation was postponed, and A suspected the money had vanished.

"This is the way you turn a Guggenheim Grant into foreign aid," said A. Gurly is the clerk at the store, and the bartender. She borrowed fifty dollars from A to get a dress to wear to the Policeman's Ball. It was a red dress, and she had looked great. She had returned all the money but ten dollars of it she had lent to Juke, who has a polaroid camera, and had a scheme to make some money with ten dollars worth of film. "A good piece to write," said A, "would be to trace this Guggenheim money as it trickled down through the little town of Anchovy. That would be a nice story."

"This bar is one of the most relaxed places I've ever been," said B. "I feel privileged that I'm allowed to hang out with this bunch of friends," said A. "It's what I've always missed—a neighborhood bar, a bunch of guys to hang out with."

Gurley didn't feel good so she wasn't dancing, but Boy Campbell was dancing with his wife to the reggae on the jukebox. *Up Park Camp*, *It Sipple Out Deh*, *Woman Is Like a Shadow*. Boy is a handsome, powerful man, probably over fifty, but looking young. A says he looks like a king. *In Dis A Time*, *Police and Thief*, *Jah Light Shining*. B danced with Mrs. Campbell, and everyone turned in his seat to watch, and applauded when they finished. "It's unusual for them," said A, "to see a white person loose enough to dance." White rum, 140 proof, simmered in the brain. "White rum is made for the black man," said Gray. "I don't drink no red rum." Everyone was dancing. "When they really get loose, sometimes late at night," said A, "they do a dance they call bondage. They start dancing as if chained up, their arms crossed, their bodies held in, and then they slowly pull the chains off. It's beautiful, and it tells the whole story.''

"I was just beginning to feel loose enough to dance myself,'' said Rafael, as they started up the hill.

That night they went to sleep drunk in a flood of stories, each one gently kissing the margins of their lives, a limitless extent of stories cresting as far out as consciousness could reach.

"Come B, Rafael,'' said George Huggins as they got up early next morning. "I show you my garden. I grow dem veg, B, and Rafael. I be a heavy gardener.'' They followed George down to the terraced garden below the house where cabbages and greens and long beans were growing. The morning light was like a net of gold over the green leaves. "Come. Now we trampoose down to my other garden, my hidden garden. Now you really come to know how heavy is George.'' They walked along the stone wall, and then down some rotted logs to a small clearing below the retaining wall, out of sight of the house and garden. In the sunlight there, each in its own small hill, were some carefully nurtured hemp plants. "This is my secret garden B and Rafael. This be ganja. A don't know about this garden, B. Don't want to know. That's how de mon is. A be a wizard, B. Only C know dis garden, B. Heavy garden B and Rafael.'' George kneeled among the plants, and pointed at a particular one. "This be Kaliweed, B. It female,'' said George. "Is that one Lamb's Bread?'' "No, B.'' He pointed out another plant with a more downy, abundant bloom. "This one maybe grow to be the Lamb's Bread. Dat be strong weed. Good weed.'' He moved on his haunches to some scrawnier plants. "Dese be male plants, B." He twisted the stem of one in his fingers till you would expect it to break, then let it go so it slowly unwound. "Dem like boys, B. Mon must twist dem, so dem become strong."

Lamb's bread is strong. You eat a brownie made with it and time begins to open its gaps. "I feel like I'm living every moment as if it's already the past," said A. "This is like instant nostalgia, like I'm witnessing the narrative of the present."

After breakfast they took a ride up the coast, and at a certain point began to drive past the huge landholding of John Connally. It went on forever: little estates, clubs by the ocean, pasturefuls of polo ponies, a lush golf course soaking up precious water, a few neatly embalmed old white men in white pants swinging golf clubs under the palm trees out of a scenario by Scott Fitzgerald. A feeling of death was on this land, something moribund conjured by the voodoo of American money. "When they say Henry Kissinger is relaxing in the Caribbean, this is what they mean," said A. "This is the money for foreign aid, and how it's earmarked for underdeveloped countries. It would be imprecise to call folks like John Connally buzzards. A buzzard won't eat living flesh, this one does." Connally's land goes on for miles, kept as green as money. "If Manley's government takes this one away from him he'll just lean back and tell his lackeys to find him another little country he can buy." Connally's Eagle's Nest in the tropics, for the Bebe Rebozos, the Abplanalps. A sty to house the super-rich, so disinherited, isolated with their money, immobilized, calcified in their accumulations. Jamaica entombed in this insidious, alien luxury.

"We shed a tear for dem," said C, as she took over the car for her trip to Jerry and I-ya.

By that evening the cruise ship with the blue stack was gone. B imagined Emily Monthaven steaming towards the Virgin Islands, or Trinidad, or home again where she knew that once and for all she would have to do something about her own life, and that meant doing something about her mother.

A stirred his rum and lime. "I still haven't finished that story about Errol Flynn." He stopped as C pulled in from the bush, and got up to meet her in the carport. Rafael sat down in the seat A had vacated, and helped Cathy read the text of a story from her picture book. Tess, the oldest daughter, almost thirteen, watched them from the living room. Lisa came up behind Rafael and hugged his head. "You're so nice, she said. "Oh, Lisa," said Tess. "Oh yeah," said Lisa. "A sixteen year old and an eight year old. Who would ever believe it?"

Something was wrong with C's tape recorder so they couldn't hear the choice conversation she had promised to bring back. "She talked about the cookbook and she said some things that if I heard them right are just amazing. Amazing."

"What things?"

"There was some stuff about excrement, about shit, that I didn't understand. Maybe I didn't want to. But it sounded very peculiar. And then, you know, we were talking about food, about eating, about I-tol cooking, and she was saying that it was better not to cook at all, that raw fruit was best. And I asked her what was the ultimate food, was there one thing you could eat, one basic thing, and she said, 'I-nana'. She would eat bananas. But she had to be ready for it, and she wasn't yet, but that was the ultimate: To eat nothing but bananas.''

Early next morning B watched a John-crow perched on top of an electric pole. It waited for the sun to come over the hill and warm its wings. When the light hit it stretched the wings, to dry them in the sun. The sun lit the bougainvillea, and the hummingbird sipping at the paw-paw near the pool, and the John-crow flew, sunlight under its wings. A emerged, and Tess, and Rafael, and the four of them drove off for Accompong.

Accompong is a Maroon village in a region of steep hills and narrow valleys called 'the cockpit'. The Maroons were escaped slaves who early in the seventeenth century, with the help of the Arawaks, began guerrilla warfare against the Spanish, and continued later against the British, ambushing them in the difficult terrain of the cockpit. They were invincible rebels, a big thorn in the colonial paw. Cudjoe, the founder of Accompong, was a great leader, courageous, a strategic genius. In 1738 he put his X to a treaty with the British that made the Maroons free and independent, the Maroon towns sovereign within Jamaica, and paradoxically the Maroons themselves were enlisted in the hunting down of fugitive slaves. ''It's difficult to understand how they could do that,'' said A. B noted that in the banana plantation they were driving through the bunches were covered with blue plastic bags. ''Cudjoe's story would make a great movie.''

They stopped for a Dragon Stout and a Red Stripe beer on the way and several people recognized A from the last time he was through. A young man, carrying his beautiful year-old son, greeted A cheerfully. Another, who said he just got back from working in the States, ran to get his polaroid when he saw Tess. A man with a greying beard, a cloth fedora on his head, appeared in the doorway. "Oh, A, how nice, yes, to see you again. And your friends, oh yes, how nice in the vibes of dis place." Another Rastafarian, always recognizable by the rap.

"I-ray, Simit. How good to see you," said A. "This is Simit. A while ago I spent a lovely day with him, smoking and just talking and being with him. He's such a lovely man. His name is Smith. They say Simit."

"O yes. How nice. And now we have this time to be together in peace and love, and to talk and be and have good company. O my goodness."

"Doesn't he sound like Grady on Sanford and Son?" B asked Rafael.

"I knew he sounded familiar," said Rafael.

Simit continued on with them to Accompong. "Now I remember who that guy was," said A as he started the motor. "Who?" "That one with the kid. He's the guy who ripped off George Huggins' harvest. Now I remember. George, and a friend of his named Colley, had harvested a big crop of weed near Accompong. They expected the sale to set them up for a year. George was going to finish his house. They took turns guarding it, but one night Colley fell asleep outside the old mill where they'd hid it, and when he woke up the stuff was gone. George is sure that guy was involved in stealing it. You can see that he's kind of oily and ingratiating. I knew there was something I didn't like about him. They do that, steal from each other, some of them. George says that's what holds everyone back."

"His kid was sure beautiful," said B.

"Colley took the loss hard. He acted just like I would in his position. He tore his hair, berated himself; but not George. He just flowed with the loss. The thing happened. He let it pass. It could have meant a whole new room for his house, but he let it go. He's a high man, a totally remarkable man."

"I-n-I be good buddies. George me good friend. Oh yes, oh my goodness," said Simit.

There was an aura of 'state visit' around their arrival in Accompong. A was well known there, received like a foreign dignitary. Colonel Martin Luther Wright welcomed them by the porch of his blue stucco house, and in their honor ordered a feast prepared of roast yellow yams. "But we have no salt fish," said his wife. "There's no salt fish anywhere," said the Colonel. "Yellow yam is best with salt fish, but it's good without it." When A asked about the Maroon drum he had ordered the Colonel took him aside to ask how much he was going to pay. "Thirty dollars," said A. "Let me get it for you. He'll only charge me twenty-five," said the Colonel. They agreed to come back for the yams and went on to George's house. He had gone back to MoBay that morning to take care of a toothache, but his wife was home. They entered the one small room where the couple lived with six kids, to see the new baby. B understood what the loss of the crop of weed had meant. They could have more than doubled their living space. He also understood why George spent so much time away from home, or with A. "You know," said A, "George and I are like brothers. We have a very intense exchange, and he also has an intellectual relationship with C but for me his wife is like a shadow. I have never had a conversation with her.'' They stood looking at the half finished foundation of the unbuilt addition to the tiny house. A closed a deal with one of George's sons for a black-billed parrot he wanted to keep in his study, then they headed across town, up the dirt main street, with its shacks, tin roofs pitched like the roofs of miniature British country cottages, breadfruit and aki trees, banana bush around them, past a small, sparsely stocked store. As they walked they gathered a retinue of curious children who followed them almost to the house of Mann O. Rowe. That was who A really came to Accompong to see. He was an old man, the unofficial historian and Secretary of State for Accompong. He was dressed in some old army clothes, a crushed felt hat, his glasses slipped down his nose, the bottoms of the lenses stuck to his cheeks with a film of sweat. A was surprised to see him walking since he had been suffering from gout last time they were together.

"You're walking good, but you still can't drink."

"I take a drink, A."

A sent for a flask of white rum as Mann Rowe arranged chairs around his table so all the men could sit in council. the old man's funky look belied his deep sense of decorum, and his innate dignity. He was proud of his own eminence as a literate man, and an historian. He laid a plastic folder on the table that contained the original document, of which he was keeper, of the 1738 treaty with the British. B read it clause by clause as they drank the white rum, and Mann Rowe talked. He braided an incredible rope of history, songs, superstitions, stories, quotes from Shakespeare. He was an herb doctor, and included some of that, and the children and women watched from the doorway, and A offered occasional official state advice on how to conduct Maroon affairs, and it was all punctuated by the musical incantations of Simit: "Yes. Dat be heavy monners, dat is troot. Troot. For dis we know, dat by de rivers of Babylon, where I lay down, and very well, remembered Zion . . ." And he went on saying the psalms according to Bob Marley.

The roast yams were laid out on the table at the Colonel's house, their aroma subtly sweet, their texture like packed snow. A paid the colonel for the drum, which Simit took in hand and immediately started to play. The young woman who had roasted the yams signalled B to follow her into the bedroom. He walked by a bulletin board full of pictures of the colonel in an oversized dress uniform, complete with epaulettes and medals. "Read this," said the young woman, and she handed him a note. "I love you and would like to correspond with you so hear is my address. P.S. give me your address. P.SS. Write me as early as you can." She was serious, stretched out on the bed, not smiling. "Do you want to take my picture?" she asked. "You can." She combed out her hair, put on a bright, flowered smock, and led B around to the back of the house. "Who's that?" asked A as she passed. "She's a good-looking young woman. Is that your daughter?" "My niece," said the Colonel. "There are three of them about the same age. Very difficult to find husbands for them these days."

"I'm really glad you were there," said A, as they drove back to Montego Bay. "When I'm there alone I get completely spaced, as if I'm in a movie or some fantasy. It's not a real world for me. Even though we didn't speak much, just eye-contact with someone from my own reality helps me to ground myself.''

"That's what travelling, or living abroad is always like to me," said B. "It's living in someone else's story. You're moving on some else's time.''

"I'm in such a curious position with these people," said A. "I'm like a roving ambassador." Simit played the drum and sang in the back seat. The parrot squawked a few times, then settled in a corner of his cage. "Did I tell you that on New Year's Day I hired a van to take the leaders of Maroon Town to Accompong for their celebration. It was the first time they had met each other. Can you believe that? It was like my own shuttle diplomacy. The Maroons are in a unique position in Jamaica. They're like folk heroes, and you can't but think that if they could just get together they could exert an influence, if not on Jamaica as a whole, at least to improve their own conditions. They were really nervous about riding, because whenever they travel it's in an old car or truck that always breaks down. But I had rented a brand new VW van, and it was getting dark just as we were approaching Accompong, and they began to get really high, and to play their drums and sing these Maroon songs that were right out of Africa. I had a tape recorder going, but I haven't been able to listen to it yet. But coming down into Accompong as the sun was setting, the VW van full of chanting and singing, it was another world. I can't imagine ever writing about it.''

When he got home A told C the following story: "Twenty-five dollars for the drum. Five dollars for the parrot. Ten dollars donation to the church. Five dollars to George's wife for the baby. A couple of flasks of rum . . ." The long story of the Fellowship dollars.

Some large bats flew in and out of the light on the terrace. Another cruise ship lit up, this one with two yellow stacks, brushed against its moorings. A swirled the ice cubes through his rum and lime, and clipped the head off a good five-cent cigar. His back was to Montego Bay, and he watched his kids watching T-V. Rafael sat down to read in the light of the terrace. Moths were called bats in Jamaica, and these bats that flew in and out after the insects attracted to the light they called ratbats. To say they flitted would be imprecise, and it was inexact to say they darted. They ratbatted around the edges of illumination.

"Do you ever save clippings from newspapers?" asked A.

"I use the newspaper sometimes," said B. "I write down phrases that strike me in the Chicago Tribune, for example, and see what configurations come up. It's all meat. Having stories to write keeps me alive. It's my psychic survival. I use anything."

"I have boxes of clippings that I pull things out of from time to time. It's useful; in fact, I don't use it enough."

"There are two stories from the South Bend newspaper that stick to me. One was about a sixty year old woman in England who tried to get her eighty-six year old mother to commit suicide on Mother's Day by convincing her to swallow a fatal dose of sleeping pills. The other went something like this—'The mystery will never be solved, of the lion barely breathing found this morning in a drainage ditch in weakened condition, wrapped in a tattered blue blanket.' Those two stories seem to fit together for me. I don't know if I'll ever write them, but they seem to be copulating in my mind.''

They could hear C talking to Juke in the kitchen. This was an evening of dominoes on the terrace and the boys were coming up the hill. ''Before they get here let me try to finish that story about Errol Flynn,'' said A. ''I was up to the butcher's wife on the yacht. Okay. The doctor's son kills the woman. That evening the butcher arrives at the yacht to retrieve his wife, and they present him with the body and tell him to dispose of it. Of course, no one there but himself knows it's his own wife, and he's too frightened and ashamed to say anything. He takes the body. The doctor's son goes back to medical school, prepared now to save lives. Errol Flynn and his friend continue their party. That is, anyway, the butcher's story, the testimony he gave at the trial.

''Do you believe it?''

''It's a great story, anyway.''

Benjy and Gray carried a table onto the terrace. This game of dominoes isn't like the child's game. They play partners—Juke and A versus Benjy and Gray—and there's a lot of heavy intimidation and psyching out. ''I be here to play heavy dominoes, A. I heavy. I heavy.'' Gray slammed a double three down at the end of the line. ''Block.'' A was left without a move. ''Ahhhhh,'' said Juke. ''Dat be heavy monners, mon. Heavy monners. Me partner is strong,'' said Benjy. ''You heavy, Gray,'' said A.

B finds a light in which to read the manuscript of A's new novel. He calls it THE PLUMBER. It's the story of a character named A who in the course of trying to dope out the nature of a complicated man, a plumber by trade, probably based on A's real father, he begins to know himself better. B was too distracted to read. He kept looking out at the lights of Montego Bay there in the lower galaxies. Emily Monthaven, he thought, was quite a bit closer to home now in French Lick, Indiana. They would surely be home on Mother's Day. Her mother had the custom of staying in her room on Mother's Day and expecting Emily to serve her. Although she wasn't as feeble as some people her age, her arthritis did make it difficult for her to move, and she was weaker than she had been just ten years back, when she could work in her garden all day. She really hadn't tasted a good zucchini or tomato since she had turned eighty and had to leave the gardening up to Emily. Even if she could move around fairly well, on Mother's Day she liked to be served. And she deserved it. She'd raised seven children, virtually by herself. Every mother deserved it. "These eggs," she shouted, and Emily rushed back into the room. "You'd think by now you'd have learned how many minutes it takes for a three minute egg. This is nearly hard-boiled."

Emily pushed a fork through her mother's egg. It was just right. "This isn't hard-boiled, mother."

"I hate to chew an egg, and you know that. I like to swallow it. An egg is like an oyster. But it has to be hot." She put the tray back in her daughter's hands. "And it's Mother's Day," she said as her daughter left the room. The door is slammed. "There should be some flowers on the tray. Some lilacs."

"Block, mon. Dat duppy you see last night warn you about dis? Heavy dominoes. Heavy." Gray had just made another strong move. Juke looked disgusted with himself. "Dat no duppy," said Benjy. "Dat a ratbat come to confuse dem dominoes."

B put down the manuscript and headed for the dining room where the parrot sat in its cage on the table. "You're not asleep," said Cathy as B passed in front of the T-V screen. "Yes I am." B put his chin in his hands and stared at the parrot. The parrot shifted from foot to foot and stared back.

Emily emptied the valium into a cup. There were about one-hundred and twenty capsules in all. She dissolved ten of them in her mother's fresh pot of tea. That would be a start. The timer rang at three minutes, and she rushed the eggs under the cold water, and then broke them into a small bowl. The toast was golden, just right. She buttered it and put a little saucer of marmalade on the tray next to the cup filled with valium. She wanted everything to be just right for her mother's last Mother's Day. She laid a fresh pink and red carnation between the toast and eggs.

"You know how much I hate carnations," said Celia Monthaven, smiling, obviously pleased. "They remind me of Edsel Pruitt. He always wore one when he came to see me, and you know what he was?" She squinted at her daughter. "He was a bounder." Emily pretended to pay no attention, but it bothered her every time her mother reminded her, as she had been doing since she was seventeen, that men rarely took notice of her.

Her mother lifted the cup of Valium. "What are these?"

"That's your arthritis medicine," said Emily.

"So much of it?"

"The doctor wants you to take a large dose for Mother's Day, so you can feel good enough to go to the auction."

"I have never gone to the Mother's Day auction, and I don't intend to now. They're a bunch of damned Baptists."

"We are Baptists too."

"I am a free thinker," said the mother. She took a sip of the tea and grimaced. "What's in this tea?"

"Mother, stop complaining. Happy Mother's Day."

"I think you're trying to poison me, with all these pills, and there's something in this tea."

"Mother, take your medicine. You're suffering from the delusions of old age. This is the doctor's prescription."

"It's Mother's Day, and my own daughter is trying to poison me. Tell me where I made my mistakes when I brought you all up." Celia Monthaven looked out her window, and at the dressing table next to it where the pictures of her dead husband and her murdered son were still draped in black. And the portrait of Haile Selassie, Lion of Judah, she had bought in Jamaica just on a whim, from that scary man with big beard and ringlets who came on the ship. The picture leaned against her mirror, and she liked it, the last really noble man who had alerted the world once to tyranny, so cruelly treated in the end, just like herself. Celia Monthaven actually began to cry. Emily left the room. The chips would fall where they could.

Dominoes was over, and Benjy sat down across the parrot cage from B and tried to play with the bird. He made small noises and stuck out his finger. "Dis bird still wild, B. Smart birds. When me was a boy, me trap dem."

Benjy's delicate features were usually cast in anxiety and sadness, a persistent desperation from being out of work and poor in Jamaica, but he was clearly delighted with the little parrot, his brown face bright as a little boy's. "Dem very smart. Me trap dem in trees. Hit dem with rockstone and knock dem down. Den I tell you how smart dem be. Dey lie dere like dey was asleep, till you go to grab dem. Den dey grab you finger. Hurt you, B, den fly away. Smart birds. And dere be a woodpecker, B. You know him, pecks de wood. You go to grab it and it do dis." He pulled his lower eyelids down with his index fingers. "Pull you eyes open. Peck you eyes. Really, B. Woodpeckers. Dem birds smart."

"You know it's damned hard to write fiction," said C, in the kitchen. "Especially if all you've ever written is poetry." When she was talking seriously C liked to settle on the kitchen counter with her legs folded under her. A poured a nightcap of rum over some ice and prepared to have this conversation again, that he'd had before.

"You've written about six pages. You can't know anything from that much writing. You have to get cracking," said A.

"You'll have to admit that it's damned difficult for me being married to you and trying to write fiction."

"This conversation again."

"I don't know why I stopped writing poetry. That's satisfying for me. I don't know why I told those people at Goddard that I'd agree to write fiction for this quarter."

"When you signed up for the Goddard writing program you knew why you were doing it," said A.

"Right. I want to get the certificate. I want a license."

"Stories are everywhere. It's all fiction," said B. "But writing it is hard, for anyone, for A, for myself," said B. There's even a story here, he thought.

"Then you have to go with the program or quit," said A.

"What I resent. I mean, I guess what I resent is that you have ten years of experience on me, A. You are ten years ahead."

"That is ridiculous. No one gets ahead."

"You are. I resent those ten years. You have to respect that."

The story is of husband and wife, of roles in marriage, of ambitions early and ambitions later, of woman's upheaval. The story of our times.

Early next morning they headed for Martha Brae, a small river outside of Falmouth, where tourists went to ride on bamboo rafts. They were going further upstream, to ride the rapids all the way down Martha Brae on inner tubes. No one but A and C's friend, George Butler, who was leading this expedition, had made the trip before. He had discovered the ride when he was a boy, and his family would picnic on the river. He said it could be dangerous. George Butler is white, his family an aristocratic white Jamaican family, that along with other rich, and that means white, families, is trying to get its money out of the country around the severe restrictions imposed by the Manley government. His family is part of the white exodus. George Butler surveyed the river. "There's thirty percent less water than there was the last time I came down. I didn't realize it would be so dry. I came down in May before."

They plopped their tubes in the water, lay down on

them on their backs, and slowly paddled downstream in the sluggish current. "Only George Butler would say that," said C drifting next to B. "Thirty percent less water. It's like a stock-market quotation."

"You know," said A. "George kept saying that Jamaica used to be wonderful, and it was probably going to get good again, so when C was riding through town with him she asked him what he meant. 'I'll show you,' he said, and he pointed at a pastry shop. 'You used to be able to get the best pastries there. And in that store,' he pointed somewhere else, 'the finest cloth from all over the world for almost nothing. And there, the most exquisite chairs.' That's what it means to him," said A. "For the privileged class virtue resides in good taste. They substitute taste for morality. Fitzgerald wasn't wrong. The rich live in their own reality."

The sun flashed through the dense foliage as they slowly floated down on their backs. High bamboo swayed and clattered in the wind, and dropped its bloom on the water that irritated the skin when they paddled through it. "The truth seems quite sinister when you think of the enormous piece of property that John Connally appropriated, or even when you think of that Errol Flynn story. Let me give you the rest of it." A and B floated side by side. This could have been Tahiti. This could have been South Vietnam. "The old guy who told me the story was actually the one who had discovered the body in the blue grotto. The butcher had been claiming that his wife was out of town visiting relatives. She had been gone for weeks. One day the old guy, he was a boy at the time, was fishing in the blue grotto, and he saw something under water. He dived for it and brought up a piece of her body. They found the rest of it here and there around the grotto. The whole thing turned out to be the butcher's wife. At first he denied knowing anything about it, but then he had to admit to it. The body wasn't just hacked up, but was expertly butchered at the joints, so it was obvious that he at least had disposed of it. The story I told you was the one he told in court. I think Flynn even testified. Of course the butcher took the rap, but it's hard to know what's true. I think it would made a great detective story.''

"I love it," said B.

"I've even thought of using a detective from New Hampshire in it.''

"That's a great story. I think I'll steal it from you.''

"That would be great," said A. He laughed. "You could tell it to your rubber ducky." He paddled on ahead.

The shallow water made the ride more extreme. Either the current was sluggish and they had to pull themselves along, or the low water sped over the rapids and they got cut on the rocks. George Butler led C and some others around the shallow places through the grass where they picked up thousands of grass ticks on their legs. A, B and Rafael kept to the water, or the dry river-bed. they dropped down through some rapids that spun them around, ran them under a cliff, beat them against the rocks, and whipped them out through a whirlpool before it calmed down. A's back got slashed. B got cut up on his arms and legs, his bathing suit ripped open. "I feel like we're in a scene from DELIVERANCE," said Rafael as he spun by. He pointed to the sky where several John-crows were crossing back and forth. That adds a melodramatic touch to this story, B thought.

High up there those John-crows crossed the narrow band of sky that separated the bamboo growing on one bank of the river from the bananas growing on the other. This was putting it quite accurately. B leaned back on the slowly moving water and with a feeling of mild anxiety watched the configurations of buzzards and thought about Emily Monthaven, who waited for more than an hour before returning to her mother's room. Her mother was gone. She had drunk the tea, and at least half the valium had disappeared. Emily felt a thrill of nausea in her belly. If her mother really suspected she was being poisoned why had she swallowed all of it? This was more like suicide, and that made Emily more like an accomplice. But where was her mother? She looked out the window for a sign of her under the maples or near the ornamental plum. One of the big bay windows was open. Her mother had probably climbed out. The sill was only three feet from the ground. Emily put on some clothes and ran outside. Their house was on about three acres that bordered a large woods. The old woman could be anywhere. Cars passed infrequently, especially on weekdays, so it was unlikely that anyone would have seen her. Emily felt as if she couldn't get air into her lungs, yet she thought they would explode. Her cotton smock was stuck to a film of sweat. "Mother," she called, very softly, as if she was afraid the old woman would hear and answer. She hid behind a corner of the house as a mailman pulled up to their box, left something, and pulled away. As Emily walked to the mailbox she thought she heard a moan. The mail was just an advertisement for a tour, this one to her liking, to the Pacific, the Galapagos, Easter Island, Tahiti. As she turned back to the house and looked up from the brochure she saw the figures lying in the culvert by the roadside. One of them was her mother. It was her mother resting in the embrace of a dwindling lion. The lion could scarcely breathe, starved as it was, its rib-cage squeezed almost through its hide. the old woman pressed against its belly, her skirts lifted, her pelvis moving very slowly to the embarrassment of Emily. It was a mystery how it got there, this dying lion wrapped in a tattered blue blanket.

Three weird white males floating down the Martha Brae on inner tubes were observed with amazement and then with some amusement by some boys spear-fishing off the banks. They ran along the riverbank, waving their spear-guns and shouting obscenities in patois.

Around the bend the current picked up over some treacherous shallow rapids. They could see C and George Butler waiting at the cleared raft landing by the next bend in the river. A made it down, and so did Rafael, but B's tube slipped from under him and Rafael had to catch it downstream, and he had to cross the rapids, ripping more flesh on the rocks. Six buzzards waited there on a fence in the last patch of sunlight by the bank. That his thigh and arms were bleeding made him feel like meat. He was exhausted meat. He looked into the John-crow's eyes. A curiously childlike shine to them. They were alert, but unimplicable. They watched him. He moved. To say they were wise would be sentimental, just as to say 'ominous' or 'sinister' would be melodramatic. These buzzards relaxed in the sun. 'Innocent' was the word that lay in his mind. Their red heads bobbed a little on their red necks as they watched a bleeding white man stumble from the rapids to the bank near their perch. Even to say 'they are waiting' would be inaccurate. The author hasn't yet become their meat. They have no role to play in his story.

Death Of The Band

for Philip Glass

He felt two small hits as he listened to the music from the bandshell, as if he had been struck by some pebbles; in fact, if he hadn't glanced at his shoulder and noticed the blood that was seeping through his t-shirt he wouldn't have paid any attention. Now he had two wounds.

One listener behind him tapped on the back of a bench with his umbrella, one slept. A scantily dressed girl turned away when he caught her eye. There was no one else on the benches. Then he saw the composer, cradled in the lowest branches of a large maple, aiming his gun. He gestured for Arnold to move aside. Arnold moved, embarrassed to be in the line of fire. A parabola of dusty light suddenly filled part of the hollow in back of the musicians, then clouds covered the sun again and the composer commenced firing rapidly into the bandshell.

The gun had a silencer, but the audience could hear the shells ricocheting inside the music. The affect was thrilling Americana. Then the musicians began to fall. It was in their contracts that each of them keep playing until he is hit in the head, which happened on the count of seven for some, three for others. Once all the players had fallen the performance was over. It was then that Arnold, who had got out of the way, began to feel guilty for the death of the band.

Peter leaned back against the tree trunk and cradled the weapon in his lap. This was the first piece he had written following strictly his ideas of irreversible subtraction. The performance had been exquisite, as good as his music could be played. The instrumentation, the live performance, the composer as performer: everything was coming together. A nice surprise was the role the audience took on its own, like a tragic chorus. This was a dramatic dimension he couldn't have predicted. Peter himself had worn the maple tree as if it were a mask. It had become more than drama. It was a ritual, and he was the shaman. How interesting. No way to predict it. It was worth all psychic hernias that one got dealing with the art world in the seventies, just to make these few discoveries about one's own music. He sat in the maple tree mask and enjoyed the little applause and fondled the instrument he had played so well. It was just a 22. Everything had become the music, even Rumi, his sound man, backing a van to the stage to get the equipment. They had to get out fast. The bandshell was to be used again that evening for a free performance of the Pro Musica Antiqua.

Arnold passed through the zoo to the south end of the park pressing one of his wounds. The hit on the shoulder had just scored the flesh, but the one that had pierced his back was still bleeding. He could touch the little slug lodged between his ribs where the flesh had stopped it. If he took it to the hospital that would involve the police, and endless explanations, and put his favorite young composer through a lot of paralyzing legal rigamarole.

And he might have to explain about the band. He didn't know how to deal yet with his responsibility in that regard. He had moved out of the way. Would the band still be alive if he had stayed put? How to answer that one? He propped himself against the park wall and slowly slid to the west side. Maybe now he had become just part of the music, turned loose in the city. Now he didn't regret skipping work, because he had got to witness a rare performance of the music he loved, a premiere performance, that had moved him greatly, that had become a part of him in these two wounds that complicated his response, a slug lodged in his ribs like a dangerous bit of information. But he hadn't figured it out yet, just how he felt about the death of the band.

The Detective touched the bodies with the toe of his wing-tip shoe. Eight of them, all longhairs, each hit in the head by a small caliber bullet. It was neat, the work of a skilled marksman, so clean, very little blood spilled. He didn't want to flatter anybody, but this was good work. He knew right then that this one would go unsolved. He'd do the paper work, but no arrests here. It would blow his statistics. His rate of convictions was already too high. He was becoming a better detective, but he didn't want them to expect too much of him. They'd start to push him. They'd want to make him a Lieutenant. He couldn't take that. Out of respect for professionalism he'd let this one go unsolved. The hitters he ran into these days all had long hair, so either way this was some kind of low-life snuffed. He pulled out a pad to write down a number 8, and noticed that an enormous crowd had gathered. "The turkeys are gathering," he muttered, his voice amplified by the bandshell. The audience applauded. "Bullshit." He turned his back on them. He didn't like this kind of caper, where he ended up on a bandstand. He hated the public eye. He liked the old-fashioned idea, so hard to come by in the seventies, of a murder in a boudoir.

They came from the rowboats, from Bethesda fountain, from the merry-go-round, from the zoo, and they kept coming, climbing down over the rocks, busting through the bushes. This was amusing. This was human interest. This was the biggest crowd the bandshell had seen in years. "Everywhere is punks," said The Detective, scanning the audience. They applauded and cheered and whistled. Ice Cream wagons, hot dogs. Pretzels. Balloons six feet long. Sparkling yo-yos. The networks arrived. Camera buffs by the dozens joined the police photographer, calling out f-stops and shutter speeds.

The Detective knew it was time to leave it with his men in blue. He scrutinized the bodies draped over the music stands one last time. One thing he had learned for sure from the spiritual practices he pursued to help ease his mind in this tough line of work was that none of these deaths meant anything at all. That was something of which he was convinced. Not even a drop in the cosmic bucket. He couldn't worry about individuals any more. They were a lot of skin stuffed with punks as far as he understood it. That was why he was becoming a better detective.

Arnold still had the key to Betsy's apartment, though they rarely saw each other any more. He let himself in. Betsy was a pisces and a liberal, full of cloying displays of generosity that he found tiresome; but at this point the prospect of Betsy wiping his brow and loving him a little was the only good possibility he had. Her apartment was sloppy as usual, dishes piled in the sink, soiled clothes on top of everything. He put his finger on the lump between his ribs. The bleeding had almost stopped and the pain was down to a dull ache. He scrubbed out one of her pots and boiled up her French paring knives. He felt remarkably clear, and unafraid of what had to be done. He wished there was someone with a video port-a-pack to record his excellent moves. He ripped an old sheet into strips and boiled them, found Hydrogen Peroxide in the medicine cabinet, laid the strips of bandage over the bathtub, and sat down on the toilet seat with a paring knife. Betsy's knives always had a surgical edge. He thrust out his rib cage, keeping a finger on the lump of lead, and then touched the point of the blade to his flesh, punctured, opened himself between the ribs. The slug squirted out over the bathmat as if it had been waiting to complete its trajectory. He felt as if he had suddenly shed twenty-five pounds. The stinging of the peroxide was wonderful. He rose with it as if from dream to dream. He hadn't needed a hospital. He didn't have to tell anyone about the death of the band. He could hang on to the wonderful feeling Peter Glucks' concert had given him.

He went to Betsy's bedroom, messed up as usual, vaginal cream open on the night table, applicator fallen into yesterday's underwear on the floor. He sat on the bed and thought about telling her everything, because Betsy would understand, because at one time the deepest bond between them was a mutual love for the new American music. He leaned back on the pillow as the pain struck him, and he passed out.

"You people are as prejudiced about us as we are with you. You better believe it. You don't have to be so condescending with me," the Detective told the girl who had joined him at a table in the museum cafeteria. Betsy blushed. He was probably right. She had no business asking if he was a cop. She touched his sleeve. "I'm sorry. Sometimes I don't think before I speak." He sure looked like a cop, but sort of attractive.

"I don't want to implicate you as a hippy, but you ought to be aware that hippies have their own prejudices." Since he had started occasionally snacking at these museums he had been getting a lot more ass, and that made him a better detective.

"I'm sure that's true," said Betsy. "The hardest thing to see sometimes is yourself." She detected a surprising sensitivity in this man, and he was alive, tuned in, not like those people she usually spent time with, bored, stoned or frightened. This man was refreshing.

"People find out I'm a detective and they right away have some ideas like 'Excitement,' they think. 'French Connection.' Like I found eight musicians, or something, shot through the head in the bandshell this morning and I bet you instantly think, 'Heavy. Adventure.' "

"Eight musicians?"

"I don't know musicians from toll collectors. Maybe they were joggers. But they were all shot through the head, and what that means for me is another long boring routine. A routine. A good detective has to appreciate a routine. I am in love with boredom. Here." He takes Betsy's hand and presses it to the gun under his jacket. "What do you think that means? Anything?"

"I think it's horrible to have to live with a gun all the time."

"It's a routine. It's like your tampax. I use it once a month. Most of my work is paper work. I file reports."

"There were really eight musicians killed in the park this afternoon?"

"It's a new American hobby. Mass murders. You're lucky it isn't California. Eight is a drop in the bucket there. What's your name?"

"I'm Hilda," said Betsy. She didn't think it would be cool to give a detective her real name. She liked the strong, thick hands on the table, the cleft jaw like two small boulders.

"You live around here, Hilda?"

"I live across the park."

"I don't like to beat around the bush, Hilda. I got a tight schedule. Let's go over there now. You know what I mean."

Betsy looked away, as if she needed a moment to decide, but her mind was already made up. It was a thrilling and slightly kinky idea. The Detective got up. "No offense meant. If you don't want it I'll understand. But let me pay for your tab." She let him do it, the first time in years she had let a man pay her bill. She slipped her arm in his as they left. No one had any idea who she was. This was the strangest thing she had done since she was a teenager. "I don't know if those guys were musicians or not. They could have been parkies . . . interns . . . foreigners . . ." She pressed close to his body. They left the museum through a display of South Sea artifacts.

"In most places they won't let you hunt with a

crossbow,'' said the salesman.

"I'm not going to hunt,'' said Peter Glucks. The instrument was fiberglass, very fancy, fitted with a brass sight and trigger, and a small brass winch to draw the string back; but it wasn't what Peter had visualized.

"Where do you intend to use this weapon?''

"I'm not sure it's really what I want,'' said Peter. "Do you have anything made of wood, like polished cherry or birch?''

"I haven't seen one made out of wood for years. It's not practical. Where will you use this weapon?''

It was something more medieval that he had in mind, something carved and elegant. "It'll just be a small hall,'' he said. "No more than three hundred people.'' The piece was scored for viola da gamba, harpsichord, recorders and hunting horn, all of them amplified. It needed a special environment.

"I'm sorry,'' said the salesman. He took the crossbow away from Peter Glucks. He wasn't going to be the one who sold a deadly weapon to a madman. "I don't think we have what you want.''

Peter didn't protest. This was the kind of resistance to his art he faced wherever he turned. He was used to it. Things would work out. When the time came to perform the piece he'd have his instrument. He would face more troublesome problems when he returned from his European tour. He had a recording session then, and that was infinitely more problematic with his new music than a 'live' performance. He was thinking about videotapes, recording the new work on videocassetes. That would make this new music a star. He left the Sporting Goods store. The crossbow idea wasn't so touchy. A more delicate problem was his piece for koto, piccolo, and blow-gun.

"Shit," said Rumi, when Peter got back to the van.

"What's wrong?"

"We got another damned ticket."

"Well," said the composer, philosophically. "I suppose we'd better pay this one."

Betsy gasped when she saw Arnold lying in the mess in her bed. He had grabbed the tube of contraceptive cream as he was passing out, and had squeezed it all over the sheets. "I'm not the neatest person," she told The Detective, who was snooping in every corner. She slapped Arnold's face. He was really out.

"I'm meticulous," said The Detective.

"Are you casing my joint, or something?"

The Detective stopped at the foot of the bed. "Is this the junkie you live with?"

"This is Arnold. He's a good friend."

"I deduced as much," said The Detective. "But does Arnold stay or do I go or what?"

Betsy lifted the bedsheet and saw the dry blood. "He's been hurt," she said.

"We've all been hurt," said The Detective.

"Get some cold water," she said, feeling Arnold's pulse. "I wonder what happened." The Detective shrugged and went for water.

"Your kitchen is for pigs," he said, returning with a bowl. She swabbed Arnold's forehead with a wet rag. "Look, Hilda honey, either he's out of here in ten minutes or I'm leaving."

"Come on. Have a heart. The man's hurt."

"Sweetheart, a little blood is no new thing from my point of view. He looks okay. He moves."

Arnold opened his eyes. "Betsy," he said, touching her face, leaving a smear of contraceptive cream on her cheek.

"What are you doing in my apartment, Arnold?"

"Dying," he smiled.

"Who shot you?" she glanced at The Detective.

"Not interested," he said. "I'm off duty. This isn't my precinct." He went back to the kitchen.

"Peter Glucks," Arnold told her.

"The composer?"

"It was part of the music, the way he ended the piece."

"Shooting you was music?"

"It wasn't like that, like it was me he shot. I was between him and the band, and he was shooting the band. I don't know if I was part of the music or part of the audience. But I moved out of the line of fire and then he shot the band. He shot it in the head. It was wonderful."

"What did it sound like?"

"I mean it was horrible, but you felt that it was some important music, and I was involved in it. I mean I was morally involved. That is a real innovation. It was my choice to move or not . . ."

"He shot everyone in the band?"

"What's all this Liptons?" shouted the detective from the kitchen. "Haven't you got any good tea?"

"Who is that?" asked Arnold.

"He's a detective. I brought him here, we were going to ball, but I didn't expect you . . ."

"Don't tell him anything. Nothing. Don't say I'm here."

"He knows you're here. What can I say to him?"

"Say I was bit by a dog. Say I was in a fight. This music is very important to me, Betsy. It's turned me around. I can't explain it yet but my whole attitude to myself and music is different. I'm . . . I don't know."

"Arnold, this detective found eight musicians dead in the Central Park bandshell today."

"I know, Betsy, and I'm trying to understand if it was my fault."

"How is it your fault?"

"Betsy, I moved out of the way after Glucks hit me. The band might still be alive if I hadn't moved, I think. Maybe not. But I have to figure it out."

"O Arnold," Said Betsy, wiping up the vaginal cream. "Only a Jewish person would worry about that. You had a Jewish mother."

"What difference does that make? I even took the bullet out of myself. Look." He exposed his wounds as Betsy headed for the kitchen.

"He's really been shot," she said to The Detective, who had finished looking in all her cupboards.

"I don't want to hear his story. All I know is you don't have a decent cookie in the place. And you buy this gummy peanut butter."

"He says he was shot at the concert in the bandshell. By the composer. By Peter Glucks." She enunciated very carefully, with great solemnity. "Doesn't that ring a bell?"

"Honey, everything rings a bell in this city. Nobody's to blame. Nothing's wrong. Everything's wrong. Everyone's to blame. Everything happens here and we don't need an explanation. It's all criminal activity. Nothing causes anything. Everything causes everything. That's the rules. Now why would a girl like you fill her breadbox with Wonder Bread? That's murder. That's suicide. You're just lucky I'm off duty.''

Arnold stood in the door of the kitchen as straight as he could. He was white as a slice of bread. The wounds throbbed a little but he felt okay. "I . . . I think I'm going to leave. You guys want to use the bed, so go ahead. I'll go home. I feel pretty good. I just want to talk to Betsy for a minute." He took Betsy's hand and led her out of the kitchen. "I'm sorry, Betsy," he whispered, "that I've driven you into bed with detectives." Betsy was touched. She and Arnold once had a very intense thing going. Tears dampened the corners of her eyes. "Relationships. Fuck them. I'll always love you somehow, Arnold," she said. "It's all so impossible," he said, and went out the door.

"Aren't you going to do something?" she asked The Detective as he stepped out of the kitchen.

"Just shut up. It's not your business." He came at her down the hallway. "Shut your woman's mouth." He twisted her arm and pushed her against the wall. He grabbed her head and dug his thumb in just under the jaw. No one had ever hurt her like this before. She could feel his fist in the small of her back. "Look, I know now your name is Betsy, not Hilda, but I'll let that go. You're lucky I'm not on duty. Just stay out of my business and stop trying to make this into a movie. Now do your little trick for me."

She believed she hated him, but there was nothing else she could do. Her hand grazed his cock as she turned. It wasn't even erect. That made him more dangerous. She

knew she'd better do it with him now, even though
Arnold had wasted all her birth control. At least she'd
learned from this experiment that her prejudices about
such men as The Detective had some foundation. She'd
never make a move like this again, but for now it was too
risky not to fuck. One consolation was that if it did happen
to her, abortions now were cheap and easy.

After that day time passed at a certain pace for
everyone: endless for Arnold who was going through the
deepest changes; frantic for Betsy who cursed her luck
when she missed two periods; for Peter Glucks time
seemed not to pass at all; and The Detective put time aside
and monotonously assembled evidence.

Arnold never left his room. Once he had consumed all
the food in his cupboard he started a long fast. He had a
sense of purpose; there was something he needed to do.
That concert had changed his life, a great compliment to
the young composer. His two wounds became two scars,
a permanent inspiration to Arnold. He turned his friends
away at the door. When his office called he hung up. His
longest phone conversation was with Betsy, who for three
quarters of an hour described her abortion to him. "Is that
all," he asked, as soon as she stopped talking. He wanted
to remain alone and silent. "Yes, but I . . ." He hung up.
After that Betsy changed the lock on her door. She realized
that for her Arnold was a lost cause. He was getting
thinner, contracting around his two ripening scars. They
were the fulcrum of his new understanding, a petroglyph
incised in his flesh. They held like amulets the special
charms of his new understanding, that the music was
something outside the mastery of an instrument, or

knowledge of harmony and counterpoint. He was reaching for a new, ineffable reality where art and experience coincide. He practiced the guitar every day. He hadn't played for years because he hated to hear himself. He had always been lousy, and a worse singer; but now it pleased him even to sing. And so what? He'd get through it. He was still terrible, and the hours of practice didn't help. So what? He realized now that the art wasn't in the guitar or the ordering of the sound or the invention; it was somewhere else, somewhere he was grinding himself to go, somewhere he had first been given a glimpse of when he witnessed, even participated in, the death of the band.

The Detective continued to piece it all together, just for the exercise, for the art of it. It wasn't happening too slow, and it wasn't happening too fast. His mixture of indifference and devotion made him a better detective. Long hours got him home late and he fell asleep with his service revolver on. When he woke up his mind was full of thoughts. Were they true? Were they false? He was being led to several inevitable conclusions. Did they matter? He was glad to be alone. He took off the revolver and the clothes and put on some pale gold pajamas. He set a cushion on the floor in the center of his living room and lit a joss stick. "Fuck the lotus position," he said and crossed his legs. Almost as if he had flicked a switch he emptied his mind of thoughts, erasing a whole week's work. His lids floated down, his pupils floated up. Men and women. Good and evil. What the fuck? Hot and cold. Colors sifted through and stabilized as pure white light in his skull. It was all the same. He had a job to do. Work and play. Guilty and innocent. A clear pleasant bell began to tinkle in the void he was attending. It entered his position through the left ear.

His new music made Peter Glucks' life more complicated, and most of what he spent his time doing had nothing to do with making music. The hassle of booking concerts, setting up tours, arranging accommodations, all fell on him since he wasn't popular enough yet to afford a manager. His work was classified, unfortunately, as 'serious' music, and serious music didn't make bucks. So the chores were his, and he actually enjoyed it, even shopping for the peculiar instruments. Now he had a wonderful old crossbow, with quarrels made of ebony and brass. More complicated was that he had to continually rehearse new musicians. He never thought he would find players enough willing to perform his new music, considering the consequences; but that wasn't the case. Every week at least two or three would show up at his loft with a viola or a clarinet and ask to be in the band. They all knew what that meant, but they wanted to learn the music and as one older player said, "It's safer than walking the streets in the city these days." And everyone played the music with enthusiasm and dedication. A whole new breed of exciting young musicians was finishing their careers playing his music. It was thrilling for Peter, and only his sure sense of priorities prevented him from turning it into a power trip. "No. No thank you," said a very talented flautist when Peter offered, as he always felt obliged to do, to buy the man dinner before his performance. "I'm fasting today, anyway."

He had finally found the bass clarinetist he needed to complete the band for his Chicago concert: two electric pianos, an amplified violin, a trumpet, a singer, and the bass clarinet. The voice was a new notion. It didn't totally work yet, but there was something very rich about it. The fall of a singer might make the performance a little too much like tragedy. That wouldn't work. It had to be a delicate balance. But it was only February 14, and he had till April to get it right. The singer was really good, and good looking. She had been a model once, and had studied voice for years, had specialized in lieder. And there was something about her that touched him personally, but he couldn't let himself get involved. He had too many plans. It would be unprofessional.

The singer answered the doorbell. Arnold was there, dressed in his fatigues. He hesitated a moment, squinting into the light, and then stepped inside. "Is this Peter Glucks?" His voice quavered slightly, as if too finely tuned. "Right," said someone sitting at the piano. Arnold set his instrument case on the floor. That he was moving very slowly made everyone pay attention to him. There was something new about Arnold's manner, something fine and ascetic, a pure glow. He could be someone you almost feared, but someone you also aspired to be.

"I want to audition for the band," said Arnold.

"That's weird," Peter said. "You're number eight today."

Arnold looked at the singer. "What's your instrument?"

The way he said it made her blush. "I sing with the band," she said.

"I love you," said Arnold. "I want you to help me."

"This thing is growing so fast it's scary," said Peter

Glucks. He pointed at Arnold's instrument case. "If that's a guitar, man, I'm sorry. I've never really written a piece for guitar. There's the pop-country-folk stigma that keeps me away from it. I know that's just in my own head, but I haven't really dealt with it. But I really do appreciate that you came to see me." The composer laid his arm somewhat patronizingly on Arnold's shoulder. "I really have no use for guitar, but leave your address in case I write something."

Arnold slipped the composer's arm off his shoulder and stepped back. He unbuttoned his shirt and slowly opened it to reveal the two gleaming scars. "Do you recognize these?"

The band closed in for a look. Peter Glucks ran his finger down the scars. "O how strange," said the composer. "I almost forgot that piece. You were in the bandshell. You were heavier. Weird. There was something in that first piece that I still . . . wow."

"It's lovely," said the singer, kissing both scars.

"Thank you for coming by, man. I'd almost forgot how that piece worked." He ran the backs of his fingers up the piano keys. "The music never ends. Ideas just grown one out of the other." He tapped his forehead. "I can't believe how fantastic."

"Do you want to hear me play my instrument?"

"Of course, man. I'd really dig to. I might do a piece for guitar. Who knows. I'm open to anything. Go ahead."

In the fluorescent light everyone seemed made of enameled steel. Arnold unsnapped his case. "I don't sing very well," he said to the singer. "Can you come and sing with me?" She smiled and crossed the room to stand next to him. He lifted his instrument out of the case. As soon as she saw it the singer sang. Arnold stepped in front of her and put the butt of his instrument to his shoulder. The singer burst into her own rendition of East Side/West Side. Arnold opened fire. "All around the town," sang the singer. There wasn't time for the composer to even sit in on crossbow. The whole ensemble fell in every direction as they were lunging for their instruments. It wasn't the greatest performance, but it was Arnold's first, and he played as well as he could. The responsibility for the death of the band could now unequivocally be laid on him. He embraced the singer and they backed out the door. She was still singing and he lightly patted the beat on her arm. Something special had happened between them. They were a new duo, a direction of their own in the new music. The elation made them laugh when they hit the street and lost their voices to the traffic, thrilled with their discovery of each other; and they skipped away to Chinatown, singing and holding hands.

NEW STORIES

One Pinch Plut

A few weeks ago my son came back to live with me. He's twenty-three. That's what they do. Everybody says so. They try the world for a while till it gets rough on them, and then come back to live with you and try to figure it out. All in all he'd been doing okay, studying in Asia, making good money as an English teacher. Life was easy for him, but he came back anyway. Maybe it was for these letters. Almost twice a week he'd get a letter from Bismarck, North Dakota, from a woman named Marianna Golf. A strange coincidence. That's the name of my mother, his grandma. She's dead three years. I dropped her ashes off the bridge into the Hudson, just like she asked, with a red rose.

Maybe he trusted me not to read his mail, or just wanted to tantalize me. I don't know why he did it, but he left these letters stacked on the arm of the chair he sat in while he watched T-V. On Thursday I handed him the ninth letter, which felt cold to the fingers, as if it sealed in a piece of bitter winter I always imagined dominates the weather there.

- You get a lot of these letters from North Dakota.
- Are these from North Dakota?

I don't think he was being disingenuous as that sounds. We've been real candid with each other, especially since he moved back in. We talk so much about everything, advise each other on careers and love, so you could think we were friends or brothers rather than father and son. His natural gentility and reserve, enhanced by his having lived among tradition-bound Asian people, was the only thing kept some distance and decorum. That was why he gave me the funny look when I said, - Strange that whoever your correspondent is she has the same name as grandma.

He didn't respond, probably thought I was being too nosy. He pointed at the MTV he was watching and said, - Huey Lewis and the News, that's not real rock and roll. That's more L.A. plastic. That's what kills me back here in America.

His evasion made me more curious. Whether it offended manners or not I wanted to know more about those letters. After all, he had two grandmothers, but I had only one mother, Marianna Golf. My right to find out about this was more important than anybody's privacy. I was the kid's father, I figured. Not too long ago I lay down the rules for him. It was my right, my duty to examine those letters. That was the way I thought. When you're obsessed with curiosity you can rationalize anything. I picked up one of the letters while Ray was in the bathroom. He had never opened it. I looked at another, and another, all nine of them. My son had opened none of these letters from Bismarck, North Dakota. When he sat down again with his Chinese novel, *The Dream Of The Red Chamber*, one of the classics he was reading in Chinese, I had to mention the letters again.

- I know what's in them, he says. - So why should I open them? I couldn't answer that. I stared at the stack, and then at him, his eyes already burrowing into the Chinese characters.

- But who do you know in Bismarck, North Dakota has the same name as my mother?

- My grandmother, he mumbled, with the tone of a rebellious teenager. - She had the same name as your mother. He smiled as if he knew he had me hoodwinked. This pissed me off, made me feel even self-righteous as I lifted the stack of nine letters and carried them to the kitchen while he was at work. (He had a job as a night-clerk in a hotel, and I know he had adventures there he never talked about.) I steamed the letters open one by one. The messages were hand-written in the form of recipes; for instance:

MOM'S POTTED BRISKET OR DECKEL & KASHA

3 lb trimmed thin-cut brisket	1 can tomato sauce
1 large onion, minced	1 or 2 cloves garlic
salt, pepper and paprika	(crushed)
1 pinch plut	carrots (optional)

Wash and trim meat, sprinkle well with coarse salt & let stand for one hour. Rinse well to remove all salt & let water drain off. Heat a pot or skillet with a little salt sprinkled on bottom to keep meat from sticking. Put meat in pot and sear, turn meat and sear on other side. Use small flame. Add minced onion & garlic & pepper. When onions are a little brown add tomato sauce & enough water to cover meat & let cook on low flame for 1 hr. Turn & let stew on other side for 1 hr. longer. Taste gravy & add salt to taste. Add more water to top of meat. Let cook another 15 min. Remove meat to large dish. Slice in 1/8 in. slices. Cut on slant against grain. Put back in pot (add carrots). When meat is soft - finis! Follow instructions on Mrs. Wolff's kasha box & add 1 cup of kasha to 1 quart of water (salted). When water is boiled down add gravy & mix in pot until thick enough to serve - ENJOY!!

Or the letter of June 6:

MOM'S BORSCHT

6 or 8 beets	sour salt (citric acid)
juice of 1/2 to 1 lemon	1 small onion
2 raw eggs	sugar or sweetener
1 pinch plut	1/4 tsp salt

Boil beets in 2 qts water (scrub beets first). Cook until soft. Peel. Grate beets on shredder and put into pot of beet water. Grate onion & add. Cook 10 to 15 minutes longer. Beat eggs in bowl. Fill glass with borscht and slowly add to eggs while beating eggs and borscht is hot. Do same with one more glass of hot borscht. Stir while adding egg mixture to pot of borscht. Boil whole potatoes and enjoy. - Serve cold with a dollop of sour cream (smetana to you).

August 12 was potato pancakes (latkes), and so on. Each letter was one of my mother's recipes, written in my mother's handwriting. The only thing I didn't get was the '1 pinch plut' that appeared in the list of ingredients for each recipe, but never showed up in the instructions.

I resealed them all and snuck them back onto the arm of the chair. This was a puzzle, a deep quandary for me. I didn't want to think about it, but it was on my mind every minute. My mother was not only dead, but her remains had been dumped, in the presence of sons and nephews, off the bridge, and the last we saw of her was a grey streak on the green slimy Hudson headed for the statue of liberty, for the Atlantic, trailed, as per her request, by one red rose. Were these letters a hoax she'd arranged for just before she died? Could it be herself alive in Bismarck, North Dakota, her death a hoax? Why that cold northern city, and not Miami Beach, where she enjoyed to go when she was alive to escape the cold? We had no connections in Bismarck, North Dakota. I'd never even heard of anyone who lived there. The next day, another letter. I didn't even bother to look at it. I could guess the contents: maybe apple strudel, maybe the perfect matzoball. Marianna Golf, my mother, was a powerful Jewish mother. Her power lasted even after her death. My son was wise to leave the letters unopened.

The last year and a half had been good for me with Kistner Real Estate, not that it was my doing, but that I was given some previously dead territory in Long Island City just when the situation was beginning to open up, and I was able to move a lot of space quickly, so when I asked for a month off they let me have it without much convincing. 'A death in the family', I explained, not mentioning it had happened three years ago.

At seven A.M. on Monday I got on a Trailways for Chicago, and there connected with a Greyhound for Pierre, South Dakota. Leave New York and you sink deep into exotic U.S.A., stars and stripes and polyester U.S.A., junk yard and shopping mall U.S.A., Pizza Hut and Burger King U.S.A. From Pierre I picked up a ride North at a truckstop, with a driver headed for Fargo to drop off a load of furniture, and latch on to a load of pigs for St. Paul. He was an ex-biker, Douche his CB handle. I never learned his real name. His rig had a monster stereo system on which he was playing new age music so loud you'd think George Winston had soul. He had never been to Bismarck and didn't know anything about it.

- I'm going there to find my mother. It was good to say it to someone.

- Goin' there no more to roam, he grinned. - I found my momma in French Lick, Indiana. He changed the tape to Waylon Jennings. I could hear the outlaw leaning on me, pushing me deeper into the America where I felt more like a tourist than a native.

To avoid approaching Bismarck from the interstate I got off at a town called Moffitt. Enter from the South, something told me. I hitched with some farmers, slow going, slept one night in a corn field. This was a pilgrimage, not a pleasure trip.

I don't know what your take is on Bismarck, North Dakota, but entering on foot from the South was for me a revelation. This did not look like any North I could ever imagine. The entrance to the city is flanked by two enormous towers that from the distance could be mistaken for grain elevators, but up close you see they are giant cages, surrounding the jungle environments, thick with a mockery of snakes, shy snickering monkeys, six-headed insects, cats with neon teeth, hyenas of war, elephants with a hundred legs, wild dogs barking in the four directions, kudu nailed to the cross, giraffes built of telescopes, all animal eyes peering at me from behind gross cabbages that made this jungle a garden. The turrets were loud with toucans and parrots and birds of paradise, ranking and reranking like an army at peace. Pale rabbits flew from tree to tree. Fruit bats giant as men and women hung sleeping from the superstructure that left openings so large any beast could escape onto the prairie if it chose. Bismarck was shining over there in the pearly light of thin overcast, as if it had been built of mercury and other opaque liquids held in flasks of lucent skin. Holy moloney, I thought, if New York City looked like this, selling real estate would be a dream. What a place for my mother to end up. I had no sense of right or wrong.

From the cage to my left a jaguar chuckled, its tooth flashed, paw extended just to stroke, not to scratch me as I entered town on hands and knees through the low arching tunnel that was Bismarck's access from the South, as if it was an igloo or a playhouse for children. I entered on Thursday but lost count of the years after that.

They weren't authorized at the Post Office to give out addresses for the postal boxes, but one of the clerks handed me the phone book, and suggested I check in the yellow pages under M for Mother. Her name was there, Marianna Golf. I found a phone booth in a supermarket parking lot, and dialed her number.

- O! Is that you, Larry? I'm in shock.

Definitely my mother's voice. - Mother?

- What then? You think one of your girl-friends? Everyone sounds the same to you. You never call me unless you need something.

Dead or alive my mother was the same. - Mother, you're dead. That's why I haven't called.

- It's always easy to find an excuse. I know all about you. Are you coming over?

- How can you talk to me, mother, when you're dead?

- Bring some breadsticks when you come, but not like last time. Those were too big.

- I know you're dead, mother. I threw your ashes off the Tappan Zee bridge with a red rose just like you said.

- The Tappan Zee? You threw me off the Tappan Zee?

- How did you get to North Dakota?

- What do I know where I am? I never go outside.

That was true. The last twenty years of her life she stayed in her room, except to go to the doctor or the hospital.

- I specified the George Washington. That was my last request. It was in the note. I'll never make another request.

- I'm sorry, mother. I'm sorry. The bridge was closed to pedestrians.

I could hear her pause, and then the exasperation and resignation in her voice. - Just bring a chicken, a nice roaster, nice and yellow, but not too fat.

After her last request my mother found a way to make some more requests.

The supermarket was the most complete I had ever seen. Of breadsticks alone there were seventeen styles, the long, the stubby, the twisted and the knobby, the sesame and poppy-seed, the cheese flavored and onion flavored, the whole wheat, the buckwheat, the pumpernickel, the vitamin enriched. A mile of chickens. You could buy them by the twenty-six breeds, by the young or old, by the organic or inorganic. There were smoked chickens, dried chickens, kosher chickens, chickens in parts, liquid chickens, chickens alive, strutting and pecking in cages behind the counter, chickens that glowed with health and self-confidence, chickens that glared at you and clucked curses in your face. I picked out a live one that looked at me from its cage as if I should turn to stone. In a few minutes it was dead, plucked, cleaned, and steaming in a plastic bag, and I was on my way to my mother.

There were several tons of mothers in the lobby of the small hotel at my mother's address. They sat in a circle, knitting on one huge stocking cap, big enough to warm the moon.

- Hello, mothers of the world, I said.
- Hello, my son, said they.
From the outside the building didn't look so tall, but

my mother's room was on the eleventh floor, just where
it had been when she lived in New York City. Her room
was the duplicate of the old place in Manhattan, same
smell of lavender and lemon oil, same adjustable bed,
same easy chair, same formica table, a room full of pillows
and blankets in a jungle of potted plants.

- Mother, don't fool around, I said as soon as I saw her.
- We all know you died. You can't be in North Dakota,
unless I'm hallucinating. Am I seeing things?

- Seeing things! With the drugs you people take of
course you're seeing things. Did you bring the
breadsticks?

It was her old voice, thin, cracking at the end to tug
your sympathy. - I even brought a chicken. I handed her
the breadsticks. - But I'm curious, mother. What are you
going to do with a chicken? Dead people don't eat, do
they?

- These aren't the breadsticks. These are too hard. I
don't have my teeth any more. I love my children with
my life and what do I get? Too big, too hard. I can't chew
something like this.

It's not a pleasure to hear a dead woman complain
about breadsticks. You want to say, what difference does
it make, you're not a functioning human being any more?
But that woman is your mother and you're afraid to insult
her, so you keep quiet. She stood up, uncertain on her
legs, and grabbed hold of my arm to balance herself. - Give
me the chicken.

- It's heavy, I warned her.

She threw me a dirty look. - Everything's heavy.

Chicken in her arms she headed for the refrigerator, wobbling like a newborn filly in her pink chenille bathrobe. The place she had grabbed on my arm was heating up, and it started to glow like something radioactive. What is happening, thought I? Is this real life any more? The question was no longer what was she doing in this place, but what was I going to do in North Dakota?

She wobbled back to her chair holding a dish full of something tricky, some little capsules or beans, that she started to finger when she sat down.

- So mother, you haven't answered my questions.

- Ask me, bubbela, whatever you like. I'll answer all your questions.

- I'm not saying I don't miss you, mother. I do; but you're dead, as I know better than anyone. Aren't you dead?

She gave me her most skeptical look. - And if I am, what's the big deal? A lot of people are dead. Your father's been dead for longer than me. You got a case against the dead?

- But why North Dakota? Dead or not, I don't know what you are doing here.

- George Washington was the father of our country, she said, straightening up in her chair. She looked dignified, indignant, proud.

It took me a moment to get the gist of her comment, that I'd thrown her off the wrong bridge, and that's how she ended up in this alien city. I was overcome with shame. - Mother, I'm sorry. The George Washington was closed to pedestrians. They were making repairs. Who knows how long that would take? Cross my heart and hope to die, mom. So I had to throw you off another bridge.

- The Tappan Zee?

- I did everything else according to your instructions. The red rose, the finest red rose I could find, cost me seven dollars just one rose.

- I'll never make another request, and you know it.

- O Yeah! How about breadsticks and chicken?

- What kind of son are you? Did I bring you up this way? To count the request of a dead mother against her. The George Washington I know, but what do I know from the Tappan Zee? Who was this Tappan Zee? Was he some foreigner? So here I am and you hock me with chicken and breadsticks.

My fault. My fault exactly for doing what I thought was the only thing I could do at the time. I threw her off the wrong bridge, so that's why she ends up in Bismarck, a town with the name of a foreigner. My fault. I felt it in my heart. My own mother here. I started to sob. - Mother, I'm sorry. Mother, I didn't mean to do that. Mother, forgive me. Mother, I was wrong. Mother, I'll never do it again. Mother, I'm gonna change. Mother, I don't know right from wrong, I don't know my ass from my elbow, I don't know shit from shinola. Mother, I'm sorry. Mother, I didn't mean to do that, I didn't mean to say that. I didn't mean to hurt you so bad. Mother, forgive me. Mother, I slit my wrists. I put a bullet in my brain. Mother, I run my car off the cliff. Mother I pull my knife on a stranger, and in the prison yard me gang-banged by big bunch, and I like it for you. Mother, I shoot smack in front of your eyes. I shoot crystal meth. I freebase along the razor's edge. Mother, I'm sorry, I get hepatitis for you. I hijack the Boeing for you. Give me ecstasy. Give me angel dust. Mother I throw away my head for you. Mother, I marry the girl next door for you. Mother I go down to eat pussy of the girl next door to the girl next door for you. Mother, I beat my baby for you. Mother, I write poems for you, I write novels for you, and then I eat the pages. I burn the pages and eat the fire for you. Mother, check the blisters on my tongue. I've got herpes for you. I am your syphilitic son. I hide in the wilderness so you won't be embarrassed. Mother, forgive me.

While I was talking she clicked her television on, and sat watching the president convalesce after his operation. - Cancer of the colon, she said with contempt. - You know how many diseases I had? You know how many heart attacks? I should be in the Guinness Book of World Records. Nobody knows what I suffered. She sighed deeply and played with the little pellets in her bowl. On T-V the president had a similar little bowl. My mother held the dish out to me, its contents rattling in her shaking hand. - I want you to take this.

- I can't take that from you, mother. You're dead. You're not responsible for your actions.

- I don't have any use for it any more. I want you to have it because I love you. I love my children.

I took the dish. Its little beans looked alive, about to hatch, like eggs. - What is this, mother?

- It's plutonium, bubby, what do you think? It's the real stuff, worth a lot of money.

- Mommy, I don't want some plutonium. What are you giving me?

- Now they're trying to outlaw it. Take my word for it. This will be worth a fortune, my son.

I wanted to let it go, but I couldn't. I couldn't disappoint my mother. The damage was already done anyway. This little dish of plutonium can kill 500 billion people a minute, mommy. One piece of it the size of a herring virus is enough to give cancer to Wilt Chamberlain, to a sumo wrestler.

- Get a shopping bag from the doorknob over there, so you can carry this. It's a fortune there. You just hold onto it. If not you, your children. I never see them either.

I was sick of reminding her she was dead, my poor mother. She's from a generation that still believes science solves all the problems. That's why she hoarded this plutonium, though who knows where she got it. And it struck me as I went for the shopping bag what that plut was in all her recipes, a pinch of plut. What hope was there with a pinch of plut in every recipe? I couldn't give the stuff up. I'd already hurt my mother enough throwing her off the wrong bridge. The damage was already done. I felt a little better with the stuff out of sight in a shopping bag. The bag was from Bloomingdales.

When I turned back a change had come over my mother, a change I imagine sometimes comes over the dead, only the dead. This was fascinating. What I'd taken to be her old decrepit body was losing substance and starting to glow. I moved to get a closer look. She had become transparent, a transparent parent, and some things moved within her as if she was a fish tank or cloud chamber. This was really interesting. I moved so close my nose was almost touching. Within the form of my mother a thousand bald eagles were flying, changing direction in unison, back and forth, up and down, by mysterious signals as a school of fish changes. They flew in formations around an enormous dolphin that swam and played within whatever element my mother contained as if it were water. At a distance within her some creatures, like expanded roaches were digging tunnels in the earth, pausing to warm themselves by a campfire. Just as I pressed closer to better make out the flags they were flying there I felt a blow to my chest as if I'd been hit with a club. Mother, whom I'd known as a woman so weak she could hardly walk without leaning on an arm, had got up and had jammed me with a front kick.

- Get away from me, she shouted, her voice fresh as a schoolgirl's. - Get away from me, you womanizer. Don't you come near me. Womanizer. Womanizer.

Her kick had nailed me to the wall. Where had she gotten the strength? She kept coming at me like a black belt gone berserk. My own mother. Maybe this was what they call the infinite strength of the dead? I'll tell you something I learned, anyway. A dead mother packs a hell of a wallop. Her punches and kicks came so swift I couldn't see them. I couldn't have hit her if I wanted to. All I wanted to do was get out of there, but she blocked the door. I would have died right there, but I felt these tugs at my shoulders, and like a zeppelin I left the ground, hoisted by two cherubim with gorgeous wings. They had the bodies of young Judy Garland, and the faces of Alfred Hitchcock.

- Don't forget the shopping bag, said my dead mother at the last, and she handed it to one of the nubile winged Hitchcocks as we flew out the window.

- This has been too much for me, I said. This can't be Bismarck, North Dakota.

- You are where you think you are, they said in unison. - By now you must be very hungry.

That we were flying around was no stranger than anything else that had happened. It wasn't very high, just above rooftops. But it did seem strange the way my escorts looked. - Why do you have that body and that Hitchcock face?

- However you want us to look, that's how we look, honey. They spoke again in unison. That was a puzzler, no fantasy of mine, a Garland-Hitccock combo. - You must be very hungry, they repeated.

They were wrong. I'd eaten very little since my pilgrimage began, but I wasn't really hungry; however, in the interest of getting back to earth, I thought it might be good to sit down and look at some food. - You kids know a good restaurant in town?

We came down in front of a place called Sybil's cafe. They lingered just a moment, as if they were waiting for a tip.

- Thanks for the rescue.
- We don't save you from any but yourself.
- Philosophical birds.
- From now on you listen to your momma.

They flew away, leaving the shopping bag by my side. Down the street a man and boy came out of the Ben

Franklin, the boy with a toy gun, the man with a new leaf
rake. A woman with green pants fed a parking meter and
started to walk my way. I looked up. Intersecting con-
trails had crossed out a blue sky. - Good morning, someone said out of the blue. It was the green pants. Her smile
was horrible. I entered Sybil's cafe and sat down at the
counter. Next to the coffee-maker a calendar hung with
all the days of August crossed out. I wondered how
September was doing. The waitress, it was Sybil herself,
noticed my interest and flipped the calendar. September
was crossed out too.

  - I don't like to forget, so I do that in advance, she said.
  - How far in advance?
She laughed and brought me a cheeseburger and fries,
slice of tomato, onion, and lettuce. I was the only cus-
tomer in the place. She brought me a Pepsi. After a while
she watched me watch the plate.
  - Aren't you going to eat?
  - I think I'd rather watch.
  - You are a strange one. What are you doing here?
  - Where?
  - Bismarck.
  - So this is Bismarck.
  - North Dakota. What are you doing here?
I grinned at my burger. - I'm womanizing.
  Her tired face took on a sudden glow. - Shoot, you can't
do that in Bismarck.
  - I came to see my mother, but I don't think she lives
here.
  - She doesn't? Then why'd you come?
  - I came to womanize.

- You are crazy. Bismarck is no place to do that.

- Everywhere I go, I womanize. I lifted one of the fries and opened my mouth. Sybil opened hers as if to help me take it. I put the fry back down.

- Crazy. Crazy. She went off wiping the counter saying that word and grinning. Two more customers came in, farmers wearing caps with Case insignias. They knew Sybil, and kidded her a lot. She came back to my end of the counter and whispered, - I hope you stick around.

I did stick around, and I went off with Sybil after she closed her diner, and once it got dark we went to a drive-in, big screen on the wide American prairie. And while we watched the chain-saw murder I womanized. All night long I womanized.

- What's in the shopping bag? she asked once.

- It belonged to my mother. Just some plutonium.

- O. She looked into the bag. - That's the strangest plutonium I've ever seen.

I looked into the bag. She was right. It was strange.

All through the night I womanized and womanized. I womanized in the morning, and through the next days and on. While I was doing that Sybil was doing something too. All night long Sybil was doing something too; I don't know what it was, but she was doing something.

Four Zippo Stories

LOOPED IN OAXACA

The time to leave was here and gone. Another cup of Mezcal, senor; in fact, bring us a jug. The borders of Oaxaca have been closed and we stay here forever, alas. We were almost away. Drink up, Zippo, my love. Tomorrow, suddenly, is not another day. For instance, that shawl you bought yesterday, you weren't going to wear it till you got home; well, put it on. And those old pants, mine, so sexy and baggy on you, that you wore for a joke here in the mornings, we thought we'd toss them to make room in our pack for yet another gorgeous serape, that luckily we haven't paid for. Now they're your private pants. That serape money will have to last, if bucks is still money in Oaxaca. Let's relax and drink another 'copa'. The exits are sealed, and it's too late to stop. This is politics. How do you feel? I feel peculiarly politically motivated. Seven days have passed since we first heard, and seven jugs of Mezcal. That's enough, I say, no more of this. Ahimé, Zippo, too late. 'More of this' is all we get. More tortillas. More salsa. More frijoles. More marimba, bimba. Gringos forever, Zippo. More and more molé. Have another copa. And senor, you are my best friends in the world and I love the whole world and the world is my great friend, amigos. Now let's fight. Quick, Zippo,

immediately start to draw something in your new
sketchbooks, particularly Oaxaca, particularly that
Oaxaca you knew before you ever saw this Oaxaca.
Oaxaca in your mind as you remember it when we were
still free of what we know now that the borders are
closed. What else is worth doing now? This here is a little
copa of Mezcal. Show what it was before it closed on us.
I will write a caption for your illustrations as best I can,
and in that way maybe we can get some rescue, bug out
of this place, but not before we finish this jug, baby. Such
a sweet trap, this. So relaxing. And God bless you, next
jug of Mezcal. You drink this down to the worm. Did you
draw the worm? How about a tree in your Oaxaca? Live
oak? Palm tree? Jacaranda in bloom? Is the senora there
carrying her wicker tray of watermelon wedges on her
head? Do the stone-masons work all night long to finish
the Zocalo? Jojoba bush perhaps. Does this policeman
stand under the tree in a bead of sunlight? Standing in a
blue uniform without shoes? Did you put some noisy
trucks into it? Do the tabacaleros march into your picture?
Are they on strike today? When do the cops break them
up? Does the waiter have a glass eye, the one who brings
you something else, until you figure out that you order
something else if you want to get what you want? Will
you put seven different flowers in it? Is this the orchid
family? Is this your family, panicking in the states? Does
that horn honk under your colored pencils? Does that
machine on the Zocalo quit when the militant speeches
of the campesinos begin? Does justice enter your picture,
with honest wages? Does this drawing rectify for the
campesino the devaluation of the peso? Is the gringo

threatened? Can we run down a street that fills seven pages? Ahimé, Zippo, who can draw it fast enough, write it quick enough to escape as I thought we could before they actually closed Oaxaca around us. This is where art ends and life begins, or vice versa. Cripes, Zippo, draw some food, quick, I'm starving. Some frijoles and blandas at the train station. Did you get the train station in yet? Do your trains run on time? One train each evening? One train to Mexico? One jet to the world?

TAKING THE CAVE MAN SERIOUSLY

"So there they are, in that well known zone, and all of them are floating on lines."

"You talk like hockey."

"It's no game, man. It's someone's life."

"Sounds just as primitive."

"Listen to me, man. I'm talking magenta. I'm talking from day before dowdy to suddenly electric blue eyeshadow."

A white limo pulls up in front of the club and three men step out. The most elegant is a woman dressed like a man. Her name is Myrtle, a name she hates. She hates her parents who named her Myrtle, and thinks it must have been out of spite because they wanted a boy. Though she is dressed now as a man she nonetheless insists they all call her Myrtle. Him Myrtle. She likes Him as a name. Horace admonishes them not to register revulsion or astonishment once they get inside. Horace is a name one can resent as well, though he never thinks about it. That's his name.

"How big?"

"I'm talkin' great big. I mean the woman fills the whole entrance. I'm talkin' ample."

"Now you're getting real descriptive."

"Really. But you should get the whole picture, man. Him too, moving like a mink, banging away. All of them floating on lines."

They press the bell and wait. Claude gazes at Myrtle. He has difficulty seeing her as a man, though she is all spit and polish. He can't call her Him, because he sees her only as the woman he loves. Thus can love penetrate the most wilful disguise. Him is the woman he continually undresses with his eyes. Horace explains that once they get inside they will see people in bizarre situations, ordinary people doing things strange. It is incumbent on them, Horace admonishes, to be nonchalant, keep their cools, to avoid a twitch.

"Flabbiness, I mean gross. At one point she rolls out her tongue and licks all the interior; I mean, grundgy. I mean this is your average contented homemaker on the rampage."

"Why should I be interested in this? I watch a lot of sports. I'm not that kind of person. I use my time with absolute precision."

"A big fat tub of warts slides across the floor on her tongue. You'll change your mind. I've seen it before."

"I think you hate women. You always have to remember your mother is a woman. Why can't you talk about ordinary people?"

"My mother is not an ordinary person. these people are. It's the men too. No one is exempt from the little secret stuff closeted away here and there. That's why this is so great here, and when all of them are banging on lines, floating in that well known zone . . ."

"What well known zone? Sometimes you talk like a millionaire."

"Sometimes I feel like a millionaire, buster."

They ring again and once more. The wait makes Him
(Myrtle) even more nervous about passing. Only Horace
of the three of course has come here before. Claude came
along of course just to be with Myrtle (Him). Him (Myrtle)
is on the verge of suggesting they forget it and leave, when
the security window opens and she is hit by a puff of air
that smells of something oozing up for millenniums to
reach the surface of the earth. A face with the complexion
of a smashed goldfish appears in the square aperture.

"Well I have to admit that once I met a person, a
woman like that, who did something like that. A nice
woman, of superior intelligence. I liked her."

"I'll bet you did."

"Her first boy-friend was the worst. Before they did
anything he liked to burn garbage in front of the TV. And
she was right there too. Right in that zone."

"Which zone?"

"You know. Same zone. Banging on lines. Floating. But
then she married a guy who applied his computer
knowledge to making pasta. Now he rivals Ronzoni."

The door opens for Horace, Him (Myrtle), and Claude.
Horace steps over the threshold. Myrtle (Him) and Claude
hesitate. They have never smelled an interior so absolutely
musty, and for one insecure moment Him (Myrtle) takes
Claude's hand and squeezes it. When she lets go she feels
a bang of courage and steps over the threshold into the
well known zone. Following Myrtle (Him), Claude floats
on a line of inexplicable joy.

LOOK MAYAN TO ME

The Calumny is not a lie. Sunshine is the blanket of the poor, some say. Not I. I say this Calumny is a tropical fruit that abounds somewhat in a broad band of tropical sunshine. "You know something funny," says Zippo, "about you? Is that you look Mayan to me." "I know I do," I say to her as she takes a walk. So succulent, this fruit, but dangerous. Deadly, in fact, but for a brief period each year when it tastes lush as the zapote, reliable as an apple. A period of forty-five minutes each year, usually in late August or early September. I ate this fruit too soon and so I am going to die. But first I will go crazy, senor. The flesh of this fruit is a passion of the tropics. The youth assigned to monitor its ripening begins its vigil in July. In the first week of August crowds crowd under the trees. They discuss the first taste of it, dainty as the essence of ferns, giant ferns that made grandiose the age of dinosaurs. Were we there at the time, senor? Quién sabe? Only the epicarp tastes like this, a golden layer just under the skin, that has an indefatigable crispness, like fresh lotus root. True! But only when the Calumny is picked within the first seven minutes of its brief maturity. Maturity we know as an ephemeral period of safety. You kiss the skin, an ochre velvet dappled with azure, before your incisors pierce that firm layer, a gentle snap through like the moment of release of your lover's resistance. The shade, some say, is the air-conditioning of the poor. Not I, senor. This tree manipulates sunshine to intensify the heat of midday. This tree is known to me in particular by the name of Borges, to whom I now humbly dedicate this

account, telling it to you from a bench under a live-oak
in the Almeda de León in the city of Oaxaca in the nation
of Mexico under a rain of fragmented seed-pods on this
eleventh day of March in the year nineteen hundred and
eighty-two. Algunos balloons have escaped into these
trees and hang there despicably inedible as the fruit of the
Borges, if we accept that as the name of the tree we
describe. O where are the children now who once owned
'globos'? Do they remember those trees that recaptured
their balloons? The 'vendedor de globos' chirps by now,
whistle in his teeth. Some of his balloons have long legs,
to make them resemble the octopus or 'pulpo', that looks
so white, boils up so delicious served to you in a cradle
of lettuce sponged lightly with lime. A child here presses
his face into an ice-cream cone as if it were his mother's
breast, and gazes into the tree. Could one of those balloons
have once been his? Quién sabe? Within the crisper layer
of this fruit the mesocarp is another surprise, a flood onto
the tongue, so much liquid like brimfuls you would expect
to cascade down the chin and lap at the feet in floods, but
this isn't liquid, it's like a textured gel, with the taste,
those who have experienced both can testify, of the palms
of human hands, supreme delicacy in more sophisticated
cannibal cultures, sweetened with licorice, as is the custom in many of those places. Don't eat this, however,
except during that forty-five minute period that comes
usually in August, but sometimes in September; and it can
happen at midday, or in the morning, or the evening,
though it hasn't yet happened between the hours of 10:30
P.M. and 2 A.M., a blessing in disguise because it means
three and a half hours rest each night for the young people

assigned to watch the Calumny. Time for them to ask
questions like, ''Why are we sent to war?' and 'Who are
those shadows that claim to own the world?'. Sometimes
one of them makes a mistake, as I did, being a foreigner,
and that one dies, as I surely will. But first I will go crazy,
senor. These deaths come as an affirmation for the living
of their own vitalities, of the quantity of life breasting in
each of them, while they wait for the fruit to come into
its time, their time. Therefore the death is a cause for
celebration, my death a carnival at the foot of the Borges,
as if everyone is sitting on this bench, dreaming up this
yarn, this cocktail out of its own language, dead myself
to everything but the wistfulness of writing this as if
speaking to someone, and suddenly in front of your eyes
the dark face of a girl child, beautiful as a pure note played
behind you on a flute, f-sharp on a panpipe blown by a
wind scattering lips, and she says, wistfully, ''Chiclets?
Chiclets?'' Who can say *no* at that moment? Do you think
I am crazy, senor? One always wants to speak to someone,
to say *yes*, *yes*, to Zippo, for instance, back from her walk,
as if what you say now can be a palpable result, the
produce of what you have taken to call your 'work':
''¡Hola! Zippo. This Calumny is the fruit of the Borges
tree. Taste it. Gorgeous and deadly, but here it is, and
worth a bite.''

THE ATTACK OF THE CONCEPTUAL ARTISTS

Uncle Davis opened the door and Bushmill pounced on him. Across the street, behind the hedge, Adelaide Herkimer was buying a baby girl from Narcisso Gutierrez, a native of Bogota, Colombia, in this country illegally, selling drugs and babies. Inside the houses a herd of elephants crossed the Serengeti from one Baobob tree to the next. They crossed in each of the eight houses except in the one at the end of the tree-lined street called Plum. It was a dead end. This last house, a Cape Cod gothic built in 1947, was wired with soft music of the kind called 'mood'. Derek Elliott lay there indoors on the thick pile carpet dressed in eight pairs of bikini underpants. His life-size inflatable doll lay beside him, plugged into a wall socket so its torso and limbs, filled with a fleshlike gel, would heat up. Bushmill tugged on the sleeve of Uncle David's uniform, and pulled him into the living room. He nudged the old conductor into his favorite chair, formed long ago into the concave of his slump. An ad for Arrid flew from a nest in the Baobob. Bushmill fetched pipe and slippers, then lowered the sound by remote. "Uncle David's here." The voice of Sophie Frielich reached the TV from the upstairs bedroom. Uncle David dimly recognized the voice, but didn't expect to hear it coming from the TV. "I hope you understand you have to leave now. Uncle David's here." Adelaide Herkimer carried the baby into the house, through the vestibule and living room, into the kitchen. "Hubba-hubba goo goo," she said to the baby, and lifted the lid of her canning cauldron coming to a boil on her six burner gas range. "Gaaaa," the baby smiled at her. "Gaaaa," responded Adelaide. Derek did forty-three sit-ups to the music, and twelve push-ups on his fingertips. The beautiful doll squirmed on the carpet as its innards got hot. Uncle David's pipe swung listlessly from his tired mouth. Bushmill jumped onto Uncle David's lap, licked his ear, jumped off again. He did that seven times during the evening. Sophie Frielich sang Rossini in the bedroom while someone smashed all the bottles on the bathroom floor. A tigress pounced at Uncle David from the TV console. It pounced in seven houses on Plum Street. In the eighth house Derek held a conversation. "I have achieved a certain position now. I have made my way and it wasn't easy. Of course, I'm handsome, and that helps. Now I have this house." The inflatable doll appeared to be doing a sit-up. Now at least she was hot enough. Only the baby in Adelaide Herkimer's arms sensed that something was not right. But how does a baby express this uneasiness? It hasn't yet learned to speak. It could cry, but to this baby that seemed vain and self-indulgent in the light of everything else that was happening. Bushmill loved it when Uncle David started to snore. He switched off the sound and bounded gleefully round and round the chair where Uncle David sawed his wood. The badges on his uniform were luminous in the subdued light. Sophie Frielich despaired of ever dealing with the complications. Derek Elliott unplugged the doll and lay down on top of it. It was a rented doll. They rolled over and the doll lay on top of him. "You feel heavier tonight," he said. "You know we haven't been the same since the abortion. I feel as if I don't know you any more." The doll cooled slowly. Adelaide Herkimer lifted the lid. Now it was boiling. She dangled the baby over it by the back of its diaper. "Steam," said Adelaide. "Steam. Steam." As if she wanted the baby to learn the word. The baby's eyes flew open. It had never felt something like this before. "I'm sorry, said Derek Elliott, "for the mess I made." Narcisso Guitérrez swung his rented Camaro onto the expressway and headed south. The lights of an American city yellowed the Eastern horizon. He suddenly felt sad. It suddenly felt peculiar to have a feeling. He hadn't expected his life to turn out this way. To pounce or not to pounce was Bushmill's dilemma. Uncle David slept in his own chair. So deep the sleep that he didn't hear the footsteps of the _____ approaching the map of El Salvador on the console from the rear.

- -

Please read the instructions carefully before you fill in the blank, then tear off along the perforations.

Why I Left Emile

We decided to move our bunch to Boulder, Colorado in 1959, and I was the one chosen to scout up a house that could accommodate 15-28 of us at a time. I was tapped for the trip because as usual I was out of work. After my father got mashed in a coal mine accident in 1956, a mine outside of Wilkes-Barre, Pa., I couldn't hold down a job anywhere, anymore myself; I mean, what for? Not for them. I was close to Emile at the time because I took care of him. I kept his car running, kept food in his house, answered his mail, left him free to think and grow, for all of us. He was our teacher, mentor, whatever you want to call him. I suppose these days you might call him a guru, though it wasn't like that.

Emile chose Boulder to bring together his East and West Coast followings. He thought the time was right to consolidate, and do our work near the mountains, which were potent, he said, with electromagnetic force that could purify our mental processes and make it easier for us to receive the teachings he had to give. All this sounds familiar, just like life in Boulder nowadays; but Boulder was nothing like the New Age wading pool it is today, and back then we were unique, ahead of our time. Boulder was an agricultural town, more midwest than west, with a small state university, and no particular pretensions, despite its beautiful location. Looking at the town back then I would not have expected anything spooky or supernatural, certainly nothing like the story that follows.

I was one from New York. Emile chose a woman named Hilda Dropsies to come with me. I knew her only casually, having seen her occasionally at our meetings. She had expressed her desire to broaden her involvement, so Emile assigned her to the Boulder house-hunt. She immediately quit her job as a legal secretary on 57th Street. Emile believed in the importance of man and woman, the completion of that circle of energy, the balance of that opposition and union, in order to get anything of value done. I went for that idea. Despite all the romantic disasters in my life, I'm always ready to be with a woman.

The bus from Denver dropped us in the center of town. Quiet town. Pearl Street, I thought, was a nicer name than Main Street. The clerk in Valentine's Hardware suggested a big, funky old hotel called the Boulderado. It was a rundown place, but I liked it. The lobby was full of old retired guys, permanent residents, ex-miners or farmers getting by on their social security, their savings, their pensions. Hilda and I took separate rooms. We had worked it out across the country as a friendship, with an occasional stiff hug in honor of Emile. I liked her fine, but she was a twitchy woman, with sad black eyes that, when she sat with you, looked from place to place, as if she expected some personal injury coming at her from there, then there, then there. Her fingers were stained from the Camel cigarettes she smoked passionately—as if she drew nourishment from them that had to be filtered through fire.

I can't say I ever really relaxed with her.

"You folks here on business?" the desk clerk asked. He wore a ton of Navajo jewelry. I had never seen so much. He had taken on the responsibility of supporting the whole Navajo nation. He lifted his arm, loaded with turquoise-studded bracelets, two rings on each finger, and plowed his brillantined hair with a silver-edged, tortoise-shell comb.

"Not really business," said I.

"Not much business here," he grinned.

"We're looking for a house."

"Town's full of houses."

"We need a big one."

"Plenty of big houses." He leaned over the counter to look around the lobby. "Why don't you buy this big hotel?"

I noticed an old Oriental gentleman watching us, sitting erect on the edge of a worn, overstuffed chair. I smiled at him as we walked to the stairs. He didn't smile back, but eyed us through thick, black-rimmed glasses.

"What's the grin about?" Hilda asked as we went upstairs.

"That Japanese guy looks like Tojo, like a stereotype from a World War II movie. 'Back to Bataan'."

"I don't see anything so funny," she said.

She was right, as it turned out. There was nothing funny here.

I washed up and grabbed a few winks, then returned to the lobby to wait for Hilda. The stuffed leather chair I settled on was so hollow that when I let go into it I thought I would keep dropping to the center of the earth. Across the lobby four old guys played dominoes, slapping their tiles with gusto onto the marble-topped table.

"You want buy house?" Tojo appeared at my right arm. It felt like a sneak attack, I was trapped so deep in the chair.

"We're looking," I said.

"You come with me," he said.

"We need a big house."

"Come with me."

I was going to protest that I had to wait for Hilda, but she appeared just then at the top of the stairs. She had to pull on my arm to help me get out of the chair.

"Long way down," Tojo smiled when I straightened up to look down at him.

He took us to an enormous house, the kind of 'estate' they called a 'white elephant' at the time, that later became known as an investment property. It was a white one, set behind a rusting iron fence, three stories high, badly in need of paint. A wide porch wrapped around three sides, a driveway through a sheltered entrance on the east side. The windows, a few of them broken, flamed in the afternoon sun as if something was burning within.

No one lived there, no one had cared for the place for years. The lawns were brown, weedy, untended. Apple trees to the west hadn't been pruned since World War II, and the place smelled like an old cider barrel on this warm October afternoon.

"Looks just like what we want." Hilda lit a fresh cigarette with the butt of her last.

"Just what you need," said Tojo.

"I don't know yet," I whispered to Hilda. "I've got a strange feeling about this place." Something about it looked forbidding, unhealthy; a pale pulsation of the light on its surface gave me the creeps. The sense of alien presences, woeful deaths.

Hilda was amused. "I bet you think it's haunted. See, that's because you lived in city apartments all your life. We've got houses like this in Paramus."

"You go inside now," said our Japanese guide.

"Doesn't it feel weird to you at all?" I asked her. "Right here." I put my hand on the center of my chest, where my heart was flying around like a caged bird.

Hilda gazed at the burning tip of her cigarette as if to show me she could stare into the flaming mouth of hell. "I might be a nervous person, Tony. I'm sure you noticed that, but I'm not superstitious. That's why I'm attracted to Emile. His work is practical."

"Go inside *now*," Tojo insisted.

He left us on our own. We walked up to the porch. I took a deep breath, and pulled the door open. Fermented apples in the dry Colorado air gave way to a damp underground smell, pungent with cordite, as if this were a mine where they had just blasted. She walked right in. "Do you smell that?" I asked, as I followed her, but she was too enthralled with the place.

"God, there'd be room for everything here. I love it."

"Funny, it feels crowded to me." I don't know why I said that. Except for a few sticks of furniture, the rooms were almost empty.

Hilda pulled her hand back and I tried to take it. "There you go." She lit another cigarette. "You must really believe in ghosts."

"I never thought much about ghosts," I said. "But

something about this place gives me the willies.''

"Well I happen to like it a lot.''

I followed her into the library, and stopped to look at some glass cases full of carefully labeled samples of coal. Hilda opened a door on the other side of the library, and stepped through. She poked her head back and waved at me to follow. "Get a look at this,'' she said.

"I've seen enough,'' I said. "I want to get out of here.''

"Come on, Tony. You've got to see this. This is amazing.''

I crossed the library and looked in. She was right. Amazing. I covered my eyes as if lightning had flashed in front of me, the room was so white, lit by sunlight driving through the big windows to the west, a shock after the somber, moisture-stained wallpapers in the other rooms. This room was trimmed with rich, rosy, unvarnished mahogany, the floor a pale glowing hardwood I didn't recognize, covered at regular intervals by Japanese tatamis, each flanked by a ceramic elbow-rest or pillow. At the west end of the room, its edges burned out by the sun beating directly through the window, was a Japanese folding screen, the landscape image painted on it bleached by sunlight. Behind the screen was a shrine—statue of Buddha, string of beads, incense burner. A thread of smoke unwound from the burner. I noticed the sweet, sandalwood smell only after I saw it. Why did it fill my heart with sadness, lay my soul open with dread?

"So super,'' said Hilda, an uncharacteristic grin on her face. "Whoever lived here must have had an Oriental hobby. I can't wait to call Emile and tell him that we found this place.''

"I just want to get out of here."

"This is a perfect meeting and recollection room. I want to see the upstairs too."

I let her do it alone. As I walked back to the hotel her phrase, 'an Oriental hobby,' kept firing in my brain. At the hotel one of the old guys playing dominoes had got so excited he had a seizure and his buddies were tending to him on the couch.

"You just don't worry about Fred," one of them said to me. "He's a gritty old sourdough."

I didn't see Tojo anywhere in the lobby. Behind the desk the clerk was waving his ringed hands around as if he were directing traffic only he could see. The old guys picked Fred up and headed upstairs with him. "We're used to this," one of them said as he passed me. As they hauled him up the stairs Fred was singing 'Autumn Leaves' at the top of his voice, as if every minute of his life was an audition for something else. Tojo stepped out from under the stairway.

"You like house," he asserted.

I had a thousand questions for him, but none of them was ready to come off my tongue.

"We love it," said Hilda, coming up behind me. "It has the perfect feeling."

"You sleep there tonight," said Tojo.

"N . . . n . . . n . . . not me," I stuttered.

"What a terrific idea," Hilda said. Whatever she was, I was just the opposite. "Can we really sleep there?"

"Hai!" said Tojo, a word I figured meant 'yes' in Japanese. "You sleep there tonight." It sounded more like a command than an invitation. Tojo turned and walked away.

"Hey, wait," I shouted after him. He turned.

"I . . . ," but my questions still would not unfold themseles as words.

"I'm going to do it," Hilda said. "I know you don't want to, but I can't let your superstitions rule the way I work for Emile."

I sighed like an old man.

"Hilda," I said. "Hilda, listen to me. We've already paid for our rooms in this hotel." I was just saying that to say something. It was a lame argument. I didn't know how to communicate my fear. I reached out to touch her shoulder, but she pulled it back like a snail sucking in its antenna. "Listen, how do you explain that that incense was burning?"

"That's easy," she said.

I knew her answer as soon as I asked the question. Tojo lit it earlier. Plenty of explanations for everything. I was making a mountain out of a molehill.

"Okay. Okay," I said. "Look, Hilda, why don't you let me have one of your cigarettes."

"My what?" She looked at me as if I was crazy. As far as she knew I had never smoked a cigarette. Her hand shook as she tapped a Camel out of her pack, then offered me the one from her mouth for a light. The smoke tasted good. It numbed my tongue. If she was going to sleep in that house, damn it, I would have to sleep there too. That's the stupidity of being a man.

We sneaked pillows and blankets out of the hotel and headed for the house as soon as it got dark. It was overcast, but the moon behind the clouds gave everything a cool, pearly glow. I felt too weird to be anywhere that night.

That underground smell made me sure I didn't want to be in that house as soon as I walked in. Buried alive, like my dad. I switched on the flashlight I'd bought at Valentine's just before it closed. When you feel as strange as I was feeling you thank God for a hardware store. Hilda wanted us to sleep in what she already called our conference room, but I convinced her to lay our blankets down near the front door.

I shone my light around the room before I went to sleep and noticed the page of a newspaper folded on the mantle. I slowly unfolded it. Just a number 2 was left of the date on the top of the page. An article was framed there by four elegant, tapered brush strokes done with a calligrapher's pen. It was a brief note about an explosion underground near Saguache in southern Colorado, at the Orient mine, that entombed 112 Japanese miners.

"Next of kin unknown," the article said.

That phrase hit me with a wave of cold and, trembling in my clothes, I slipped down next to Hilda. She was already asleep. I don't remember ever wanting to hold someone in my arms so much, to feel another heart beat next to mine; but Hilda had her back to me, and I knew it would be worse to feel her freeze up when I tried to pull her close.

I waited for sleep to come. It struck me how fresh that page of newspaper looked, not even yellow, though the accident described must have happened at least seven years ago, probably earlier. I must have finally fallen asleep, though I don't remember closing my eyes. At a certain moment in the drift of pale presences through my sleep I acknowledged that my eyes were wide open. I thought, "Dawn." And how I welcomed it, until I realized the light around me came from somewhere inside the house. Hilda coughed deep in her sleep beside me. What I had taken for a wheeze accompanying Hilda's cough I realized was the note of a strange flute coming from another room, and the sound of a plucked instrument. I sat up. The scent of sandalwood had cleansed the air and made my soul uneasy. Hilda was curled like a caterpillar in the palm of a hand. I covered her with my blanket and stood up. No more sleep for me.

I lit my flashlight and shined it on the walls, though everything was already lit with an eerie light. I'm no exception. I'm pulled to walk the edge of terror with everyone else. My heart was loud as a drum.

From the library I could see the door cracked open of the room beyond. The light from there was bright as the afternoon sun. I shined my dim torch into it as if to erase it, or perhaps illuminate something about it. Not a chance. I clicked off my torch and stepped slowly towards the lighted doorway.

"Tony?"

I heard Hilda waking up in the parlor. Another voice in my head told me to leave it alone. Best not to know some things. Turn your back and move on. But the fool I've proven to be swung the door wide.

What I saw, I saw; or better to say my eyes felt what they felt, and it emptied my heart with grief. There were the shadows of two musicians behind the screen, playing sad music. On each of the tatamis a Japanese man in kimono sat motionless on his heels while spirits swirled around the room in constant motion, spirits of Japanese miners dressed for work, faces blackened, lamps glowing on their hard-hats. I could feel the pain of these spirits adrift in an alien land. They were all awhisper in Japanese, and I felt my own spirit ready to bust its physical trap and whisper with them.

As each approached me, his woeful face like a wind in my face, I heard him say my name, Antonio Galatina—my name in Italian. Do you know how it feels to hear your name repeated in the realm of the dead? Each sorrowful spirit revealed itself to me with Antonio Galatina on its lips like an incantation. I could not count them all.

"Tony," Hilda said from behind me. I turned to her.

"Did you ever see so many?" I moaned.

"No," she said.

"Do you see them?" I asked.

"No."

"You gotta see them. They're all right there." I pointed back through the doorway. The play of phantasms had flickered out, but for the tatamis where some had sat, the ceramic pillows in disarray. Dawn was settling in , the room a little less than dark.

I couldn't speak.

I returned to the hotel and lay down to violent dreams. Like Jacob I wrestled the power of light come down in the forms of angels.

When I went downstairs hours later I found Tojo sitting alone in a corner on a straight-back chair. I stood in front of him for immeasurable moments before he looked up at me.

"Those spirits," I asked, "in that house, were those the spirits of the miners, the Japanese miners buried in the Orient mine?"

"Hai!"

"And do they haunt that house forever?"

"Hai!"

"And other houses here in Boulder? Do such spirits haunt them as well?"

"Hai!"

"And this hotel? Even the Boulderado?"

"Hai!"

That horrible affirmation. The dread in my heart. There was no escape.

"But why?" I asked a final question. "Why Boulder, Colorado?"

He hesitated a moment, then grinned slightly and motioned me to lean closer so he could whisper in my ear. He said something to me that I do not want to repeat now, for the irony and the sadness would be lost, considering the kind of place Boulder has become.

I climbed up to Hilda's room to tell her we were leaving. She had just laid the phone in its cradle when I pushed the door open.

"I talked to Emile," she said, "and I described the house to him. He loves it. He wants us to go ahead with it. I'm excited."

"You talked to Emile?"

"I couldn't find you," she lied. "Emile thinks the place sounds just right. It's perfect to talk to him. He gives such strength. You should call him."

I couldn't say anything. The devastation inside me was expanding to fill the whole world.

"Look, I know how you feel about it, but you're wrong," Hilda went on. "It's only your superstitious nature, and I'm going to show you that." Though she already held a freshly lit cigarette in her right hand, she picked up one burning in the ashtray and sucked on it. "I'm going back to that house tonight, and I'm going to sleep there again in that room you find so freaky."

"Hilda do you know what day this is today?" was all I could say.

"What day?"

"It's October 31. It's Halloween."

"Tony, look, Tony. I'll call Emile, and you can talk to him. It would do you some good. I told him about your reactions, and he reminded me that his teaching laid open the residual superstitions of our culture, the obvious folklore superstitions, the subtler marketplace superstitions, so we can reform our total beings. That's what recollection and reformation is all about. Look, I'll get the number for you." She lifted the phone off its cradle. I pressed her hand back down.

"Don't call. I can't speak to him right now."

I passed the rest of that endless day in my room, waiting, dreading the evening. I watched out my window as Hilda left. She walked briskly, puffing pale smoke into the deeper darkness.

"I'm a man," I thought. "A man. A man. What good to be one? How can I let her go there by herself?"

I sat on the bed, looking at the walls folding in and out of themselves, and then I said aloud, in a voice that was almost my father's, "Porca miseria, porca putana America." I folded some blankets around a pillow and followed Hilda to that accursed house.

She was inside when I got there, probably in the room

itself. I wasn't going in unless I had to . I laid my bedroll under a big old maple tree and stood for a moment, my arms spread against its trunk, my cheek resting on its bark, listening to its old life. That made me feel better.

I lay down and watched the full moon, the solitary moon, as it crossed the sky. Not a sound. I didn't sleep.

The light hit with a thud at the side of my face. I didn't want to turn to look at the house, but there it was, the windows blowing out with light as if an electric storm had erupted within, a ghost storm without thunder. My lungs filled with lead. I closed my eyes and gathered into my soul the whole world of terror, then I opened them again until I was blinded and ran for the door of the house so convulsed with light.

I flew through the door. Light exploded around me, throwing me to the floor. I crawled, as I had trained to do in the National Guard, on my belly through the parlor and the library, towards the door of that room beyond, feeling all around my body these concussions of light, more terrifying because they were silent. My belly still to the floor I arrived at the sill of the door of that room and placed my hand on the bottom corner and pushed. The door was held shut as if by a heavy wind, so I slid forward pressing my shoulder against it to force it open. The door opened and opened on a scene so horrible words on a page can't begin to evoke the terror. There in the room, the room was exploding. Hilda slept on the floor. the Japanese miners were working the phantom seam of coal in there, and that mine was imploding, blowing out the bodies of the miners, faces twisted with pain and lamentation, the room full, an endless capacity for dying, bodies

ripping apart, wrists and heads and knees and fingers
flying loose, my ears full of a single unbearable note of
woe, not just from the spirits of Colorado miners awash
in there but everyone, and my father, and you and me,
and all the vaporized halls of Hiroshima and Nagasaki
emptied here in a swollen tide of grief.

What can I say to tell you what I felt to witness this? I
am still witnessing it, alas; and so are you, you in your
little boats, waiting for the flood, stranded in the drywash
of my dreams.

Hilda was still in there, now pressed, flattened against
the ceiling, still sleeping under her blankets, blessed
woman.

How could she sleep?

I ached for the arrival of dawn as it came on, sweet
dawn, filling the room with its weary glow. Hilda slid
slowly, imperceptibly down the wall to the floor, where
she rested, still asleep.

"Hilda, wake up," I whispered. "It's morning now." I
shook her lightly.

"What?" she asked, her face still buried.

"Morning," I said.

"Good morning," she said, turning to me, her face and
hands blackened as if she'd slept all night rubbing on a
seam of coal.

"Did you see anything?" I asked.

"I slept good," she said.

"Look at yourself." I helped her up and led her to a
mirror on the door of the library. "Just look."

"I'm all smudged with dirt," she laughed. "Isn't that
strange. The room is so white. Where do you think this

black came from?"

"Who knows?" I said. "It's very strange." I couldn't begin to talk about what I'd seen, not then.

"I guess stranger things have happened." She stared in the mirror, rubbing her sooty cheeks.

"Didn't you see or hear anything at all?" That was the last question I could ask.

"I guess I sleep too well in this house."

"Good," I said. "I'll see you back at the hotel."

I returned to my room at the Boulderado and packed my bag quickly and went down to the lobby to find Tojo. I wanted another word with him before I left, but I didn't see him anywhere. I waited for the desk clerk to get off the phone. He made a note on a pad, then looked at me, laying his turquoised hand on the counter.

"What can I do for you?"

"That Japanese guy—the one who's always around here—did you see him today?"

"What Japanese?"

"You know the guy. He's usually in the lobby."

"Some kamikaze son of a bitch? I wouldn't let no Japs in here."

I looked around. This was hard to take.

"Listen, bub," he went on. "They put me on a death march in Guadalcanal, fed me worms, piss water. They beat the skin off my back. They cut off my toes. I'm lucky I'm here at all. Sometimes I don't think I am."

"Okay," I said. "Okay." That was true. It was true.

"Forget what I said," he said.

Hilda came through the door as I turned away from the desk. "You got your bag," she said. "You're going back to New York."

"Don't think so," I said.

"You should stay here, go through what you're going through and get through it."

"Yeah," I said.

"I'll be at least another week, to start preliminaries, once I get the earnest money. Emile says everything will be great. He says we did good."

"Hilda," I said, and paused.

"What?"

I sighed, "Butt me."

"What?"

"Give me a smoke."

"You're picking up all my bad habits."

"Just a cigarette," I said.

She stepped into my arms, the first and last spontaneous affection I ever felt from her. Then she drew back and tapped a Camel from her pack. Her dark eyes were really sad. I touched her face. She lit my cigarette. "This feels like Humphrey Bogart and Lauren Bacall," she said.

"Wrong," I said. "This don't feel like anything at all."

Hilda puffed her cigarette. I felt like I could cry. She reached up with her small, tobacco-stained fist and brushed me across the chin. "Here's looking at you, kid," she said. I didn't think that was funny at the time.

I didn't go back to New York, but headed for Canada. I wanted to leave the USA for a while, head for the Northwest Territories—Whitehorse, or even on to Fort McPherson. I never got that far north. From Vancouver I took a little narrow guage to Lillooet on the Frazier River in B.C., a tiny town cupped in high mountains. I knew inside myself you couldn't escape, that the spirits are everywhere. Even today if I go to a Japanese Restaurant and overhear the chef talk to the waitress that simple "Hai!", so dreadful to me, yanks my spirit from my flesh to set it drifting alone through the endless damaging of ghosts. Nothing is lost in the records of the spirit. No one is free of the misery invested by those who came before, because whoever that was is always yourself. All you need do is close your eyes and the whispering begins.

Lillooet, B.C. Just to be somewhere where there were few people, where the past was not so grievously dense and powerful; and far away from Emile, of whom I speak now with respect and pity, who claimed he had it figured out, that he would move us in to the city of Boulder.

I see him now only in a recurring dream, where I search for him with my flashlight. The clerk from Valentine's follows behind with some spare Eveready batteries. When I find Emile I shine my light on him. He is in the form of a great frog with the face of a Lhasa Apso, sitting on an enormous and hideous chocolate cake, resting on four crates of imported Sake, riding on the back of seven appaloosa stallions down the heart-line on the palm of an enormous turquoised hand. Emile sees me and his throat pulses. I am frightened, like the prey. His mouth opens, and he loosens his tongue, not the light, sticky flicker of a frog, but a plush, vermilion carpet rolls out of Emile's mouth. His eyes wink once, and he barks at me like a frog, words that make me laugh and tremble. "Do not pass. You take the next step."

Zion

The kid slipped out of the waiting room and went upstairs. Down there the family waited for the father to die, the brother, brother-in-law, friend, business associate to die. It was the kid's father kicking off. He was twelve. He hated the stupid emotions. This was a veteran's hospital in Hunt's Point, in the Bronx. The corridors were full of wasted men poisoned and smashed from several wars staring out at nothing from their wheelchairs. His father lay in a room by himself inside an oxygen tent, still slightly breathing, asleep as he had been for what seemed forever, as if to be awake for it was too much, when the transition out of, the awakening from the waking dream finally came. Even at twelve the kid felt that everything that went on was a dream, an unstable surface of emotions, obligations, obsessions. "Cry," his aunt had said, her eyes red with her own phony weeping. "You should cry, get it out of your system." What system? He didn't have a system. The kid would not cry. He sat on the plywood chair by his father's bed, alone with him in the yellow room till he no longer smelled the ammonia and medicines.

The oxygen tent that surrounded his father was of a transparent but cloudy material that seemed to him the stuff out of which the dying man was slowly fixing his ghost. A frail, blue-veined hand dangled from under the tent, by the edge of the mattress. The kid took the hand and held it, a soft accountant's hand, left hand that had held the tennis balls he threw up to make his accurate, tricky serve when he won the city singles championship. That was his father he had never known, his healthy father. From the time the kid was five the father's heart had begun to betray both of them, so he never got a chance to learn tennis from him. He would never get to know him as a kid who goes through adolescence battling his father gets to know the man. A father's role was to be sick, to provide the family with an ailing heart. He held his sleeping father's hand. It felt dry, but slippery as the skin of a snake. These are the last breaths of my father, he thought—one, two, three, four. Downstairs was the family hysterics. Aunts and uncles sobbed, surrounding his mother. One uncle threatened to dive out a window with grief; but his father's breathing was calm as the steady hiss of oxygen replenishing itself in his tent.

He felt his father gently squeeze his hand, and he looked at the face within the tent. The father's eyes slowly opened, and opened a smile on the dry lips, as if the face were a parched garden suddenly receiving water from an unknown spring. The kid smiled, "Hi, dad," he said. The father smiled wider and winked at the kid, as if they were sharing a joke, shut one eye and opened it again before he turned his head the other way, closed both eyes, opened his mouth, let out a peculiar noise, and died.

That wink would last the kid for the rest of his life, it was the last transmission from his father. The whole cycle of his life, his ability to play with the world, his attitude towards the fate of anyone, of himself, hinged on the

conspiracy of that wink. It was a joke. All of it. He
dropped the hand, got up, went into the nurses' room,
and sat down. The nurses knew who he was and ignored
him. He waited about ten minutes, keeping his secret
knowledge that his father was dead, relishing the fact that
it was a private joke, between himself and his father. A
Puerto-Rican attendant came in, looking a little upset, said
to the nurses in an accent barely understandable, "Room
two hundred six, he pffft!" He illustrated the 'pffft' with
a forefinger slicing across his throat.

*   *   *

As I throw my camping gear into the back of my truck
these images of my dad's death thirty-eight odd years ago
come to me for no reason I can figure. Am I a lucky man
to have watched him die before I got old enough to wish
him dead? Before I had the chance to think he was a jerk
in his American Legion hat? Before we did battle over
ideologies? My own sons are beyond that age now, perhaps. You never know about your own kids. Maybe they
know how stupid you are. Maybe they sometimes wish
you were dead. Maybe you press them into a battle they
wouldn't engage if you weren't there, if you had passed
on politely, with a wink, before they reached the dismal
age of competition and conflict.

On the other hand I enjoy having my sons around, a
great luxury these days to be so close to some men who
call you 'dad'. Avrum is the oldest one. I ask him if he
wants to take a trip with me to Bryce and Zion. He's
named after my dad, whose name was originally Abraham,

which he changed to Alexander. I never found out the reason for this, except that I vaguely remember hearing he wanted to avoid the nickname, Abe.

- Where is Zion, he asks.

I take out the maps and show him where I'm headed.

- It looks like a great trip, but I have to work. I don't think I can take off.

So I drive alone to Zion. It's probably better. What is going to happen will probably not have if any of my kids comes.

It's a long day into Utah from the Eastern slope of the Rockies. I get to Green River at about 3:00 P.M. and nine miles west of it I turn south on route 24, one of the roads to Lake Powell. Memorial Day weekend is just ending and the traffic is coming the other way.

When I go to the Southwest, south of the thirty-ninth parallel, I am stunned by the sheer mineral beauty of our planet. It's all food for the soul. Vermilion, ivory, blue-green, chocolate, yellow striations of buttes and mesas, in forms frivolous and tragic, forms of loss and victory, forms of lovers, enemies, shadows of desire and revulsion that all solidify and then disperse in the mind as the sunlight moves, changing the shapes and tints of the world. The landscape is so old the soul acknowledges it from a realm of formless eternities, and offers you a sense of completeness, well-being so deep you can't even think of it. The car seems to float down the road, and I am ferried by my spirit participating in these slow changes of form and color on my way down route twenty-four.

I suppose I'd be less romantic about it if I lived there, trying to work all that dry mineral beauty to make my

living. When the Bryce family gave up to the federal
government what now is the national park that has their
name Mrs. Bryce's only comment was: "It's a hell of a
place to lose a cow." In the distance I see the road enters
a cut between two mesas; and there it seems to fan out
and flow like a river. I blame it on my astigmatism at first,
but as I get closer I see the river moving where the road
should be. The light has taken on that late afternoon angle
and golden tinge that usually clarifies. As I get a little
closer I see that it's a river of cows, and floating on that
river is a line of big boats. I stop to train my astigmatic
eyes on this vision. Boats on a river of cows, here in
Marlboro country. Ben Franklin didn't have an aphorism
for this. DeTocqueville might have predicted it. It was
beyond Chateaubriand, but Blaise Cendrars could have
thought it up. If I write about this, I think, no one will
believe me. What road? What cows? What boats? What
afternoon? What drugs? What planet? I get back into my
pick-up and drive down towards this apparition, slow up
behind an old black Ford pick-up as we approach the herd.
These dawgies are being driven to higher country pasture
up the highway. There are a lot of cow-kids on horseback
herding the cows, and one older cowboy with a whistle
and several dogs. And the boats are there, there in the
midst of the herd, afloat on the beshitted hindquarters of
the cows. Big Chris-crafts pulled by Winnebagoes slowly
move through the herd on their way home from Lake
Powell, the drivers grumpy, their windows rolled up,
their air-conditioning on full. Kids lean out of the windows of the pick-up in front of me to pull the tails of the
cows as they pass. I wave at the cowboy and he winks at

me. If one of these dawgies shits on my truck, I think, I'll become a vegetarian. Continue on to Zion, vegetarian baptised in the cycle of beef production.

I stop in Hanksville at Shirley's Rock Shop, where route twenty-four jogs west. The store is in an old false-fronted building off the highway. Shirley himself hovers politely as I check the variety of rocks, artifacts and souvenirs on his shelves. He's a balding, grey-haired man, with friendly blue eyes and soft hands of a shopkeeper. He wears plaid shirt and denims and polished work shoes.

"Business is down," he says. "The store used to be full of Germans, French, Belgians, and they used to spend their money. But with the dollar the way it is over there they can't afford to vacation here any more. You used to go into a campground and think you were in Germany. Go out to the parks and you never heard any English." He pauses, and looks around. "I used to run a grocery store," he says. "But a rock shop is a lot better. When the power goes out the rocks just sit there, don't melt like ice-cream or spoil like produce and meat."

When he sees me looking at some pots on the shelf he taps my shoulder and says, real paternally, "Don't get those if you want them for old. They just look old because they're imitations. Now take these arrowheads and spear-heads. They don't come from around here. The rock is too hard around here. I go to South Dakota to get these. They're from the Mississippi basin where they flaked flint, made these real crude implements. When you find them from around here the work is much finer."

He answers the phone, then returns to see me looking into a glass cabinet with some small jade bears gripping

salmon in their mouths. I think they might be eskimo or
aleutian, and ask him how much they are. "The small ones
are six, and the big ones twelve. They're made in Taiwan.
It's real good jade. And them baskets. They call them
willow baskets, but they're not willow. This time of the
year the Indian women come through to get willow for
their baskets, but they don't actually use willow, they
gather squawbrush, or stinkbrush, or skunkbrush we call
it. Grows by the river. Has a real strong smell. They get
it in the spring, when it's tender, and they can bark it easy.
They call it willow, but it's just stinkbrush."

I realize this man is just the opposite of a good salesman,
and I like him for it, but with his disclaimers I can't think
of anything I want to buy in his store. "I better head out,"
I say. "It's getting late. I should find a campground."

"I never go to a campground," he says. "Too noisy. I
just pull off somewhere next to the river. As long as you
got what you need." His last piece of advice as I go out
the door.

The mallows are in bloom behind the hill where I turn
off by the river, just east of Capitol Reef, their red
blossoms translucent as blood spilled in water. I never saw
these pale blue blossoms of sagebrush before, and there's
some small cacti opening limpid violet blooms, and vetch
flowering by the road. All these flowers surround me as I
set up a bed in the back of my pick-up. Perfume of river
and sage rises through the dry air around me. I go down
to the bank and squat by the river and watch the stones
that live under the current. The hills on the other side
look edible, made of halvah, in the last touch of sunlight.
My father used to bring home some halvah occasionally

as a treat, its texture of sesame seed, oil, and sugar, as friable as good earth. I think of my own sons as darkness gently lays blue quilts on the canyon. Why can't this world, the world I inherited from my father, and pass on to them so screwed up, be always rich for them with these balmy moments. That would be a patrimony. I crawl into my truck and fall asleep, thinking my father never experienced this landscape. There was a place we went about thirty miles north of New York City he liked to call God's country, but he never felt the easeful benedictions of these dry breezes.

The road from Grover to Boulder, Utah, just opened after the winter, crosses some beautiful mountains; and from Boulder to Escalante you are airborne, crossing the Escalante canyons on a narrow saddle, steep drop on either side, over these turquoise and puce and beige canyons. This is an orbit. This is another planet, not the one of our ancestors, but a planet hospitable to some beings made less of flesh, more of spirit.

I ride into Bryce among the Winnebagoes, this holy landscape reduced to recreation, many grouches with cranky kids, checking out the magic as it moves past their windows. I'm doing the same, a grouch myself, and the magic makes me even more so. The quote from Edward Abbey inscribed at Rainbow Point misses the point as it celebrates the observation that this southwest landscape lays bare the millenniums of geologic history, so we can actually see that history, which is true enough, and wonderful; but it describes the earth as if its function is to reveal information about itself, to support our scientific prejudice, a prejudice that perpetuates its exploitation.

What we have to do to survive is to reaffirm our relationship with other mysteries embodied here, that we can
never conquer, the subtler spirits in this landscape, spirits
that keep the gentle aspects of our life in balance, spirits
that calculate every moment what to reveal in their
endless play with our minds, their game of essence and
perception. "There's the light," I shout. "The light!" I
stand there bonkers over the bleached midday canyons.
Light is the subtlest mutagen. Makes each moment
emanate as a new moment. "Without it, nothing," I shout.
"Nothing without the sun!"

I am crazed in the cockpit of my truck riding into Zion
between the Winnebagoes and the Airstreams. "Never,
never," I say to myself aloud, so loud I can feel it echo
around my head. "Never has a landscape so potent with
mystery and spirit been entrusted to such spiritless people,
such empty rituals. Tourism! Tourists! Myself included.
Myself infuckingcluded!" In the campground my tent is
surrounded by the RVs. I can see them through their
curtained windows watching television as the light on the
hills dances backwards. One large family down the road,
many RVs, several campsights, pits a big barbecue and
harsh Coleman lanterns against the night. The
grandparents sit in cushioned folding chairs and watch
their grandchildren play war among the trees and trailers.
I am the ultimate grouch of the vacation syndrome. One
of the kids runs hollering up the road towards my tent.
He gets suddenly quiet when he sees me sitting at my table
in the dark, and stares at me as if trying to figure out if I
am real. "Buzzy, you get back here," his mother calls.
"We're going to roast some marshmallows."

I stand up. "I'm a ghost. I am a ghost," I say as I step towards the kid. He runs back to his family and tells them he's seen a ghost. They pacify him with marshmallows, but in his little Buzzy heart he knows that he has seen a ghost, and he will always know it, and it will make a better person of him. Buzzy was once my name, given me by my father, a name I refused to let anyone use after my father got sick.

Next morning I stop for a hitch-hiker. He is a young man, wearing no shirt. He tells me he spent the night before camping on the west rim. We live in the same town in Colorado where he goes to the University. He's an earnest kid, who has already taken some rough shots. "I got run over by a car," he says. "I'm trying to recover. That's one reason I'm spending time out here. I'm trying to heal myself." His back and chest covered with acne make it look like his accident encouraged previous internal abuse to escape to the surface. "The west rim was so beautiful. You have to be careful about water. Today I'm thinking about going up the East rim, but I don't know if I should or not, or maybe just go home, but the fresh air is good for me. How can it do me any harm? When will you be going back?" He gives me a wistful look as if he needs some fathering.

"I'll be here a few days." I am intentionally vague because at the moment I feel I don't want to be father to any kids but my own; in fact, I want to be alone; in fact, I could use some fathering myself.

"I haven't made up my mind what to do. I could go up the East Rim, but maybe I should go home."

"I think you should go up."

"You think I should?"

We walk together on the trail along the North Fork of the Virgin River, through what they call the hanging gardens. Purple and yellow columbine curve out of the ferns clinging to the wet face of the cliffs. Towers of the canyon, vermillion and ivory, mass above us. This is not a difficult walk, not too long, quite level. You can hop out of the Winnebago and make it there and back in your espadrilles. Back into the RV, turn on the TV.

The trail ends at a bend in the North Fork where the river widens. Three young Germans splash in the water there off a gravel beach. They like to hear their German language echo in the canyon. My young friend studies German and speaks it okay. He wants to talk to them. I was around for World War Two, and still have trouble talking to Germans. When I see them drinking water from the river I suggest my friend warn them about giardia. At first they protest the water is so clean, but he reminds them that you can't see bacteria, and that this one is unfriendly, and there might be some danger. They come over, tall blonde aryans, two males and a female. Friendly as dobermans.

"How do you like America?" my friend asks.

"It is so big," one answers in English. "Germany is not so big. Here you have more . . . more . . ." He searches for the word in English. "More . . . lebensraum. More lebensraum. How you say it in English?" That word hits me like a swastika across the face. I step back and let my companion finish the conversation. Lebensraum. Hitler's word. One of Hitler's ambitions for the Third Reich. These German youth are too young to feel the dark resonance of it. I was much younger even than they are now when it was happening, hobnail boots across the bones of Europe, splashing in the blood of my Jewish people. Twentieth Century. Human race in retrograde. I look up at the enormous, slow, pink, vermillion, ivory towers of our planet in late afternoon light. How easy to be stone, how indifferent, how subtle the heart beating in its chambers. Zion. City of God.

In Springdale there's a restaurant called The Bit & Spur, run by what looks like a persistent vestige of hippydom. They serve good Mexican food. If you live in the Southwest long enough you can do without your French and Chinese cuisine, but you can't do without an occasional good Mexican feed. Jalapenos, chiles, blue corn meal, cilantro, keep the fires stoked in your interior landscape. It makes you proud and grateful to be feeding yourself in the USA.

"Is this restaurant a commune?" I ask the waitress as she sets down my chile rellenos. She's an attractive, slightly cross-eyed lady with a bandanna around her head, rosy-cheeked, very cheerful, moving gracefully in a hippy sack dress tied at the waist with a Guatemalan belt. She looks like a fugitive from the sixties when young people tried to find an alternative to raising kids in what they saw as the tyranny of the nuclear family, to raise them communally, to live communally in peace and love and drugs and rock and roll. This has all been dissipated now, communes disbanded almost everywhere. The nuclear family, the Levittown experience, seems happy in retrospect, better than the chaos that devolved from epidemic divorce and communal rancor. Even Stephen

Gaskin's farm in Tennessee is dismantled now, and sold off in private parcels to those few who wanted to stay; Stephen Gaskins, the most paternal of hippy gurus, who once theorized that the only way to save the planet was for two thirds of the US population to voluntarily become peasants. I suspect it hasn't happened. Now most of the children of these communes have degrees in real estate law, computer science, dance therapy. They vote for Ronald Reagan.

"No," the waitress says, cheerfully. "This is just a small town. There's a lot of love in the food."

After dinner I go into the bar, among some ripening drunks, to watch the NBA playoffs. A young Aussie, who's been hitching around the world on his grand tour, is drinking tequila as if he's in a competition. He puts his arm on my shoulder, says something incomprehensible, calling me 'mate'. Then he tells me he is twenty-two and his dad doesn't know where he is and doesn't give a bloody fuck. He started travelling when he was nineteen, and his father didn't know, and his father is bloody alright, and his father doesn't bloody care about a bloody thing.

It starts raining, what they call a Baha storm, not expected this early in the year, and it rains through the night, and when I wake up before sunrise the mists are down in the canyons and just begin to lift as I start for the trailhead, to begin the climb, a short steep one to Angel's Landing, then the long trek the rest of the way to the west rim. The trail starts to rise gradually, then goes up through a red canyon and turns into a ladder of steep switchbacks carved against the face of the cliff that takes you to the turnoff for Angel's Landing. I rest at one of the turns and a couple overtakes me. They're a pair of vigorous hikers, in their thirties, wearing shorts and boots well broken in. We continue together up the canyon. They are French people, speak English pretty well. He's in the states for a year, working for a computer company in Silicon Valley. They immediately start bitching. "Why," he asks me as if I'm responsible. "do they pave the trails here?" It is true. For about nine miles the trail to the west rim is paved, probably an old CCC project, so no matter how you struggle, how exhausted you are getting up there, you notice that someone got there before you with a bag of cement, some gravel, and sand. Pink sand.

"We are from Grenoble," says the woman, a short, wiry, vigorous person. "and we are accustomed to walking in zee mountains, and we never pave zee trails. Eet ees more dahnjeroos. On glisse. On glisse. Eet ees slippery to walk on zee trails when zey are paved. Eet ees crazy to pave zee trials. Why do you pave zee trails?"

I start to give them the history of the New Deal, and the necessity of putting people to work at that time, but they aren't listening.

"And we know this is a very beautiful country," says the Frenchman. "but we are not so impressed with the petroglyphs and Mesa Verde. They are not so important."

"Oui, yes," the woman continues for him. "You don't know when zey were made. You don't know. Maybe last week. Maybe just two-hundred years ago. In France we have zee caves. We have Lascaux. Zee Dordogne. You know zee Dordogne? Zat is zee seed of humanity and culture. Zey are a much older civilization. And zey are more refined and sophisticated zan zees petroglyphs, zees puebloes. From a much higher civilization.''

"Well, why don't you go back there?'' I think, but I am too winded, and too chicken to say it. "Go back where you came from. Back to your caves, Frogs. This is America. Love it or leave it.'' In the face of some French superior critical attitudes I become all American.

They turn off to climb to Angel's Landing and I keep going for the west rim. I am alone on the trail, crossing the pink bedrock, and rising after some miles finally by long switchbacks along the white cliff of the west rim. Everywhere, gripping little cracks filled with soil, paintbrush and columbine grow out of the rocks. A couple passes me, descending with packs. They have spent the night. I am sorry I didn't pack gear to spend the night myself. I climb into the woods near the top, to the first spring, the first fresh water on the trail, and then keep going to the trail along the rim. The whole of Zion assembles its promontories and canyons below me. I give up on words. There are no photographs possible to express the privilege of being here. When the trail levels off at the top I catch a glimpse of someone else. To see him touches me to the bone. A thrill of recognition. Who is he? How did he get here? You can see the whole trail on the way up and I saw no one. This is an older man, walking in front of me down the trail. How peculiar. How familiar.

*   *   *

The guy continued slowly on the trail along the rim of the canyon, following at some distance the older man in front of him. He forgot the fatigue he had battled as he was nearing the top of his hike. Seeing this even older man up there he was somehow rejuvenated himself. The man wore a pair of baggy denims, a green chamois shirt, a blue day-pack, and blue canvas deck shoes. He sported a cloth cap with a transparent green eyeshade. How did the old man get this far in those shoes, the guy wondered? He noticed that as the man walked he never looked off across the canyons at the feature attraction, but always into the trees, and through them into the sky full of clouds that had lifted from the canyons and now were blowing swiftly eastward. It was dizzying to look up, as if the world had been given an extra spin. The guy was struck with how familiar this older man looked from behind, his slightly bow-legged walk, his rich brown hair under the hat, just a trace of grey in it. The guy's own hair was grey already. He stopped to look out through a clearing for a moment at the wide canyons, junipers studding the slopes of the broad washes. He suddenly realized why he recognized the man he was following. It was his father, his own father whose hand he had held as he died so many years ago. He looked back to the trail again and didn't see him. He had lost him again. He hurried back down the trail to try to overtake him. There were several things he wanted to say to him, many things he wanted to ask. He thought he caught a flash of blue backpack through the brush far ahead. As far as he could remember he had never seen his father in jeans before, nor had he ever seen him with a backpack. He tried to call out, 'Dad, wait', but all that came from his mouth was a whisper.

He feared he'd lost the old man. Suddenly he felt very

tired, very old himself. He thought he could never make the hike back to the parking lot. The whole landscape looked bleached, the colors flat. He was too exhausted to enjoy anything. He walked a little further and sat down and leaned on a log near the washed-out ashes of a campfire, and he dozed off.

He couldn't tell if it was a noise awakened him, or if he just opened his eyes, turned his head, and spotted the old man again. He had entered a copse of blueberry bushes, surrounded by small trees, and dominated at one end by a huge broad old orange-barked ponderosa.

"Dad," said the guy. The old man stared up into the tree, his lips shutting and opening slightly as if he were forming bubbles, and watching them float upwards. The guy looked at the old one's face, so much like his own, that little moustache his father wore. "Dad, I'm so glad you're here. It's the last place I would have expected to find you. It makes me happy that you get to see this country. This is really God's country." His father turned under the tree, still looking up. He wanted to reach out to touch him, embrace him, but was afraid to disrupt whatever it was that allowed him to see his father. "I thought you were dead; in fact, I know you died," he said. "I was holding your hand. Do you remember? That hand." He reached out for the same hand just as his father lifted it to point up through the tree. The guy let his hand drop. "The world has changed so much, dad, since you left. It seemed much simpler then, but maybe it's never simple. I don't know. But you never heard of a world like this. It seems terminal now, like nothing can set it right." He started to tremble. Somehow it sounded so corny when he tried to say it. His father started to shuffle slowly around the tree, still looking up through the branches as if there were something up there he was trying to figure out. "I don't mean to say it's all bad," the guy went on. "You're a grandfather now. You've been one for a while. You have three grandsons. Three from me, and two more from my sister. They're men now themselves. I think they really missed having a grandfather when they were growing up. I'm sure you'd like them. You'd be really proud of them. They're good men. They're interesting people. What's hard is to give them the world the way it is. It's such a tormented place to try to make you way through it. I feel like I didn't do anything right. I could work harder to change things. It was a lot simpler when you went away. You didn't know this violence and confusion, this plain stupidity. I wish you'd talk to me. It's like there's no hope. There's no long run to look out for. Now everything can end in an instant. What can I do?" He paused and caught his breath. He'd forgotten at what altitude he was speaking. "Can't you answer me, dad? You must know something now, where you've been. Tell me. These are my sons. They're your grandsons. They're in the world so deep now, no turning back for them. Help them. I'll tell them, 'your grandfather said dot dot dot.' What? What can you tell them?" He started to follow his father as he slowly circled the tree, deliberately, seven times. He followed him asking questions, impossible questions he had never asked before, except of himself. But his father, the lucky man, had died too early, in those glorious days of hope and optimism after World War II, and all his questions had been simpler ones, with progress as the answer. What answer could he have to his son's questions?

After the seven times around the tree the guy's father stopped, and removed his day pack. He hadn't yet even looked at his son. "Dad, I'm here with you. This isn't funny. This isn't a joke. I've been talking to you. I'm ready to listen to you. Why won't you say something to me?"

His father pulled three tennis balls out of the backpack, and held all of them in his left hand. He held them in front of himself, then looked up for the first time into the face of his son. Father was smiling, a familiar smile, and then he winked, a familial wink, the eternal wink of his father. The guy sighed, that was all. His dad transferred two of the balls to the right hand, and one at a time tossed each into the air with his left as if he was serving. "Everything hangs on the toss," he thought he heard his father say. "What?" A perfect toss each time, and so accurate and strong the balls rose without touching a branch through the whole length of the enormous ponderosa. He watched each ball rise and keep rising. In the branches of the tree all the birds had assembled as if in conference with his father, and as the ball rose past them they flew up momentarily and then settled back so the tree looked like it bloomed three times from the bottom to the top in a flutter of wren, junco, grosbeak, loon, nightingale, cardinal, titmouse, jay, kestrel, hummingbird, falcon, hawk, magpie, eagle, raven, and you name them, they were there, a momentary flowering of feathers, and then they subsided, as if everything remained the same. When the guy lowered his eyes his father was gone, and when he looked up again the tree was empty, except for a squirrel half hidden and chattering at him. He looked down the trail for a flash of blue backpack, but nothing. He started for home. "Everything hangs on the toss." Was that what he'd heard his father say? Was that wisdom, or tennis? It made no sense. His dad made no sense. How can anything 'hang' on a 'toss'. Toss goes up, hang goes down. Could he tell this to his sons? "Your grandfather says everything hangs on the toss." His kids would understand it. That kind of knowledge skips generations. On the hike back to the parking lot the landscape went by quickly. Everything looked familiar. What he'd passed through before was similar, but in a different light. What had his father actually told him? Was this the truth? He could have it embroidered on a flag. Was it a joke? He could start a cult. "Everything hangs on the toss."

Parrots In Captivity

Monday morning and all the crackers are in revolt. They broke from their wrappers while I meditated and now they're flying. I'm not used t this. They hover in the skylight, releasing a fine rain of palm oil and salt. Those crackers give me the creeps. Andrew, my parrot, sharpens his beak on his perch. "I'm not of the hummingbird species. What can I do?" he says, in an unparrotlike voice. "And what if you were?" I squawk. Ilyana enters, kicking aside the peanuts of styrofoam, boxes, and bubble-wrap that fill the loft where we live. I don't know how to discard the wrappings. We live together, but she also has her own place, just in case. All three of her pagers are paging. "I didn't expect to see you up so early," I tell her. She ignores me, dropping a sheet of paper between my legs as she passes my cushion. She kneels by the stereo to press the button that ignites the CD players. Andrew has taken wing. A grey feather rides an air current into a slant of winter light that bangs through an upper window. Ilyana slides her hand into the CD slot and a green mustard glow worms through the veins of her wrist. I look over the piece of paper she so fliply flipped at me. It is dated March 8, and starts "Dear Andrew". Andrew is my name, also the name of my parrot.

Dear Andrew,

No more tic the nippies; no more heft the booblet.
'Booblet, indeed.' 'Tic the nippies' indeed. She gets a little
prezioso sometimes.

No more tongue the cock tip; no more lip the balls.

No more sit on face; no more stiff in bung. She gets
some gross, too, thank god.

No more lick the sphincter; no more nose the clit.

No more slide on thick joint; no digits in wet gush.

No more juice and jigs; no pipping at the perineum.
'Pipping at the perineum', sounds like a 40's big band
tune, like ''Stomping at the Savoy''. Let's see. What else?

No more lick the jam out; no more buttered buns.

No more. Stop. No more. Stop. No. Stop. Stop.

Ilyana loves to makes the rules. ''Rules make the world
inhabitable, and sexy,: is what she says. She likes to break
the rules too. Make 'em and break 'em. That's a motto.

''There's no feeling in the world as good as this
feeling,'' she sings into the crumb-packed air. She means
her hand still plugged into the CD. I've never seen anyone
do that before. I'm itching to try it myself, but it's
probably not for me.

''Aren't you going to answer your pagers? It could be
important. It comes from your other life, and that's always
important. That sound would drive me nuts. It does, in
fact.''

Her neck slowly bends, gaze floating to the skylight.
''Look, Andrew. Look up there.''

I think she is avoiding my question, but not so. This is
important. Something is subverting the revolution in the

skylight. Andrew. Snatching the saltine militants from their vigilance is my parrot. He is all grabs, beak and talons.

"Andrew," I shout. He hovers int eh cracker chaos, wings whirring as if he were the world's biggest example of its smallest bird. Kamikaze cookies dive at him from all angles, in vain. Not even the hairiest triscuits, nor the nimblest of waverly wafers can avoid the lightning of his grab.

"I never thought I could do it, Andrew," he mumbles, his beak full of what Polly wants. "But it was a challenge, and I was perched there, saying to myself, Andrew, you good-for-nothing parrot guy, what the hell are you doing with your life? Maybe it's time to lay it on the line. Maybe it's time to do your thing. So I went for it, just like that. And you know what? I can do it. Yeah, I'm up to it. I'm a goddamed helicopter, Andrew."

Andrew is the African Grey Parrot, a breed famous for its mimicry, for its limitless vocabulary. Though one would be hard put to attribute cognition or thought to these birds, I don't care. Andrew's example gives me courage to rise from my cushion, to abandon my meditation. Don't vomit, brothers and sisters. Meditation is my crackers, my hand in the CD slot. Meditation is my own clear feedlot in the whole garbage world. I approach Ilyana, waving her paper in front of me.

"You make up these new rules? This is for us?"

She pulls her hand from the slot and holds it between us like a sceptre, the glowing trowel of her separation, a digited feather of chartreuse flame. I am almost moved to tell her how much I love her, because I do love the lady,

but her pagers push me back. Who knows how many
lovers at that moment are aching to get in touch with her?
Hmmm! Aching to do it. Do it with Ilyana.

"Andrew, don't jump to conclusions. That's a poem.
My Jesse Helms piece. I made it for the NEA. I write a
certain kind of political poetry now. My poems have their
own rules." She flicks the page with her fingers. "This is
from my AIDS sequence."

"So are you afraid of AIDS? Getting it from me?"

"I'm a woman, Andrew—W-O-M-Y-N. I'm not afraid
of anything." She rises from her squat and pats my cheek
with her glowing member. "This is my lantern on the
reef."

"That's why I love you. Goddamit, Ilyana, do you
know how much I love your." There. I say it. It's not so
hard. Maybe it's even true.

"Why do you love me, because I'm not afraid? You
love my big shoulders? You love this?" As she waves her
hand in front of her face the glow dims like an ember.

"I love looking for your heart in all your behavior. I
love your unpredictability." I slap the sheet of paper.
"And you keep us organized. You're one hell of a legis-
lator for us. Do you love me, Ilyana?"

"Of course I do." The parrot swoops at the last cracker
enclaves. "I love a man who nurtures a parrot."

That strikes me funny, but I don't pursue it. She finally
goes for the phone to call her service and answer her
pagers. I check the time. It is late enough to go to work.
I don't want to hear her talking to whomever is on her
frequency. I dress quickly. I like clothes, putting them on,
wearing them, removing them. Double-breasted blue

pinstripe, black silk shirt, dusty pink tie, high-top wing-tipped sneakers, hiding iridescent blue socks. Andrew swoops down and lights on my shoulders. "Looking sharp, Andrew," he tells me. "I'm sure you can beat the world in that costume." He ruffles his feathers. "Just like I did." Is pride an inherent parrot characteristic, or did he pick it up somewhere? "I saw the problem and I went at it."

"You don't even know the world, Andrew. Nobody beats it," I tell him. "You look for an opening and try to get the advantage. Maybe you score a few times, but the world is not set up to be beaten."

"You do all right, Andrew," says the parrot. "you got the privileges, live in this big loft, on the top floor. You bring in mucho dinero, conchita."

His last owner was a Puerto-rican Rimilar queen, died in a sex-shop shootout.

I get to the elevator, a freight elevator that serves only my loft regularly, and is used below sometimes for heavy deliveries.

"You be good," I tell Andrew, before I send him back to his perch.

"What's to be good? I'm great already."

"If you don't I'll turn you into parrot juice."

Andrew flies away, squawking, "Parrot juice. Grawk. Parrot juice. Grawk," sounding one hundred percent like the parrot he is.

In my city the street is immediately the street and it's instantly in your face and maybe you love it, but there is no rescue from it, even if you're hip enough to sort the losers from the survivors. The eyes that check me out do a dry stroke through their rage. Drugs, crack and ice in particular, have made these denizens predictably unpredictable. No more tender junkies. Anyone can be in the way. If you're dressed as I am you should have a limousine waiting, which is the safest, which I don't. At the very least you should take a cab, which I will. The wind is cold that lifts a wave of street grime into the air. Airborne are several pages from the newspaper, three stories aloft. The headline reads, Bulgaria Buys Burger King. The cardboard sign of the victim camped in the next doorway has blown over. I stand it up and secure it with a block of wood. He had printed it with a blue magic marker. I AM DYING OF AIDS. MY FAMILY HAS ABANDONED ME. MY FRIENDS CAN'T FIND ME AND DON'T WANT TO. THE AGENCIES REFUSE MY CASE BECAUSE I AM A JUNKY. I HAVE NO HOPE AND I HAVE NO MONEY. PLEASE HELP. As I have every day since he showed up a week or so ago I put a dollar in his cup. He makes a little squeak, and a line of spittle comes to his cracked, bloody lips. I bend closer to listen. His face is blotched with exposure and disease. The last sweats of dying reek from him. His excrement and piss smell sweet by comparison. A skinny arm, covered with lesions, twists out of the pile of rags that cover him, and reaches for my face. I pull back, He says something. I close in again. "What?" I ask. His face lifts towards mine. "Kiss me," he says. "Please kiss me." His pucker is made of snake, his tongue a molten spoon. I straighten up immediately. I wonder if this is the way it has to be. All I know is that this is the way it is.

The cab takes me uptown.

As we get closer to my office, near the museum, the

crowds of the homeless and derelict, the beggars and the
dying, get absorbed into the crowds of my kind of people
who make the money. They are apparently living, and
seem to think they are sure to make a difference as they
walk to their businesses in thick overcoats, with locked
dispatch cases strapped to their wrists. I touch the taste
of that dying man on my lips with my tongue. Now that
I have tasted death I am sure of death. The rest of my life
will be a long story of death, death, and death. As a word
it's more soothing than 'money', softer than 'love', more
welcome than 'kicks'. Maybe death is a renovation, like a
trip to the body shop. In the first place I never requested
its opposite. The newspapers are full of it, we never get
enough. I once thought death was a semi coming at me in
reverse, but they tell me that death is like corn on the cob.
I love corn on the cob. I would also love a bath in hot
mustard.

Daredevil couriers race by on sleek bicycles, with
message packs on their backs. The air is full of numbers.
Numbers rain down from the skyscrapers. I pay the cabby
on the corner and walk to my building, across from the
museum. I am later than usual, but expect my daily
encounter with the man who for the last few months has
lived under the arch of the shallow colonnade of the
church. "I'm an artist," he always says. "Can you help
me out till my next exhibition? I used to live in a tent in
the park, but they threw us all out, ya know. All the artist
are back on the street now, ya know. A dollar, or whatever
you got lying in your pocket." I often mention that I used
to be an artist, maybe to engage him in a conversation
about the arts, but he won't be swayed from his routine.

"A dollar, or whatever you got lying in your pocket," he repeats. And then when he get it he says, "Thank you, sir. You've helped a starving artist today. Joy to you." Today he isn't on the street, but I see him crouched inside the colonnade, holding a sandwich to his mouth, his hands in grey gloves cut off at the first joint, body bent under a tent of greasy blankets, and I approach him there with my dollar in hand. This has been the toll I pay to cross the street and enter my building. I hold the dollar out, and he doesn't reach for it, but looks at me through delirious pale brown eyes that shine through deep wells of disappointment. "I can't take it," he says.

"It's a dollar for a starving artist," I say, hoping he doesn't think I am mocking his routine.

"I can't take it now. I'm on my lunch break."

I don't know what to say. I look at my watch. "It's not even eleven o'clock and you're already on your lunch break."

"You think this isn't work? You try it some time. This is a day's work I do here. You run your business, I run mine. Now I'm on my lunch break."

I don't know what to do with the dollar. I lay it down at his feet and shrinks away from it. "Look, can you help me out?" I say. "I've got to get across the street and every day it costs me a dollar. Help me out and take the dollar so I can get to work."

He grins exposing the egg salad covering his teeth. "You full of shit too, man."

"I can see lights lit in the Trump Tower. Deals are being finalized."

He inflates his cheeks and waves his head.

"Look, I used to be an artist."

His laugh sprays egg flecks on my wing-tipped sneakers. "And I used to be a green beret, a nasty motherfucker. I'm still that nasty."

"Take the dollar."

"What time is it?"

"Twenty to eleven."

"Okay. Leave it here. If it's still here in twenty minutes, after I'm done with lunch, call it even. If it's gone, then tomorrow is a two buck trip."

A squad car pulls up by the curb. "Let him be. He's my own brother," I say. "I'll take care of him when I come back down."

My office is small, a room in a suite of offices on the fifty-first floor. Several of us have taken rooms in this suite, and among us we pay Hilda, the receptionist, who sits at the desk in the entry and takes messages when we're out. She hands me mine as I pass her, hardly looking up from Jude The Obscure, which she has been reading for more than a year, since she started to work for us. Even in this suite of offices I am a small player. My room has its desk, its two chairs, its small couch, its framed prints from the museum shop at street level below. I am a member of that museum, a member for life. Death is a member of that museum. At one time I expected my own work to be exhibited there, but I lost interest. Never got to do what I could call my own work. At least the money is my own. I was happy to discover the real nature of money. Not currency, money. Art is currency, and some of the artists get to use it to pay the bills, but not all of them. Money, ont the other hand, is a virus that spreads throught he telephone wires.

I have ten telephones in my office, and three fax machines. I learned how to trap the virus with my fax machines, and I do that every day. I come into the office and make calls on each of the telephones, and then the three computer terminals along the wall start to display numbers, in various configurations and graphs. They are buying and selling. Whoopee. hooray, and alas. I monitor the flow and keep score. If you think this isn't work, you try it some time. I create the medium for cultivating this virus, which begins to arrive to its own satisfaction in documents on the fax machine. My wisdom is not to cultivate too much. Too much is a disease. Enough is a condition of equilibrium. I set a goal—twice the maintenance payment on my loft is enough for any day. The elegant day is when I arrive at that figure just before I am ready to pack it in. Sometimes I don't quite get there, or reach a negative amount, but that is all to be expected, and counted in to the monthly balance, which for the last few years has always been in my favor. the virus and I are compatible, and that is why I said goodby to art. Goodby art, hello death.

Some days I make my quota early, once or twice a week, and when on those days I have nothing left to do, and don't want Hilda to see me leaving early, I sit in my office writing down this story. I write just a few sentences at a time, sometimes a few words is all. Only certain words are appropriate to my story. I see it has mythical proportions, with am oral that soon will be revealed, as soon as I finish and write it down. It's about a character whom I call Ronald Reagan who this time plays a megalomaniacal orthodontist hungering to possess all the mouths in the world. HE wants to crack open the mouths of everyone so that he and his cohorts can replace their fillings or crown their teeth with his own device, a microchip installed in the amalgam that will allow him and his close conspirators to open and close each mouth at the whim of the conspiracy, only to utter phrases consistent with their standards of crazy-for-the-rich democracy and the American way. He has terrified the population of the world, and they are fleeing the cities for the Maine woods, the Hindu Kush, the Australian outback, Hudson's Bay, and other places more remote, placing great pressure on these fragile ecologies. Well founded rumors have it that Ronald Reagan has placed in fixed orbit over the world's largest cities a fleet of demonic satellites, each of them carrying forty-three ton tubes of Fixodent. Each of these is remotely controlled and he threatens to uncork it all if the populations don't voluntarily come to his chairs. If not he will worm the adhesive down on all the avenues and alleys of the world, to hold whole populations in place, with no gaps or air spaces, while his DDS armies circulate with their drills. Ronald Reagan does not allow for anesthesia. The French, who have just succeeded in widening and prettifying their Champs Elysees, are outraged. They say, 'incroyable' and 'un disastre'. The Germans, anticipating a reopening of the once majestic Unter Den Linden, are reuniting and reforming the Waffen SS in the face of this threat. They are ready to goosestep again, into outer space if the order is given. The Brits stiffen their upper lips. No one will violate the sovereignty of their decaying molars. The Chinese will wait to see just what kind of dentist this Ronald Reagan is. To some in Africa and Asia the idea sounds plausible, better than absolutely no dental care, but they can't see the madness of it. The Japanese manufacture the chips for the dreaded Ronald in their Korean factories. There is only one person, one possible hero, rising from the population, able to lead the masses against this threat. Her name is Tracy Chapman. She won't take this shit, because her generation is about to inherit the world. She puts on a wig made of green, yellow, and black polyester fur, and starts to wage her own campaign, gathering followers that sing her songs accompanied by acoustical mouth music. She will win in the end, she has destiny on a leash. Winning is a rule I make whenever I write a story, although I don't know how she does it yet, because I haven't got to the climax. Ah, the climax, brothers and sisters, the climax. I don't know how good this story is. It might be very publishable. To me it feels profound. Writing it is a spiritual experience. I write it out of inner necessity, in the face of you know what.

This evening, as I step off the elevator, into what is usually the comfort ad solace of my own space, I feel that something is different, something is very wrong. For one thing, Ilyana hasn't left. Her coat is still on the rack. On monday mornings she almost always leaves, to spend a few days at her own place, often till the next weekend. Another sign is the pickles. They have escaped from the fridge, have uncapped their own jars, and are slopping through the bubble wrap, scattering styrofoam peanuts in briny glee. Goddam pickles on the loose. Chopped jalapenos gather at my feet and start to climb the high-tops. The dilly beans line up, standing on end to form a rank of defense against he playful onslaught of the pickled okra. Marinate artichokes exfoliate as an audience. I call Ilyana's name, get no response. Andrew is not on his perch, and I find him in none of his usual hideaways. I hear some rustlings in the bedroom, which is an enclosure, cantilevered off one wall, reached by a curved stairway. At the foot of those stairs I listen to the bedclothes up there and realize that a pickle breakout is the least of my problems.

I remove my jalapeno hightops and quietly ascend the stairs, pausing on each step to listen for what I fear is going on in the dark bedroom. Once I hear a grunt, then another grunt. Once a little cry, and then another perfect little cry. At last I stand int he doorway of my bedroom, and when my eyes adjust to the darkness I find my worst fears are realized. That vile parrot is in bed with Ilyana.

Andrew is an African Grey, his damned breed famous for its infinite capacity for mimicry.

The wretched bird looks out from under the covers, and punctures the comforter with his beak. Goosedown erupts. Ilyana opens her eyes, sees me, and sits up suddenly, pulling my sheets over her breasts.

"I never thought I could do it, Andre, but it was a challenge. I was perched there, saying to myself, Andrew, you good-for-nothing parrot guy, what the hell are you doing with your life? Maybe it's time to lay it on the line. Maybe it's time to do your own thing. So I went for it, just like that. And you know what? I can do it. Yeah, I'm up to it. I'm a goddamed helicopter, Andrew," the fucking parrot says he's a fucking helicopter.

"It's not what you think," says Ilyana.

"I don't think," say I.

She cowers a little, as if to make me think she is afraid of what I might do. Each time she moves more goosedown squirts into the air, but that's the least of my worries. What might I do? Eastern Europe has booted out the commies. A playwright has become president of Czechoslovakia, hooray and alas. Nelson Mandela is free, or not free, but out of the small prison and into the big prison with the rest of us. I don't appreciate the world any more. Mike Tyson was knocked out by Buster somebody. What might I do? The Sandinistas are down. Cuba so far is an unknown quantity. China despots make strong sound,s but we know the people are stronger. Which way Albania? My mind is excited, but my heart is tired. Do I love her any less finding her in bed with a bird, my bird?

"It's till not what you think," says Ilyana.

"I don't think, grawk."

"What is it then?"

"It's part of a dance piece. I'm working on a dance piece to go with those poems."

"What is it about? How to avoid AIDS by sleeping with a parrot?"

"AIDS grawk. AIDS, grawk."

"You're not listening to me. This is one of the movements from the piece. I will perform it with Andrew at the Alternative Space, or at the Alternative Alternative Space. I have only a month to rehearse. You walked in on a rehearsal."

"Rehearsal. Rehearsal," parroted the parrot. "I'm a helicopter. Grawk. Grawk."

"Andrew, you don't think I was...not with Andrew..."
Ilyana says. She whips her hands from under the comforter and lifts them as if in prayer, both hands glowing.
Where have those been, I wonder? The air around her is
bright with goosedown. It's a snow scene sealed in a
globe. It's love thwarted by dandruff. It's a dry moment
in the washing machine from the point of view of streaked
skivvies.

"Let the pickles romp," I whisper into nowhere, as I
turn back down the stairs. "What harm can it do?"

I assume a half-lotus position on my cushion. They have
a hard enough time, picked in their prime, then subjected
to harsh climate of brine and spices and who knows what
other caustic agents. Then they are squeezed into jars with
little space to express themselves. Why let it irk me that
the Vlasick Polish guys are racing the kosher dills across
the floor, sometimes smashing into my meditation
cushion.

I sit.

And why worry the situation between Ilyana and
Andrew? Who am I to intervene and keep them form
expressing themselves, and for what? I love them both. I
bless them both.

I sit. And I know that throughout the city, and
throughout many cities in this time zone many people
have settled onto their cushions and are sitting with me.
Let's all sit. Sit till we fit.

Noise form the street barely reaches, barely makes it
through the insulation. A fan circulates warm air through
the loft. Many people freeze up this evening on the streets.
I am not yet them. I think about the beauty of the

countryside, of the waterfalls, and the long blond beaches with their perfect waves, and I look down in my thoughts off a wild mountain into a necklace of small sapphire lakes. Once that was a refreshment for the spirit, and gave a sense of well being, but even that now does not seem to be enough, even that seems damaged by someone, by so many like myself. Maybe it's still there, and up for grabs, that elevation of the soul in isolated contemplation of nature, but probably someone is making money from it, someone like myself has turned it into profitable recreation, hooray and alas.

I sit.

From out there a scream is muffled, An argument. Was that a gunshot? Yeah. I am separated, I know, from the misery out there by my thin green veil of money. That veil is volatile. I know that too. How quickly we can be exposed and into the street, just a moment of conflagration and it's gone. I live here in a world of bubble wrap and styrofoam peanuts. Outside of where I live the pressures are unbearable, and my brothers and sisters endure their blistered lives there; inside the pressures are slight, emotional, and except for touching me personally they have little significance. But what is outside and whit is inside all is taken into the heart and weighed there measure by measure all the same, and it does weigh, and that is what is meant when the heart is heavy.

"The heart is heavy. The heart is heavy. Grawk."

STEVE KATZ

Steve Katz was born in 1935 and grew up in the neighborhood of Washington Heights in Manhattan. He studied Pre-Veterinary at Cornell University for two years, then transferred to Liberal Arts. He wrote a novel in his senior year, a draft of which was critiqued by Vladimir Nabokov, who, Katz relates, leaned over him "like the tallest dentist in the world" to advise him to read more Shakespeare, Wordsworth, Keats, and Shelley.

Katz worked for the Forest Service in Idaho and for a Nevada quicksilver miner before moving with his wife, Pat Bell, to take a teaching assistantship in Eugene, Oregon. He left the academy to hitchhike to New York, where he worked as a waiter until he could buy steamer passage to Venice, then went to Florence to satisfy his obsession with the Massacio frescoes. His wife, with his sons, Avrum and Nikolai, then joined him in the city of Lecce. Rafael, his third son, was born there. After three years in Italy he returned to Cornell to teach. There he wrote *The Exagggerations of Peter Prince,* published in 1968 by Holt, Rinehart, and Winston.

Creamy and Delicious appeared two years later, published by Random House, then *Saw,* published by Alfred Knopf, appeared in 1982, receiving significant reviews. The *New York Times* wrote, "Steve Katz . . . is a witty fantasist who can homogenize pop detritus, campy slang and hallucination to achieve inspired chaos." In league with such writers as Jonathan Baumbach, Peter Spielberg, Russell Banks, Ronald Sukenick, and Clarence Major, he helped organize the Fiction Collective, which published his novel, *Moving Parts.*

From Cornell, Katz moved to Pine Bush, New York, and wrote *Stolen Stories,* a book of short pieces, many of which focused on the New York art world, where he had many friends.

Two years teaching at the University of Notre Dame was followed by an appointment at the University of Colorado, where he still teaches. There he wrote *Wier & Pouce,* a monumental "bildungsroman" that received national attention. *Florry of Washington Heights,* a popular experiment in the conventional novel, followed in 1987. Both books were published by Sun & Moon Press.

Sun & Moon Classics

Sun & Moon Classics is a publicly supported nonprofit program to publish new editions and translations or republications of outstanding world literature of the late nineteenth and twentieth centuries. Organized by The Contemporary Arts Educational Project, Inc., a non-profit corportation, and published by its program Sun & Moon Press, the series is made possible, in part, by grants and individual contributions.

This book was made possible, in part, through a matching grant from the California Arts Council, and through contributions from the following individuals.

Forthcoming

DARK RIDE AND OTHER PLAYS, by Len Jenkin
   with a Statement by Joseph Papp; and an Introduction
   by the author
NUMBERS AND TEMPERS: SELECTED POEMS 1966-1986, by Ray
   DiPalma
CHILDISH THINGS, by Valery Larbaud
   translated from the French by Catherine Wald
THE CELL, by Lyn Hejinian
AS A MAN GROWS OLDER, by Italo Svevo
   translated from the Italian by Beryl De Zoete; with
   an Introduction by Stanislaus Joyce; and an Essay on
   Svevo by Edouard Roditi
ETERNAL SECTIONS, by Tom Raworth